Spiked

R. E. Rowling

ISBN 978-1519469021

To William Henry Reeves

For Jan

1

Bill hadn't managed to have any lunch. Carstairs had come down to his office at the local council three times to harass him about being late for the fire safety inspection at *Sunshine Soft Drinks*. But now already on his bicycle and not late Bill swung into the High Street instead of taking the back road out of town. The High Street had degenerated into a budget supermarket, a fish and chip shop, a hobby shop, a Chinese takeaway and a hardware store advertising a permanent closing down sale. The newsagents however should have something to eat. Bill propped his bicycle against a rubbish bin and went into the shop.

The task was harder than he'd anticipated. There were shelves of magazines, chocolate bars and greetings cards but no food. He came to a stop by the counter and looking suitably male and helpless the woman behind the till took pity on him.

'Can I help you?' she asked.

'Well,' said Bill, 'do you have anything sustaining that can be consumed in a hurry?'

'We've got this,' said the woman. She pointed to a pyramid of bright red cans slashed across with a black name: *Spiked*. A hand written sign beneath said: 'Promotional deal. Energy Drink. Two for the price of one'.

Moments later Bill was standing outside sampling the recommended lunch. He finished the first one standing in the shop doorway and threw the empty can from where he was standing into the rubbish bin. The second one he took to the bench at the far end of the shop window to relish more slowly. Draining the last few drops he stood up, twisted himself into a short run up and bowled the second can smack into the centre of the bin.

'How's that,' he said to his bicycle, glanced at his watch and realised that now he was late.

It wasn't a problem. A caffeinated sugar high hit him half way to the job and he arrived at *Sunshine Soft Drinks* in record time, a bit out of breath and heart racing. Susan would say that he should be more careful at his age. Although at sixty-five Bill couldn't help feeling pleased with himself as he swung into the bicycle rack at the corner of the car park. But the bicycle rack wasn't there. In fact the whole place had had a good shine up. The apologetic Fords that used to fill the old *Sunshine Soft Drinks'* car park had been replaced with aggressive new Minis and Audi Sportbacks.

Bill chained his bicycle to a newly landscaped tree, unclipped his briefcase from the luggage rack and dusted himself down. He frowned uncertainly at a sleek black sign on the wall of a new reception building. *Spiked.* Bill was puzzled. He opened his briefcase and found the letter from *Sunshine Soft Drinks* requesting an urgent assessment and renewal of their fire safety certificate, which was due to expire at the end of the month. There was no mention of new buildings or new names.

His only correspondence with *Sunshine Soft Drinks* had been to remind them that his assessment always included a talk to employees. The talk was a fudge that Bill had used indiscriminately for twenty years or so feeling that his more creative energies were best spent on cricket. Although Bill's wicket keeping form had been poor last season and it wasn't likely to be improved by the cricket club committee meeting due that evening.

He sighed and headed towards the building. A sugared caffeine low distracted him as he tried to push open a large glass door. The door opened silently and Bill half fell into a large tropical plant just as an elegant woman of indeterminate age approached him. She was wearing a light grey suit with something soft and blue underneath and something soft and blue around her neck. She was carrying a buff folder and smiled at him with lipstick not eyes.

'And you must be?' she questioned politely.

'William Reeves. Chief Fire Officer.' Bill pulled himself up if not tall then broad.

'Ah, yes - you're a little early.'

'Am I?' said Bill, the sugared caffeine swinging up again. 'I'm always a little early. I like to be prepared,' he bluffed. After his unplanned liquid lunch he would need to use the bathroom.

The woman was looking at him expectantly.

'If I could just sit somewhere out of the way for five minutes or so and go over my notes?' Bill suggested.

She hesitated.

'You'd better come this way.'

This way was into a small room behind the elegant glass of the reception area. It was obviously part of the refurbishment that wasn't yet complete. The room was currently being used as a lumber-room and piles of paper and files were heaped everywhere. The woman put her folder down and removed a bundle of papers from a chair.

'This is just fine,' Bill said, wondering why she hadn't suggested he sit in reception. Perhaps he wasn't elegant enough for the glass and palms of *Spiked.*

The woman left him, her high heels tapping importantly down the marble floor of a new corridor. Marble flooring was good for fire safety. Bill pulled his own buff folder out of his briefcase and looked at it resignedly. Was it time to retire? From fire safety bureaucracy and cricket?

He looked at his watch. He just had time to find the gents. He left his folder on the chair and went out into the marble corridor. The cloakroom, like everything else, looked new and well built. Even the toilet flushed expensively.

When he emerged a girl was hovering outside the small office cum lumber-room looking anxious. The receptionist perhaps? He hadn't noticed her when he'd arrived. The girl looked slightly less anxious when she saw him.

'Mr Reeves?' she said, looking behind her as if she, or even he, had done something wrong.

'Indeed! At your service,' he said. He sounded ridiculously old fashioned.

'They're all waiting,' she said.

Bill looked at his watch.

'But it's only…'

She waved her hands urgently. Bill felt a tight knot grip his heart. The precursor to the palpitations he usually managed to control and hadn't told anyone about yet, not even Susan. Or could it be another caffeine induced reaction? He persuaded the girl that he needed to collect his things. He grabbed his coat, briefcase and the buff folder then allowed her to hurry him down the corridor. He should have been assessing the windows and the fire exit signs as he went, but the girl was pushing him along until he found himself stepping through a side door and standing behind a lectern in front of a room full of people.

He arranged his folder on the lectern giving himself time to concentrate his thoughts before introducing himself and making the usual joke about being the chief and only fire officer in East Wolds. Then he settled himself to read the first sentence of his jaded script.

Except it wasn't his sentence. *Private and confidential: NOT TO BE SENT BY E-MAIL*, was what his eyes read, but by some miracle of reflex what his mouth said was: 'The first and most important aspect of health and safety in any organisation is fire safety and precautions.'

His eyes travelled down the page. *Why* Spiked *is going to make us the next hottest must have product.*

'Take this room we're all in now. How many of you have taken the few seconds it takes to make a mental note of where the fire exits are?'

There was a disturbance at the back of the room and the sophisticated woman appeared waving her buff folder at him.

We have three aims.

'I'm sure that a few of you have, but exactly how many of you have noticed if there are fire alarms or fire extinguishers in the room? And if you *are* standing by either of those features have you taken the time to work out how to operate such a feature before it's needed?'

To be the most talked about product.

To be associated with all outdoor, sporting and high adrenalin activities.

To be addictive.

Bill raised his eyes from the page and looked directly across the room at the woman. Her eyes were registering panic and her suit was riding up over her hips. It wasn't her buff folder she was waving at him, it was his. Her buff folder was on the lectern in front of him posing as a fire safety talk. Bill smiled benignly, pointed in a reassuring way at his lectern notes and carried on with his talk.

The woman paused, confused. The notes she had were identical to the talk that Bill was giving. She edged her way to the front of the room while Bill continued his recital. When she reached a table by the lectern she put the buff folder down.

'Your notes,' she hissed.

Bill smiled again. Tapping the lectern smugly he leant towards her and said in a loud stage whisper. 'Good job I always have a spare copy with me.'

Someone in the audience tittered. Bill launched into what he hoped was the next section of his talk.

Three simple aims.

Market the product to sell to 19 year old males. Nothing illegal in selling highly caffeinated products to adults. But aim it at children.

Advertise through sponsorship of all sporting events, sporting heroes, local and national. We get a reputation for regeneration and investment in local and national communities and association with healthy outdoor pursuits and achievement.

Spike it. No one will know.

Bill finished his talk, closed the folder and whipped it off the lectern before the lipsticked woman could make her way round the table. He picked up his own folder and put them both in his briefcase. The woman was now at his elbow.

'Let me help you.'

Bill clutched the briefcase into his chest.

'No, no' he said tightly. They both faced each other. Bill dropped his eyes and looked at his watch. 'I'd better get on with my inspection,' he said, 'I need to get back to the office this afternoon. Please, lead the way.'

The woman made no move. Her eyes passed over him in a way calculated to make him feel uneasy. But another caffeinated high was washing through him and he grinned at her with a not entirely appropriate smile.

'Which way, then?' he asked.

She turned away, dismissing him. 'Miss Summers will show you round,' she said and left him standing in the marble corridor.

The anxious receptionist appeared again.

'Miss Summers?'

She looked taken aback, but nodded.

Bill smiled. He was doing a lot of smiling. Susan said he always smiled when he felt guilty about something. He followed Miss Summers down the corridor. The gloss faded as they turned off the marble corridor into the foreman's offices attached to the production warehouse and stores.

'You're not Geoff Summers' daughter are you?' Bill chatted. She looked at him nonplussed. 'Used to play cricket,' Bill expanded.

The girl relaxed a tad. 'You mean me Grandad? He played cricket.' She smiled uncertainly. 'I think.'

Bill flinched mentally. Her Grandad. The retirement gremlins hovered again.

'You're a local girl, then?'

'Yes, most of us are. It's just top management that's been brought in.'

'Here we are then,' Bill announced, as they reached the production floor. It was busy. The production team, settled back to work after Bill's talk, seemed well organised. Things looked efficient and clean. 'It's a bit different from the old days,' Bill said, '*Sunshine Soft Drinks* was held together with a piece of string.'

The girl looked at him. She wouldn't know. A man joined them. A tall man with some weight on him.

Bill put his hand out. 'Bill Reeves, Fire Officer.'

'I assumed so. Shaun Bean.' The big man shook hands dourly.

'Shaun Bean? Isn't that that famous chap from Sheffield or somewhere thereabouts? Sharpe! That's the one.'

The observation had been made before and the man didn't look as though he enjoyed it. 'Shall we get on with it?' he said.

Miss Summers left them and Bill followed Shaun Bean while Shaun Bean pointed out all the fire extinguishers, fire doors, exits, fire hose, etc. His manner was surly and sarcastic.

'These vats, what's in these?' Bill asked breaking an aggressive silence.

'What do you think, eh? The drink of course.'

'So you make it on site? You don't just bottle it up here?'

Shaun Bean looked as if it wasn't anything to do with Bill. 'We make it here. We're a ruddy soft drink producer, what the hell else do you expect us to do?'

'If that is the case I'll need a list of raw ingredients.'

'Bloody hell. If you insist.'

'Regulations,' said Bill wishing that the man wasn't quite so sizeable.

Shaun Bean went into a small office and Bill took the opportunity to have his own poke around. It all seemed in order. He wondered why he wished it wasn't. Why he wished he could issue an unfit for use order and have the whole place shut down by evening.

Shaun Bean returned with a print out of raw ingredients and escorted Bill on to the packing sheds. The same order and hard working atmosphere continued. There were cartons and cartons of cans of soft drinks. Mountains of them. They were red emblazoned with black lettering spelling out the message and the name: *Spiked*. The same *Spiked* that he had consumed in lieu of lunch. The highly caffeinated spiked energy drink that he'd just inadvertently read a confidential memo about. A hot sweat spread from his armpits up his throat and he clutched at his chest protectively.

'Do you drink this stuff?' he said suddenly to Shaun Bean.

Shaun Bean looked even crosser. 'What the hell is that...?'

'I'm sorry, it's just, I'm not feeling quite...Do you mind if I just get on and finish.' Bill pulled himself together. Smiled. Felt dizzy and sick. Took a stumbling step towards the exit.

Shaun Bean smiled nastily and eagerly dumped Bill back in the marble corridor although his inspection was obviously incomplete. Bill was infringing so many procedures and protocols that his head span with more than caffeine. He felt decidedly edgy and he was so relieved to see Miss Summers at the reception desk that he greeted her with a rush of familiarity.

'Remember me to your Grandad, love. Could be very handy with the bat on occasion your Grandad.'

Miss Summers smiled, then the telephone went and Bill left her, hearing her trying to tone down her accent and sound posh.

Once outside and back on his bicycle Bill felt much happier. So he thought very little of a youth snooping and peering into all the car windows until the youth suddenly shouted out. Bill twisted round on his bicycle and saw the thin scrappy looking youth gawping at him. He notched up another gear and charged out onto the open road. It was possible that the shout was articulated into an, 'eh, you,' and even a brief attempt at some running footsteps chasing after the bicycle, but Bill didn't look back. He kept his head down and veered onto the old canal pathway. The daylight was already fading and although the path was still firm with a winter frost the canal was a dull sludge blotting up what was left of the sun.

As Bill bicycled he had time to think about what he'd done. He'd stolen a folder of confidential documents while representing his local council. Of course the lipsticked woman didn't know that he had the documents; she thought he just had a spare copy of his own notes. What she did know, and no doubt lots of other important people at *Spiked* also knew by now, was that she didn't have her notes. And if she didn't have her notes then they were either lost or someone else had them and the last person to have seen them was Bill.

Bill's heart lurched. He hadn't meant to steal the folder and there had been lots of occasions when he could have returned it. He could have given it straight back to lipsticked woman; he could have casually dropped it somewhere in the vicinity of Shaun Bean and perhaps got Shaun Bean into trouble; he could have snuck back into the office-lumber room and innocently hidden it amongst all the piles of papers. But he hadn't. He'd escaped with his contraband and now he was stuck with it.

He would go home, have a cup of tea with Susan and Google *Spiked*. And as he swung into the cul-de-sac where he and Susan lived he wondered how long it would take for lipsticked woman to find out his address.

2

It took 45 minutes. Which was the 30 minutes it had taken him to get home, the 4 minutes it took his vintage computer to switch on, the further 2 minutes to log onto his e-mails, the 1 second it took to delete three e-mails inviting him to elongate his penis, the 5 minutes it took to download the minutes for tonight's cricket club meeting, the 3 minutes it took him to fail to watch a You Tube link sent by his grandson and the 59 seconds it took to run downstairs from his little home office in the box room to greet Susan as she came in from work.

'There's a very posh car driving up and down The Avenue,' said Susan as they exchanged a fond marital greeting.

'A black Audi Sportback,' said Bill looking at his watch. Forty-five minutes exactly.

'A what?' said Susan.

'A black Audi Sportback.'

'How on earth…'

'You know, the ones with rings on the front that golf club people drive.'

'I didn't go looking for any rings.' She gave him one of her looks. 'Shall I put the kettle on?'

Bill didn't answer yes to this last question. He went back upstairs into his office and peered out of the window. The small spare bedroom, or box room, was at the front of the house and the window offered a limited view of The Avenue where they lived. The Avenue was a cul-de-sac of small pre-war semis originally intended as part of a larger urban sprawl but post war development had taken place in other parts of the town while further development of The Avenue had been limited to a half dozen or so detached bungalows. Bill looked out of the window but no black Audi was in sight. It didn't however mean that the Audi had gone.

Still checking the window Bill clicked on the documents for the cricket club meeting, selected print and watched while his also vintage printer copier slowly ground out four pages of meeting notes. He heard rather than saw the gate click. He pulled the lipsticked woman's folder from his briefcase and slotted the cricket club papers on top of the confidential memo at the same time as he bellowed for Susan.

'There's no need to shout.' Susan was standing in the doorway. 'Now what are you up to? And come to think of it why are you home early from work?'

Four sheets of highly confidential memo and cricket club papers fell onto the floor. Bill didn't have time to answer her. He scrabbled on the floor stuffing the papers back into the folder

'Don't bother, I didn't ask,' Susan sighed and left him to it. 'The tea's brewing,' she called back as she went downstairs.

Bill tried to get up and run after her and banged his head on the desk. 'Susan, Susan, don't let anyone in. If anyone rings the doorbell don't let them in.'

The doorbell however had already been rung. Bill heard Susan crossing the hallway to answer it, Susan's polite greeting and the soft tones of an educated male answering her. Bill charged downstairs just in time to stop the man from getting a second foot over the threshold.

'We don't want any, thank you,' Bill announced, holding the door with one hand and the doorframe with his other as he broadened into position.

Susan attempted to peer around him. 'The young man isn't trying to sell us anything. He's from *Spiked* as used to be *Sunshine Soft Drinks* and he says you might have left something in their offices after your inspection today.'

Bill was looking at the young man, who was indeed carrying a buff folder identical to Bill's buff folder and identical to the lipsticked woman's buff folder.

'No, I've got all my buff folders,' said Bill, emphasising the all.

'Are you sure, dear,' intervened Susan from somewhere behind Bill's shoulder.

'Quite sure,' Bill said.

The young man coughed politely. 'If you could just check?' he asked.

'No, it's not mine. I've got all my buff folders,' Bill repeated. Behind the young man he could see the black Audi Sportback parked outside their gate next to Susan's Honda.

'Why don't you just check? You know how forgetful you can be,' persisted Susan. 'And your things were in a terrible mess all over the office floor just now.'

'I've got all my folders,' Bill shouted. Then he smiled, expansively, broadly, beamingly. 'It's really very kind of you to go out of your way, but I'm sure I have everything I need and that you've got everything you need. Your company will be hearing from me in due course with my full report. Good-bye,' and he shut the door.

He and Susan watched the young man through the opaque glass panels in the door. He stepped back from the entrance, hesitated for a long few seconds then turned his back and went up the path and out through the garden gate. Bill waited until he heard the purring of the Audi engine and saw the car slink away towards the main road.

'Is there something you're not telling me?' Susan said.

Bill avoided her gaze. 'Little Bill,' (their affectionate name for their *You Tube* enthusiast grandson called William or Will by everyone else), 'Little Bill asked if he could come on Saturday and maybe stay the night.'

'When was that?'

'Just now, in an e-mail.'

'Yes of course, but I don't remember Carol or Ben saying anything.'

'Annie's got a pre-season coaching session all weekend. I think they've got to drive her all the way to Peterborough or somewhere.'

'Of course, that's right. I'd forgotten. I'll check my messages. Oh and Bill?'

Bill tried not to look guilty.

'Don't you think we should stop calling him Little Bill. I mean he's not really little anymore now is he? He's ten years old.'

Bill smiled, relieved that Susan seemed to have lost interest in their visitor. He looked at his watch. It was half past four. Bill had to go out to his meeting leaving the house at about a quarter to seven as it took him ten minutes to bicycle to the cricket club.

'Are you in tonight?' he asked Susan.

'You know I'm not in tonight. It's knitting club. It's always knitting club on Thursdays.'

What would *Spiked* do next? If both he and Susan were out would they break into their home? The notion seemed ridiculous, but if they did it would be professional and untraceable. Bill and

Susan had never bothered to install an alarm. He went back up to his office pondering this eventuality. He would have to set a trap. Because if someone did break into his home, albeit for just a discreet rummage, he would like to know about it. And if they were that keen on reclaiming the highly confidential memo then Bill would know that what he had stolen was important: very important indeed.

'I've become an industrial spy,' he muttered to himself. He took the folder with cricket club notes jumbled with the *Spiked* memo out of his briefcase and left the fire safety report on *Sunshine soft Drinks* in his briefcase. He fastened the left buckle properly and deliberately tucked the right strap loosely into the buckle without fastening it.

'Dinner time,' called Susan up the stairs.

'That will have to do,' said Bill.

3

It was already twelve minutes to seven. Bill was flapping round the kitchen with his meeting notes trying to find a pencil. Susan was also trying to leave the house to go to her knitting club. He found a shopping bag with Easter bunnies hopping all over it.

'Can I take this?' he asked Susan, going out of the backdoor without waiting for her assent.

'I don't understand why you can't just take your briefcase,' Susan called after him.

'It's full of work stuff,' Bill called from the path where he was trying to attach the bunny bag to the luggage rack on the back of his bicycle.

'It wasn't full of work stuff the last time I saw it,' said Susan, 'work stuff was all over the floor and briefcase was distinctly empty.'

Bill didn't hear her.

'And you're late,' she called out louder as she locked the back door and followed Bill down the path jingling her car keys.

'I know I'm late,' Bill said struggling with the gate.

She closed the gate after him. 'Have you got your keys?'

Bill was now launched into the middle of the road and cranking up the gears.

'You've forgotten your helmet,' she shouted after him, 'again.'

Bill raced onto the main road and a smart new Mini had to break to avoid hitting him.

If he cut down The Elms he might just make it in time. He careered into the middle of the road waving his right arm in the face of the Mini and sped up along The Elms. The Elms conveniently by-passed the small town centre and culminated in a snicket which cut through to the village green, home of the East Wolds' cricket team.

The Mini took the same short cut and came to a halt by the snicket and a smart looking woman in a grey suit climbed out of the driver's seat. She walked along the snicket just far enough to see Bill pushing his bicycle at great speed over a rough, wet, muddy outfield towards a battered old cricket pavilion. She returned to the car distastefully stepping over wet heaps of nature.

'That was definitely him,' she said, distaste still distorting her smart features and wrinkling her lipstick.

Meanwhile Bill flung his bicycle against the faded weatherboarding of the clubhouse, grabbed the bunny bag and pushed open the pavilion door as the church clock chimed out the hour. The others were already there passing round a jar of Nescafé and a kettle. Bill grabbed a mug and the empty chair and loaded up with two teaspoons of coffee and three teaspoons of sugar. There wasn't time to worry about his heart.

A few rough greetings were still taking place as the chairman called them to order and the usual reports were mumbled through. Bill wasn't anything special on the committee, just a member, so he had time to glance through the agenda and check if there was anything he should know about. Item 5. Rebuilding of pavilion. Item 6. Call for an extraordinary general meeting to approve plans and financing. He was puzzled; he'd not heard anything of this before. He quite liked the old pavilion.

'Bill,' his neighbour was nudging his elbow, 'pass the milk on can't you.'

Bill filled up his mug with milk and passed the carton on to his neighbour. The chairman continued. 'The time has come to freshen up, to revitalise. You'll all have seen that rebuilding of the pavilion is on the agenda, but I think it is about more than rebuilding of the building. The money, this new sponsorship we're being offered can revitalise our whole club, from the bottom up.'

Bill suddenly sat up spilling coffee on his minutes which soaked through to the *Spiked* documents underneath. Why was the chairman suddenly talking about sponsorship? And Bill hated phrases like 'from the bottom up'. He tried not to look old and cross.

'If the club is to survive it needs to modernise, it needs new members. It needs children. We've done well in the past, but recently,' and here the chairman paused and looked at Bill, 'our game has slipped, we are not as sharp as we were. I think we have, as it were, taken our eye off the ball.'

This was not right, or kind. Bill had had a trial for Yorkshire once which was more than any of the others had.

'Which I think is the perfect lead in to Item 5 on our agenda,' the secretary broke in.

17

An expectant hum spread around the table. Some people obviously knew about this already, talking at work, meeting at the pub, Twitter, Facebook, but Bill's cronies didn't; the has-beens.

'As some of you know,' continued the chairman.

Aye, and as some of us don't know, thought Bill.

'Sorry, Bill, did you have something to say?'

Bill looked alarmed. 'No you're alright, just carry on, don't mind me.'

'As I was saying, as some of you are already aware we've been offered a most generous amount of money to rebuild our pavilion.'

Money? Pavilion? More coffee was spilt.

'As we all know we have spent many years now trying to come up with fund raising schemes to repair this old pavilion but all to no avail. The last assessment we had for repairs, now when was that?'

'2009,' interrupted Bill.

'2009,' continued the chairman, 'and as you older members of the committee will remember, the building was condemned as unfit for use.'

'It's done well enough since then though, hasn't it?' This was muttered by another member of the committee.

'Yes, but it's not safe is it?' The chairman looked almost triumphant as he rounded on Bill again.

Indeed it wasn't safe; it broke every fire regulation in the book. Not fit for use. Bill doodled on his agenda and didn't look up.

'But now, as some of our younger members are aware, *Spiked* has offered us a most generous amount of money in the form of sponsorship.'

Bill gasped and choked on a cold swig of coffee. Other members aahed and oohed.

The chairman raised his voice. 'A most generous sponsorship which will not only fund the building of a new clubhouse but will allow us to recruit new members and field, for the first time in many years, a colts team and an under 21s.'

Someone started to clap. A younger member said, 'Wow'. A general euphoria crept into the old damp condemned unfit-for-use sixty year old pavilion.

'But hang on a minute,' Bill said, scraping his chair back on the rotten wooden floor, 'what if?'

The cheering stopped and everyone looked at Bill.

'I mean what do we know about this *Spiked*?' Bill doodled '*Spiked*' on his agenda.

'What do we need to know?' someone piped up.

'For a start what guarantees do we have that they'll actually cough-up the money?'

'It's not, of course, been approved yet and all these details will be available when we have the extraordinary general meeting,' said the chairman.

'I mean they're just a new company,' Bill struggled on. 'We don't know anything about them.'

'It's the old *Sunshine Soft Drinks*,' someone else broke in. 'They make soft drinks just like before. I can't see what's so mysterious about that myself.'

'But it's not just like before.' Bill looked at the spread of politely uninterested faces. The confidential memo glistened underneath his meeting notes. He opened his mouth wondering where to begin then faded to a standstill.

The chairman started tidying up his notes. 'If that's all perhaps we can move on to a show of hands to gauge the feeling towards the general principle of accepting sponsorship and taking a resolution to an extraordinary general meeting.'

The show of hands was vociferous and positive.

'I trust you'll make the necessary arrangements,' the chairman turned to the secretary, and the meeting was closed.

'Eh up, Bill, aren't you joining us for a quick drink?'

'I don't know, John, it's been a long day.'

Bill pushed his bicycle and the two men walked along together in the direction of the town centre and the predictably named Cricketers Arms. There was a silence, almost companionable.

'You think it's alright then do you?' Bill asked John.

A puzzled frown crossed John's brow. John Bailey was a fellow bicycle enthusiast who batted at number four. 'You mean re-building the pavilion?' More silence. 'It'll have to be done one way or another, I suppose.'

19

'Yes, I know,' Bill paused as they reached the road. The Cricketers Arms was one direction and home for Bill the other. Bill sighed. 'It's just the one way or another bit I'm not sure about. I mean this sponsorship business. We've never been sponsored before.'

'Oh, that,' said John, 'Everyone's doing it these days, the Headingley Carneige ground, John Smiths Grand National.'

Other groups from the meeting joined them, moving on to The Cricketers Arms, or home.

'Schools even, there's a school in Hull,' John continued, inspired.

'God forbid, East Wolds *Spiked* Comprehensive,' Bill muttered. Another silence, a thirsty one for John.

'I was there today,' Bill continued.

John looked suitably blank.

'At *Sunshine Soft Drinks* or *Spiked* as it is now. You know, checking out the rebuilding and fire safety, the usual stuff.' Bill put a hand into the bunny bag and pulled out the various notes he'd stuffed into the buff folder. 'Now, John, what would you reckon to,' but John wasn't listening. He was hurrying away towards the pub.

It was dark, and chilly. Bill wished he'd put on an extra sweater. The Fish 'n Chip shop was closed and the kids that hung around the cobbled square had gone home. Bill pedalled on up the dark street. Worried. A car cruised slowly past him and he tried to see what make it was, who was driving it. Something rustled in a garden. A bin had fallen over. He turned into The Avenue, the menace following him down the dark street. A car was parked outside his house.

Susan's. He gave a huge creaking breath and started to laugh. Espionage and whistle-blowing were surprisingly difficult. He opened the garden gate and went through his comfortable routine of locking up the bicycle for the night and checking the shed door, whistling into the black winter night. He opened the backdoor loudly and shouted cheerfully into the brightly lit kitchen. 'I'm home.'

'So I gathered,' said Susan, 'do you want cocoa or tea?'

'Ooh, what do you reckon? Shall we have some cocoa?'

Bill locked the door and rubbed his hands together to get warm.

'How was the meeting?' Susan asked as she watched a pan of milk over the stove.

'Alright. How was knitting?'

'Alright,' Susan said smiling into the pan.

'Do you actually do any knitting? Isn't there some name for it? Knit and talk or something?'

'Oh, you mean stitch and bitch? Knit and talk sounds much nicer doesn't it? Yes we knit, and talk.' She put two mugs of cocoa on the kitchen table. 'Melanie Andrews has got a new car.'

'Oh well, those Andrews have got money to burn. He made a packet when he sold off the family green grocers. What've we got now? Eh? Poundsavers or something.'

'*Londis*. You're such a reactionary, Bill.'

'Am I?'

'I do like those new Minis,' Susan continued dreamily. 'There was one just driving out of The Avenue when I came home. I wonder who that could have been?'

Bill nearly spilt his cocoa. 'A Mini? One of those new aggressive kinds? When?'

'For goodness sake, about twenty minutes or so ago. I got home just before you and you must've been home about…I give up.' And she did. She cleared up the mugs and decided to go to bed.

Bill had rushed upstairs into his office.

'Have you finished down here? Shall I switch the lights off?'

No reply. Bill was on his hands and knees in his little office examining the buckles on his briefcase. They were both fastened, properly. He rushed past Susan on the stairs and started examining the front door, the back door, the downstairs windows.

Susan had followed him back down the stairs. 'What's going on?' she said.

'Nothing, nothing.'

'That's a lot of nothing,' she said sceptically, then wearily, 'I'm off to bed. Somehow it suddenly feels like a long day.'

Bill followed her up the stairs, but he didn't go to bed. He switched on his computer and while he waited for it to log on he retrieved the official forms he had from *Spiked* and took a copy of the list of ingredients which he'd prized out of Shaun Bean.

Google.com, Spiked. A minute or so while the old computer struggled to download some images. 'There we go,' pronounced

Bill. '*Spiked©* is a UK based soft drinks company (formerly *Sunshine Soft Drinks*) which has recently made a successful entry into the highly competitive energy drinks market.'

'Bill,' Susan's voice drifted plaintively from the bedroom.

Bill continued in a painful stage whisper. 'The new company statutes were convened in October 2014 and the stated company aim is to take over a leading share of the UK energy drinks' market before marketing this new brand leader abroad. The company slogan is *Spiked Flies©*.' He went back to his search results and clicked on images. Red can. Trendy black script. His grandchildren would call it cool, dangerous, exciting, spiked.

He took hold of Shaun Bean's list of ingredients. Water, sugar, citric acid, Taurine. Google search: "Taurine, or 2-aminoethanesulfonic acid, is an organic acid widely distributed in animal tissues."

Another entry. "Taurine is a major constituent of bile and can be found in the large intestine and in the tissues of many animals, including humans."

"Taurine is regularly used as an ingredient in energy drinks, with many containing 1000 mg per serving, and some as much as 2000 mg."

He carried on down the list. Natural flavouring, sodium citrate, Carnitine, ginseng. 'Ginseng's supposed to be healthy isn't it? Susan?' Then Bill remembered what the time was and carried on reading quietly. Ascorbic acid, Caffeine, vitamins B2, B3, B6 and B12… Bill noted two things; that caffeine was an integral ingredient in energy drinks and that in the *Spiked* ingredients it was misleadingly low down on the list.

'Come to bed, dear,' said Susan. She was standing in the doorway rubbing her eyes.

'What do you reckon to this?' He handed her Shaun Bean's list.

She put out her hand to borrow his glasses and read through it.

'I hope you haven't been taking any of this stuff,' she announced crossly, 'no wonder you can't sleep.' Susan was the practice nurse at the local health centre so she knew what she was talking about.

'What do you mean?'

'They're all stimulants.'
'All of them?'
'Yes, more-or-less.'
'Apart from water.'
'Apart from water,' Susan agreed tiredly.

4

The phone in Bill's breast pocket started buzzing and then gave a big echoing shout that sounded like a synthesised guitar. Bill wobbled on his bicycle then started rummaging in his pocket and managed to fish the phone out. He clicked the button to read the message. 'Dad, hi,' said the message but Bill couldn't read the rest without glasses. He held the phone up towards the skies optimistically. 'R u', 'collecting' perhaps, 'Will. Or' illegible, or not so easy to guess. Bill pressed the telephone icon on the phone.

'Carol?'

'Dad?'

'You just sent me a message.'

'Yes. You got the message I sent yesterday?'

'Hang on a minute, love.' Bill changed the phone to his other hand and negotiated a school crossing and a lorry with it's engine running outside the High Street supermarket.

'Dad?'

'With you in a minute.' He made a one handed left turn off the High Street. 'Okay that should be better now. Less noise.'

'Dad, where are you?'

'On my way to work.'

'On your way to work?'

'On my bike.'

'Dad! Isn't that illegal or something. It can't possibly be safe.'

'Don't tell Mum.'

'You're impossible and I will tell Mum.'

'Is Little Bill coming to stay then? When did you say?'

'Dad! I thought you got my message? I just want to know if you're collecting him from school or?'

'If he's got his bike at school I'll collect him as usual.'

'I'll just leave his things in the shed. You left the shed door unlocked?'

Bill said nothing as he rode into the council car park.

'I'll take it that's a no then.'

'Just let me park the bike,' Bill said as he performed an elegant leg over seat act and cruised into the bicycle stands.

'Where were we,' he continued. 'So Annie is off on one of her coaching weekends?'

Carol said something but Bill was distracted by a black Audi Sportback gleaming in one of the guest parking slots.

'So Ben and I thought we'd make a weekend of it,' Carol was saying.

'Yes, very nice love I'll see you later.'

'Dad you'll -' but Bill had pressed the red icon on his phone and rushed into the council building. He sidled up to Sally Anne on reception.

'That Audi, parked in the guest parking?'

'Oh that,' Sally Anne moved in conspiratorially, 'fancy chap, southerner, wanted to speak to the boss. Urgently.'

'I don't suppose he had an appointment?' Bill asked and oozed his way invisibly up the stairs to his office.

His desk was neat. Three in-trays. One completed cases, one current cases and one pending cases. He emptied the papers he'd brought back from *Sunshine Soft Drinks*, now *Spiked*, and put them in the current case in-tray. He switched on his computer, which was about two models up from his home computer, waited for the slow log on procedure to take effect and watched his telephone warily. He still jumped when it rang.

'You'd better get up to my office, fast,' said Mr Fred Carstairs, OBE and chief council officer.

A stranger, male, tall, sleek, passed Bill on the stairs. He was the kind of man who kept fit and took stairs not lifts. Carstairs' office door was open. Bill knocked anyway.

'That was quick?' Carstairs looked surprised.

Bill tried not to look guilty.

'It's a bit awkward, Bill,' Carstairs said spreading out the fingers of two fat hands which rested on a mahogany desk.

Bill sat down without being asked. Carstairs being expansive was a bad sign.

'So what's the complaint?' Bill asked.

Carstairs looked surprised a second time. It was some small gratification.

'It's not exactly a complaint, at this stage,' Carstairs lowered his glasses and peered over them, 'but I understand there were some issues with your assessment at *Spiked* yesterday.'

25

'Oh, no it all looked fine,' said Bill, 'very nice in fact.'

'No, not with your assessment but with your procedure.'

'Well, Fred,' said Bill, 'you know my procedure. It is always the same. Never been any complaints before and no cause for complaints now.' The broad wicket keeping shoulders expanded.

'Well, Bill,' Carstairs floundered.

'Probably best if I just get on with the paper work for *Spiked* I should think. If they see that everything's in order -'

'It wasn't just the procedure,' Carstairs resumed with more authority, 'there was an implication that something had gone missing.'

'What?'

'The man didn't say.'

'You can't imply that something's gone missing, Fred, either it is missing or it isn't.'

Carstairs opened his mouth then closed it again. The man had indeed been very vague about what was missing.

'Like I said, I'll get on with the paper work. That'll be best,' said Bill and left Mr Carstairs OBE worrying at an old-fashioned ink pen and a blotter.

Bill paused on the stairs on the way back down to his office. He put his hand on his heart. 'Now don't you start,' he said crossly, 'it seems I've got enough on my plate without you joining in.'

At three o'clock the *Spiked* case was dropped into Bill's completed case in-tray and Bill slipped down the back stairs and out through the fire escape door which led straight into the car park. He lurked behind a bush or two and having established that there were no Audis or Minis in sight he unlocked his bicycle and raced off to meet Will from school.

'Hey, Grandad,' Will greeted him.

'Hey, Bill,' said Bill. 'How was school?' Although Bill didn't wait for an answer but carried on cycling without waiting for Will to sort himself out.

'Grandad?' Will shouted. He was puffing and panting trying to pull along side the speeding Bill. 'Why are we going this way?' he asked as his grandfather headed towards East Wolds town centre instead of towards The Avenue and home. 'Grandad,' Will shouted again, as he'd now fallen back several yards behind Bill.

Bill slowed down and twisted round on his bicycle. 'We're going to buy a can or two of *Spiked*.'

'*Spiked*? Way, Grandad, that's cool, that's way cool,' said Will, and energised by the mere thought pedalled double speed and caught up with Bill.

5

Two cans of *Spiked* adorned the kitchen table. *Extra Spiked* and *Original Spiked*. Will was beside himself with longing. 'Everyone,' he said, 'everyone drinks *Spiked*.'

'Well, you're not,' snapped Susan. The snapping was aimed at Bill.

'Oh no, they're not for drinking,' said Bill, 'they're for experimentation.'

Bill picked up the can of *Extra Spiked*. 'Here Bill.'

'William,' corrected Susan.

'Now, Billiam, let's see if we can read these ingredients?'

'Billiam, that's so cool Grandad.'

'I'll Billiam the pair of you, now move your chair round to Grandad so I can get on and make some tea,' said Susan.

'Pass me your glasses, Susan, and let's see what this stuff claims to be made of.'

'Where are your own?' asked Susan passing Bill her reading glasses.

'In my pocket,' said Bill putting Susan's glasses on.

<small>Ingredients: carbonated water*, glucose*, sucrose*, natural flavours* (apple extract, grape extract, lemon extract), taurine, carnitine, ginseng*, caffeine*, niacinamike, riboflavin, guarana extract*, inositol, glucuronalactone, pyridoxine hydrochloride, cyanobalamin. (* denotes natural ingredient),</small> Bill tried to read.

'Here, Billiam, you try?' Bill passed the *Extra Spiked* can to Will.

'Ingredients, carbated water, er cose something, natural flower...' struggled Will.

'No, no it must say 'ingredients' not 'ingredients',' said Bill.

'But I can't see it properly, Grandad.'

'Let me have a look,' said Susan picking up the *Original Spiked* can. She held out her hand to Bill and he gave her her glasses back. 'I see what you mean. You're obviously not meant to be able to read this are you? I don't buy products in the supermarket if I can't read the label without glasses on,' said Susan putting the can of *Original Spiked* back on the table.

Bill looked at his wife, impressed. 'Really?' he said. 'You check all the ingredients of what we eat? I never knew that.'

'Doesn't everyone?' said Susan getting back to making tea.

'No,' said Bill, 'no. I don't think anyone cares. It's just something you read about in the paper, but no one really cares.'

Having ascertained that the cans of *Spiked* weren't going to be opened Will wandered off to watch Cartoon Network in the front room. Susan was stirring a big pan of Bolognese sauce and Bill absent-mindedly set the table.

'What do you know about caffeine, Susan?'

'It's a stimulant.' She started to prepare a salad.

'Is that bad?'

'As a general rule stimulants put a strain on the heart.'

'So does exercise,' said Bill.

'And if you do too much exercise you get an enlarged heart.'

'Really?'

'Which isn't very good for you either.'

'But -'

'Yes, athletes get enlarged hearts.'

'Which -'

'Isn't good for them.'

'But has nothing to do with the contents of energy drinks.'

'No,' said Susan, 'but you did ask.'

'Did I?' Bill tried to focus on the problem at hand again. 'So caffeine is bad for the heart,' he said tentatively.

'Caffeine can put a strain on the heart and is linked with increased blood pressure and raised blood cholesterol and it can stunt a child's development.'

'You sound very knowledgeable,' Bill said surprised.

'It's just standard guidelines. If a child comes to me with behavioural issues and insomnia I always ask the parent what the child eats and especially what they drink.'

'And?'

Susan lifted up a can of *Spiked* and waved it at Bill by way of a reply.

Bill sat at the table silently staring at the cans of *Spiked*.

'Have we got a spare key to Carol and Ben's? Billiam, Billiam?'

Will dragged his feet into the kitchen.

'Have you still got that chemistry set?'

'Yea.'

'Come on then, on your bike. I said we were going to do some experimentation, didn't I.'

29

'Dinner'll be ready in half an hour,' Susan called after them as they raced up The Avenue, watched by the driver of a Mini parked two doors down from Bill and Susan's house.

Will led the way and Bill followed him humming, for reasons best known to himself, the theme tune from Heartbeat. The route to Will's house went via the village green, or cricket pitch, and Will took the same shortcut that his grandfather had taken the previous evening. The Mini followed them to the same snicket and the driver from the Mini got out and watched them impotently as they bicycled around the outfield and vanished through another snicket. The driver, being a southerner, didn't understand snickets. He, because it was a he this time, got back into the car and the Mini drove away.

Will's family's home was a smart detached new-build made of handmade bricks, sporting a double garage and distinguished from its twenty five neighbours by having a green door rather than a blue one.

Will took the house key from his grandfather. 'I'll go in first and fix the alarm,' he said.

The alarm threatened briefly while Will silenced it. He then ran upstairs to find his chemistry set while Bill contemplated, not for the first time and not without admiration, the bourgeois success of his daughter's existence. The picture on the hall table was new. It was of Annie holding yet another trophy.

'That's for the under 16s county tennis championship,' said Will as he presented Bill with a box stuffed with chemical wonders.

Bill strapped the chemistry set onto the luggage rack on his bicycle, Will re-set the alarm and they raced off back to Grandma only five minutes or so behind schedule. The Mini had not returned.

When Bill opened the can of *Extra Spiked* Will jumped around the kitchen in excited anticipation. Susan was in the front room watching *The One Show*.

'Let's taste it, Grandad, let's taste it.'

Bill was smelling it as it sizzled out of the can. He poured a little into a glass. It was bright red to match the colour on the outside of the can. Bill didn't remember any colorant on the ingredients' list.

'Grandad, Grandad,' hopped Will.

Bill considered the glass bubbling with red energy; it would be a relevant experiment to give some to Will...Susan put her head round the door.

'Do you mind if I watch that film I borrowed from Melanie?' she said.

Will was saved from the experiment but Bill packed Susan back off to the television with suspicious eagerness.

'Get your chemistry set out,' he said to Will.

Will put the chemistry set on the table and took the lid off the box. A large warning printed on a separate piece of paper drifted to the floor and hid under the table. The Chemistry set, not suitable for children under 14, had been a present from Bill. Will started to get everything out.

'Let's not use everything at once,' said Bill asserting his responsibility. 'We just need a flask and a Bunsen burner.'

'What's a Bunsen burner?'

'A burner to heat things up, like you have in science.'

'But I don't do science yet, Grandad,' said Will.

Understandably there wasn't a Bunsen burner in the chemistry set, but there was a flask.

'I suppose we could use the gas,' said Bill uncertainly.

'What are we going to do with the gas,' shouted Will waving the flask at Bill.

Bill glanced nervously at the door. 'If we reduce the liquid we might be able to find out how much of other substances apart from water it has in it,' he whispered.

Bill found the funnel from the chemistry set and Will held the flask while Bill poured the red *Spiked* into the flask. They both looked uncertainly at the flask and Will swilled the liquid round in it then pretended to drink from it. Bill eyed up the gas stove and the door with equal trepidation.

'It won't really work, will it?' he said.

'What won't work?' asked Will.

'I'll have to find another way,' said Bill, not having a clue how to reduce the liquid nor how to assess its contents even if he did. What had the memo said? Spike it, no one will know. Could they be putting more of substances such as caffeine in it than was legal? Was there a legal limit? Susan might know.

'Grandad, Grandad, we can just put some stuff in the liquid and see what happens.'

Will took a little plastic spoon from the set and shovelled a generous amount of a blue powder into the flask. The *Spiked* fizzed a bit and went brown. Bill poured some more of the *Spiked* into a test tube.

'Try something else,' he said.

Will, using the same spoon, tried a bright yellow substance. The liquid just went brown again. Bill got the can and put it in the middle of the table amongst the detritus of chemistry set.

'Here let me try,' he said and shovelled a large amount of white powder into the can.

The door opened. 'What on earth are you two doing?'

And chemistry set and *Spiked* exploded all over the kitchen.

Will was despatched upstairs with Susan in tow to repair the damage to him. Bill put the remains of the chemistry set in Susan's Christmas cake tin and despatched it off to the shed. Bits of glass were swept up into an old newspaper and put in the bin. The rest was scrubbed down with Fairy Liquid and Bill made a big noise with the hoover in an attempt to appease Susan before he escaped to his office. It was time to look more closely at the documents he had taken from *Spiked.*

There were four pages of memo. The first he had already read. The second went into marketing strategy. The third listed national and local sports that they intended to target.

The local cricket club is the most influential sports club in the town. If we finance all its activities we will have the whole local community dependent on us for not only their jobs but for their recreational activities as well. Spiked will dominate local lives and therefore dominate the local community. No local body will want to risk losing our patronage by policing our activities and the planning permission we will need for expansion into stage III will be easy to obtain.

The last page was just figures. He had hoped to find a list of ingredients, a recipe for how the drink was actually made. He put the papers back in the folder with the cricket club meeting notes. What did he do next? What did whistle-blowers do? They seemed to find all manner of people to reveal their secrets to but Bill hadn't found anyone yet who he thought would listen. So he decided to follow a much easier course of action and get more evidence first.

6

The next morning's breakfast was a sombre affair. The festive Saturday morning scrambled eggs was tainted by the lingering smell of chemistry set. And the cafetiére of fresh coffee sat on the table between them hardly touched.

Bill munched a large mouthful of toast and scrambled egg. 'Is there a legal limit on caffeine?' he asked Susan.

'What do you mean?'

'You know, like a legal limit as an ingredient.'

'You mean in something like this?' Susan pointed to the unopened can of *Original Spiked* which was still on the kitchen table and still mesmerising Will with temptation.

'Yes, in something like that,' Bill said.

'Not as far as I know,' Susan replied.

'But it is addictive,' Bill continued.

'Yes, it is addictive.'

'So why isn't there a legal limit?'

'Really, Bill, how on earth should I know?' exclaimed Susan. She waved the cafetiére in the air as if proving some point. 'Are you having any?'

Bill shook his head. 'But I suppose chocolate is addictive as well, isn't it? I mean all sorts of things are addictive. You could get addicted to knitting.'

'Or cricket.' Susan ended the conservation by getting up and pouring the rest of the coffee down the sink. 'Why don't the pair of you go for a bike ride,' she said.

It was a lovely winter morning. Fresh, sunny. There were no Minis or Audis lurking in The Avenue. They started the excursion with a lesson in mounting the bicycle. Bill pushed his bicycle along on his right side, put his left foot on the pedal, gave a big push off with his right foot, stood up on his left foot as the bicycle moved off and swung his right leg over the seat then sat down and pedalled on.

'Now you try,' he called back to Will.

After a bruised knee and an interruption caused by Susan appearing with bicycle helmets Will suddenly found himself in the bicycle saddle.

'I did it, I did it, Grandad,' he told the whole avenue.

The Saturday morning traffic was building up on the main road so they turned off as soon as they could and pedalled along the canal path in an amicable silence. The canal path led, inevitably, to the *Spiked* offices and factory. *Spiked* was sparkling in the sunshine. The car park was more-or-less empty. Bill sailed up to his landscaped tree and elegantly alighted from his bicycle. Will had too much speed and landed in a heap on the grass.

'Look, look, Grandad, it says *Spiked* on that big building.'

Bill looked and saw someone moving around inside. On a Saturday?

'Stay here and watch the bikes, there's a good lad. I won't be long,' said Bill already heading towards the big glass entrance door.

The door didn't open. Bill peered through the glass and caught sight of Miss Summers wandering from one pot of ornamental greenery to another with a watering can. She looked like a trapped butterfly. He knocked on the glass and Miss Summers spilt water all over the marble floor. Bill knocked again and she came cautiously towards the door. A couple of yards or so from the glass she recognised him. Bill waved and tried to look friendly. Miss Summers went to operate a remote button on the reception desk and the glass door opened.

'Good morning,' Bill said brightly.

'I thought it was you,' Miss Summers said. 'My Grandad did remember you. He said I was to say hello.'

Bill smiled. It was odd that both of them appeared to be working on a Saturday morning.

'They don't make you work on Saturdays do they?' asked Bill.

'No, not normally,' she relaxed a little and almost smiled. 'It's the London Fun Run', she added as if that should explain everything.

'Oh,' said Bill.

'*Spiked* is the main sponsor, or something like that.'

'Oh,' said Bill more interested.

'And there might be enquiries or something. To be honest I'm not really sure.' Miss Summers looked anxious again. 'But I get paid overtime.'

'Ah,' said Bill.

A silence ensued. It was Bill's turn to explain himself now.

'I just need a bit more information,' he said.

'For your report?'

'Yes, of course, my report. That's right. I need the ingredients of *Spiked*. Well, not just the ingredients.' He leant over the reception desk and eyed up Miss Summers' computer. 'Does that computer have access to Company data?' he asked.

'Company data?'

'I mean do you think you could find some information on it for me?'

'I don't know,' Miss Summers replied honestly.

'I need the recipe,' Bill said loudly.

Miss Summers looked blank. Bill edged his way round to her side of the desk and they both peered at her computer screen. It was, as Bill had hoped, logged on to a general company site.

'Here, go to technical data. That's right.' He guided the mouse. 'Now click on production, now product. Bingo,' he shouted again. 'That was easy,' he added to himself.

Because, there it was, the recipe, the recipe that Shaun Bean used to make *Spiked*. With quantities.

'Can you print that out for me, love?'

'Oh no, I can't print it out,' said Miss Summers.

Bill was taken aback for a moment. He hadn't expected her to be obstructive.

'I can't print anything out,' she added.

'Ah,' said Bill.

They both looked at the recipe. Bill could hardly sit here and copy it out. Could he? He suddenly realised what he was doing. Sitting here in the enemy camp on a Saturday morning with no good reason, illegally accessing company data.

'I need it for my investigation,' he said carefully.

'Your fire report?' Miss Summers colluded.

'Yes, I need it for the forms. I don't suppose you could e-mail it to me could you?'

'Yes, that's easy,' Miss Summers said confidently and almost smiling again.

'Send it to billreeves@tiscali.co.uk,' said Bill.

No comment was passed on the private form of Bill's e-mail address. Miss Summers opened her e-mail page, attached the document and clicked 'send' before Bill got to the glass doors. They didn't open and a man had appeared from around the corner of the building. A large man. Shaun Bean. Bill turned to Miss Summers.

'Oh, yes,' she said opening the door with the remote button, 'I keep forgetting.'

Bill sprinted towards Will. 'Better get going,' he shouted and launched onto his bicycle.

Will ran behind. 'Can I practice my mounting, Grandad?'

Shaun Bean had seen them and started running towards a small red Ford.

'Not now, Billiam,' shouted Bill who was going so fast that Will had to hurl himself onto his bicycle any-which-way and pedal furiously after him.

But the red car was faster and before Bill could cut back onto the canal path Shaun Bean had pulled ahead of them and jumped out of the driver's seat in time to grab Bill's arm as he tried to race past. Will screeched to halt beside them.

'Hay, that's Danny's dad,' he said to Bill. 'Hia, Mr Bean,' he said to Shaun.

*

'Have you had a nice bike ride?' Susan asked them as they came into the kitchen brandishing helmets heroically. 'Where did you go?'

'Oh just along the canal, you know, the usual,' Bill said.

'We went to *Spiked*, Grandma,' Will elaborated, 'it's really cool. It's a huge glass building with *Spiked* written on it just like on the cans.'

Susan opened her mouth to speak then shut it again.

'Grandad went inside and spent ages talking to a woman.'

Bill opened his mouth to remonstrate.

'Then Grandad came out in a big hurry because Danny's dad was chasing him.'

Bill sidled to the door. 'I just have to check my e-mails,' he said and ran upstairs.

It took five minutes before his e-mails finally trickled into his inbox. The most recent one was from ssummers@spiked.com. There was no message, just the attachment. Bill spent another three minutes opening the attachment and a further two minutes while his printer made up its mind to print the document. In a sudden rush the one page of industrial espionage spat out of the printer and floated to the floor. Bill checked that it all seemed to be there and then deleted the e-mail from ssummers.

Now he could learn how to make *Spiked*. He couldn't see anything that looked unfamiliar from either the ingredients list on the cans or the list he'd got from Shaun Bean but now he had the actual amount of each ingredient. It was mostly water with a big chunk of carbon dioxide to make it go fizzy and then it was more-or-less just sugar. And the ingredient was just sugar, not glucose or sucrose as indicated on the can, which might be illegal but it wasn't spiking. Next on the list was caffeine. Pure caffeine. Higher on the actual recipe than on the list of ingredients. There were two measures of caffeine, one of them in brackets. Bill had a quick look down the whole recipe list and saw that a few other ingredients were also listed with two measures. The explanation at the bottom was fairly obvious; measurements in brackets referred to *Extra Spiked*.

Bill could hear the shouts of boys playing in The Avenue. He looked out of the window and saw Will charging about with three other boys following the vagaries of a football as it went hither and thither across the street.

The amount of caffeine in *Original Spiked* was 300mg per litre. The amount of caffeine in *Extra Spiked* was 600mg per litre.

Bill clicked his computer back to life and opened up the internet. He typed in *spiked.com*. The home page was blazoned with live images from *The Spiked London Fun Run*. Bill found the link to 'our products'. There were lots of enticing pictures of various cans of *Spiked*. With persistence Bill finally found product information and, after further delving, a declaration on caffeine content. A 33.33 ml can of *Original Spiked* claimed to contain 60 mg of caffeine. A 33.33 ml can of *Extra Spiked* claimed to contain 130 mg caffeine. Which simply wasn't true.

Bill closed the website and opened up his e-mail account again to look over the other unread mails. But there weren't any unread mails. Someone had hacked into his e-mail account. Someone else had been reading his e-mails.

Downstairs he heard that the boys had just charged into the kitchen led by Will.

'Grandma, can we have the *Spiked*. We'll share it, promise, promise,' pleaded Will excitedly.

'No,' Bill shouted, fiercely, angrily.

Four wide-eyed faces looked up at him as he appeared in the doorway and Susan dropped the can of *Original Spiked* into the bin.

*

'Is caffeine more addictive the more you have?' Bill asked Susan later in between slurps of tea from a large mug labelled The World's Best Grandad. The picture on the mug looked remarkably like Bill. Balding a bit, broad open face, thick greying fair hair where he wasn't balding.

'Well, you won't get addicted from drinking this,' Susan said drawing her mug of tea closer.

'If you drank say ten cups of coffee in a morning?'

'No, unless it was those little cups of strong coffee, espresso.'

'So if you spiked something?'

Susan caught the name and looked at Bill sharply.

'And added extra coffee or caffeine?'

'Would it be addictive? Yes it might make someone addicted,' Susan said carefully.

Bill said nothing.

'Is that what they're doing at this new *Sunshine Soft Drinks* factory?' she asked Bill suddenly.

Bill nodded.

'Is that what all this is about?'

Bill nodded again.

'How do you know?' She sounded accusing.

Bill looked guiltily down at the table and slurped some more of The World's Best Grandad's tea. 'I accidentally got hold of a private and confidential memo.'

'Oh Bill, I hope you gave it right back.'

Bill tried to smile and Susan got suspicious.

'Don't ask,' he stalled her.

'And this memo thing said something about caffeine content in *Spiked* I take it.'

'Not exactly.'

'So how do you know about caffeine in *Spiked*?'

Bill paused.

'I suppose that's what all that experimenting was about,' Susan sounded scathing, 'and it might have made a spectacular mess but it didn't tell you anything about caffeine content, did it?'

Bill shook his head.

'And that list of ingredients you showed me the other night just listed caffeine. Was that list from that private memo you're not supposed to have?' she said crossly.

'Oh no,' said Bill, 'that's legal. I mean that's part of the fire assessment file from work.'

'And something else obviously isn't.'

'Susan, they're spiking *Spiked* with masses of undeclared caffeine.'

'And you know this because someone told you?'

'Industrial espionage,' Bill said unhappily.

'You mean stealing,' snapped Susan.

'But Susan, Little Bill can buy this stuff and drink it.'

'And what are we supposed to do about it?'

'Stop them.'

'Oh Bill, the whole thing just sounds ridiculous.' Susan took their mugs to the sink and looked sadly at the fridge.

'Shall I get some fish and chips?' Bill said. 'Billiam, Billiam,' he called through to the front room where aliens were just landing on the television, 'do you want chips for tea?' A noise taken for consent came back in reply and Bill went in search of money and a backpack to carry them home in.

The Fish 'n Chip shop was busy. A fellow cricketer was just loading up with five cod and chips.

'This'll keep us going 'til the AGM meeting thing,' he said as he walked out of the door past Bill.

'Meeting, what meeting?' Bill called after him

'You know, the extra-ordinary meeting about the new clubhouse.'

Had a date already been fixed? Bill hadn't heard anything since Thursday's meeting. Had he not been informed or was the hacker deleting his e-mails?

'What do you want, love?' The Fish 'n Chip woman raised her voice above the noise of frying chips.

'Three haddock and chips and three portions of mushy peas, please.' Bill turned from the counter just as Shaun Bean walked into the shop. Bill made a vague greeting in his direction and Shaun Bean said nothing. The Fish 'n Chip woman was trying to give him his change. He dropped a pound coin which spun into a far corner of the tiled floor. Then when he finally managed to gather his wits and everything else together he had to squeeze past Shaun Bean who was deliberately blocking the door.

Halfway home a red Ford Fiesta pulled alongside Bill, driving close and pushing him into the curb. Shaun Bean waited for Bill to recognise him before pulling away and stopping the car just a little way ahead. Bill had to pull out into the road to ride past the now parked car which immediately set off again. This time pushing Bill out into the middle of the road and the oncoming traffic.

Shaun Bean wound the window down. 'Oh sorry,' he said, 'I didn't see you there.'

He slowed down and let Bill go in front of him. Bill clicked up a gear or two and went at full speed. Shaun Bean crawled along behind him. Bill cycled up onto the pavement and felt a bit safer but Shaun Bean was still following him. All the way down The Avenue. Bill charged through the garden gate, propped the bicycle against the shed wall and crashed into the kitchen.

'Chips in the backpack,' he gasped at Susan and ran up the stairs.

The red Ford Fiesta was just vanishing out of view back towards the main road. Bill managed to catch his breath but his heart was bouncing all over the place.

7

After breakfast the next morning Bill packed Will and himself up and off onto their bicycles again. He could see Susan wanting and not wanting to protest.

'We're just going to the green,' Bill said, waving the keys to the pavilion at her.

'We're doing net practice,' Will added.

It was early and quiet out on the road. It was still dry and as long as they kept off the pitch they couldn't do any damage just practicing in the nets. Bill liked the idea of training Will up a bit ahead of the season. They took the short cut and pushed their bicycles around the edge of a sticky outfield where remnants of a night frost still pulled on the grass. They locked their bicycles together by the pavilion.

Bill opened the door to the storeroom and Will stood outside poking his finger through several rotten planks of wooden panelling. Bill emerged with bat, ball and stumps and tried not to notice the state of the pavilion. Will ran off with the stumps and had managed to knock them in by the time Bill joined him in the nets.

'Bat or bowl?' Bill asked. Will was already wielding the bat and practicing sweep shots at more risk to the stumps than the netted boundary.

Bill sent a few slow balls and Will got his eye in. He wasn't going to play for England, thought Bill resignedly.

'Grandad, look, someone else has turned up,' Will said, missing the ball which missed the off stump by a whisker. 'It looks like Danny.' Will waved. 'Hey Danny, I didn't know you played cricket,' he shouted over the green.

Bill turned round to see Danny who was walking across the green towards them with his dad, Shaun Bean.

Bill turned back to Will. 'Send us the ball, Billiam,' he said. He bowled a short length easy ball and watched Will anxiously standing on one leg desperate to show his friend that he could hit the ball with as much gusto as Jo Root. The inevitable sweep threatened the nets and miraculously willow hit leather and the ball limped its way back to Bill at the bowlers end.

Shaun Bean and Danny were watching.

'Hello, again, Bill.' said Shaun Bean.

42

Bill nodded a cautious greeting. 'Now then, Shaun. Your boy?' he asked indicating Danny.

Shaun Bean looked down proudly at his son and mumbled a gruff greeting to Will who was strutting towards them prodding the turf professionally on his way.

'Hey, Will,' said Danny.

'Hey, Danny,' said Will exchanging a high five.

'My grandson and I,' said Bill to Shaun, 'we're just out for a knock-about.' He wanted to say, 'What's your business here,' but the green wasn't private property.

'Yeah, good that us members can use the equipment,' said Shaun stretching his back and flexing a few powerful looking muscles.

Bill opened his mouth. Shaun Bean wasn't on any membership list that Bill had seen.

'Danny's joined the colts and I've joined the team.'

'You can't just join the team. You have to be picked.' Bill sounded mean.

Shaun held out a hand and Bill threw the ball to him without thinking.

'Better get practising then, hadn't I,' he said to Bill, tossing the ball expertly before giving it a vigorous polish along his groin. 'You're good, are you?' he continued turning to Will.

Will tried to look cool faced with the ominous bulk of Shaun Bean. 'I'm okay,' he replied.

'Get yourself to the other end and I'll send a few down.'

Will trotted back down into the net, his swagger gone.

'Anyone going to wicket keep?' asked Shaun as the ball was tossed into the air again and deftly caught.

'I will,' said Bill.

Shaun turned to Danny. 'You just watch, son, and learn a few tricks from the old man.'

Bill took his time walking down the net. He gave Will a thumbs-up and took up his position behind the stumps. Shaun was testing out his run.

'Okay, ready for it?' he shouted down the wicket.

Will nodded. He was standing as far back as he could. He'd hit the stumps if he made any attempt at a stroke. Shaun was charging down at the other end and released a powerfully fast ball which whistled past Will's ear. Bill caught it quietly behind the stumps. Will turned to see what had happened.

'I wasn't ready, Grandad,' he said. 'I didn't see it coming.'

'Here, give that bat to me,' Bill said to him.

'But it's too small for you, Grandad,' Will tried to protest.

'That won't matter,' said Bill.

Will gave him a worried look and ran up the wicket to the bowler's end. 'My Grandad's going to have a go,' he said to Shaun. He joined Danny and they both watched Shaun steaming up and sending another bowl careering up the wicket.

Bill knocked it calmly into the turf and it dribbled up the wicket to Shaun who immediately turned and set off on his impressive run-up. Bill knocked it into the turf again. And so it continued for an over or so. The boys got bored and wandered off to examine a large chestnut tree on the far end of the green. Getting a bit bored himself Bill decided to send a few over Shaun's head. It was easy, too easy. He might have been fast but Shaun Bean wasn't as good as he thought he was. Bill couldn't help smiling.

After an aborted attempt at a bouncer Shaun walked up the pitch towards Bill. 'Swap?' he said with a cursory glance at the child-sized bat.

Bill took the ball and walked slowly back to the bowler's end. He didn't need much of a run-up. He waited for the all clear from Shaun and sent a slow off-spinner up the wicket, beautifully pitched. It hit Shaun's boot. LBW, thought Bill. Shaun said nothing. Another ball and Shaun blocked it again with his heavily booted leg. Bill turned and sent the ball over the wicket this time. Perfect length. It eased past Shaun's bat and knocked out middle stump. How's that, thought Bill.

'We should get some pads and proper equipment,' Shaun said crossly. He dropped the bat on the crease and walked back up the wicket towards Bill.

The boys were beating at large heaps of moulding leaves which had been raked together in the outfield.

'Time to go home,' Bill called across to Will who immediately came running over to join them.

'Who won, who won?' he shouted.

'Oh, we weren't playing to win,' said Bill, 'just practising.'

44

Will looked disappointed. He turned to Danny who was right behind him. 'See you tomorrow.'

'See you,' said Danny.

'We'll need to put the equipment away,' said Bill rather formally to Shaun, 'unless of course you've got a key.'

Shaun scowled. 'We've got to go,' he said.

Bill wasn't looking forward to Shaun Bean's revenge. But he was whistling loudly as he and Will tidied everything away.

'You sound pleased with yourselves,' Susan said as Bill and Will walked into the kitchen, both talking at once and both crashing bicycle helmets down on the kitchen table in a way which made Susan wince.

'Grandad thrashed Danny's dad at cricket,' Will announced.

'I thought you were just doing a bit of net practice,' Susan said.

'We were,' Will chatted on, 'but then Danny turned up with his dad and his dad thought he was really good but Grandad showed him.'

Bill watched Susan struggle with pride and frustration.

'And who is Danny's dad,' she asked.

'No one you'd know,' Bill said quickly, 'a new member.'

'Then it sounds hardly fair for you to show off the first time he turns up. He's obviously keen if he's practising out of season. And in front of his boy too,' Susan remonstrated.

Bill tried to think of a suitable defence when Will piped up. 'Oh no, Grandma, it was perfectly fair. Danny's dad tried to kill me, didn't he Grandad?'

'Don't be so ridiculous, William,' Susan said, now turning her disapproval to Will.

'He did though. He sent a big bouncer that nearly hit me on the head and Grandad wouldn't let me bat any more so Grandad batted instead. And you know how sometimes Grandad makes a few uneasy shots as though he's not very good then suddenly hits a big one? Well, that's what he did with Danny's dad.'

'That's quite enough,' pronounced Susan.

'I just need to check something on the computer,' said Bill, smiling, and slipped out into the hallway.

There were no unread mails on his e-mail account and nothing from East Wolds' Cricket Club. He clicked on the internet icon and the page was still on *Spiked.com* from his search the previous afternoon. The site had already been updated. The *Spiked London Fun Run* had been a success. Thousands of people had taken part and there were lots of pictures of them smiling into the camera, basking in the sunshine, glowing with health and fitness and all waving cans of *Spiked*.

Bill clicked randomly on the page and pulled up various company vision mission statements and blurb about people in key managerial positions. He clicked on another tab, news perhaps, he wasn't sure. *Spiked* was sponsoring local and national sports men and women. He already knew that. *Spiked* was sponsoring local sports clubs as well as national sporting events because *Spiked* believed in the importance of local communities. *Spiked* was just doing a deal with the renowned local East Wolds' Cricket Club and donating a massive £50,000 in the form of sponsorship to help rebuild this once famous local club. In addition *Spiked* was encouraging all its local employees and their families to join the club in a push to revive interest and boost membership. 'East Wolds' Cricket Club has never had such an opportunity,' says EWCC chairman, Robin Dowling.

Bill clicked the control-alt-delete button on his keyboard and wondered if he couldn't just put the whole dinosaur of a machine into the bin. Along with the whole World Wide Web and all its *Spiked* sites.

8

The smell of roasting meat was cheering up the whole household. Bill and Will were sitting in the kitchen getting in the way. Bill eyeing the oven hungrily and Will eyeing the clock impatiently.

'They should be here, they should be here,' Will chanted.

'Any minute now, I should think,' said Susan. 'Bill, you still haven't put the extension in the table and when you've done that the pair of you can set it.'

'Right oh, Grandma.'

Bill started fiddling with clips under the table and Will started counting out knives and forks whilst still watching the clock. The table suddenly clicked into its extended position revealing a mess of white dried up bubbles and red liquid and at that same moment they all heard a car draw up outside. Will rushed to the door and Bill eyed the mess of failed *Spiked* experiment which had seeped through to the underneath of the table. He dived for the kitchen dishcloth just as Susan exclaimed in horror and inadequately wiped up the mess seconds before his daughter stepped into the kitchen.

'Hello, hello, everybody. What's been happening here, then?' Carol announced brightly. 'We've had a fantastic weekend, haven't we dear,' she continued turning to her husband who had followed her through the door.

'Now then, Ben,' said Bill.

Susan whipped out a tablecloth and spread it out over the table in one practised and concealing sweep.

'Oh, it smells delicious in here,' said Carol giving her mother a hug. 'Has William behaved himself?'

'Oh, *he's* been no trouble,' said Susan turning a cold eye upon Bill who was busying himself with Will's abandoned table-setting project.

Will now reappeared in the kitchen hanging on to his sister and badgering her with questions. Annie kissed her grandmother. 'Hi, Gramps,' she said to Bill.

She was wearing a red headband with black writing on it and a t-shirt to match with '*Spiked*' blazoned across her chest.

'We've so much to tell you,' said Carol sitting at the table. She turned to Annie. 'Shall I tell them or do you want to?'

Annie shrugged. A pleased shrug. An almost enthusiastic shrug given her 15 years. 'I've got a sponsorship deal,' she said. She pointed to her chest. 'With these *Spiked* dudes. It's like a really cool energy drink.'

Will was almost beside himself and had so much to say that the words were choking themselves in their hurry to get out of his mouth. Bill was just staring at the logo on Annie's t-shirt. 'I don't believe it,' he said quietly.

'And,' said Carol, 'tell them the rest.' She was bursting with pride for her daughter. There had been years and years of training and driving to tennis tournaments, even cutting down on her own hours at work to help her daughter achieve the impossible.

'And I've been selected along with just fifteen other kids to go to a sports school in the States which specialises in tennis.' She glanced at her father. 'That is in the autumn after GCSEs.'

'And all sponsored by *Spiked*,' said Bill in an odd strangled voice.

Will finally blew the block on his thoughts and the words burst out. 'I know all about *Spiked*. I've been there. And Grandad knows people that work there, like he even goes there on Saturdays. And I went with him. And we did an experiment and it exploded all over the kitchen.'

'What are you talking about?' asked Annie.

'It's a local company,' said Ben calmly.

'Really?' said Annie. 'I didn't know. That's so cool.'

'And it's red and Grandma and Grandad don't let you drink it and Grandad's been -'

'Dinner's ready,' said Susan giving Bill a curious look.

Bill looked back at her gratefully and sank onto a chair.

When they'd all gone and Bill had scraped the last of the meat off the roasting tin he went back up to the control-alt-deleted computer and opened the *Spiked* web page again. He went back onto the sponsorship pages and trawled through all the pictures. It didn't take long to find her. There was Annie, thumbs up, pictured with fourteen other young tennis stars and all spiked up with enough logos to write a book. Then he found another picture with just three girls. The three prettiest. He looked at his granddaughter. People always talked about Will being a chip off the old block but Will wasn't really like his grandfather. Will was little. A bit puny. Not particularly good at sports. Just a good kid. But Annie was like Bill. She was strong, tough, broad across the shoulders and packed a forehand with the same power that he had once used to crack off fours at Headingly, earning himself his trial with Yorkshire. If they'd had sponsorship back then he could have played professional cricket.

She was also handsome in the way that he had once been handsome, with blond hair and a broad open face that gave people confidence. The same confidence that Bill had always taken for granted but that now suddenly eluded him. He had to stop procrastinating and take action. Tomorrow.

9

'You're up bright and early,' said Susan, eyeing up an empty bag of muesli.

Bill was munching through his second bowl and slurping tea busily.

'What's the rush?'

'No rush, just things to do,' said Bill, slurping and crunching. 'Is that the time? Why didn't you tell me it was that time already?'

Bill shovelled a huge spoonful of muesli into his mouth and dashed to the sink with his bowl, scattering drops of milk all over the table. The dash continued upstairs into the bathroom where toothpaste was similarly spattered all over the bathroom mirror and then into his office where papers were randomly stuffed into his briefcase. The rush clattered downstairs and paused to kiss Susan, who was making do with toast for her breakfast, then continued outside with a bit of cursing as he knocked his shin with his bicycle pedal three times on the way to the gate. He was already half way up The Avenue when Susan appeared at the gate waving his bicycle helmet.

By the time Bill got to the council offices his heart was thumping in all sorts of odd directions. The car park was empty and the only people in sight were two cleaners and the caretaker. Bill pressed his briefcase to his chest as if that would make his heart behave and slipped past the unmanned reception and up the stairs to his office.

The done in-tray ready for filing was still full. Thank goodness Lisa, who did the filing, hadn't done any filing since Friday afternoon. Bill seized the folder still labelled *Sunshine Soft Drinks* and dropped it into his current in-tray. He then collapsed onto his desk chair and said to the office in general. 'Now what?'

'What's that, Mr Reeves?'

He jumped guiltily and his heart started bubbling and complaining all over again.

'Good morning, Lisa. Aren't you a bit early this morning?'

'Not as early as you. Anyway it's not that early.'

Bill glanced at his watch. She was right, it was already five to nine. That was close, he thought.

'Anything for me?' she asked peering into his done in-tray.

'No, not really,' Bill smiled and straightened himself up.

'It's just that it looked quite full on Friday and I felt bad that I hadn't cleared it up before I clocked off.'

'No problem, no problem at all,' gleamed Bill.

'I know that you like a clean office on a Monday morning.'

They both eyed up Bill's current tray which was now overflowing. Bill vaguely pointed at it. 'Work to do,' he said importantly.

'I'll just take these few bits then,' Lisa said digging to the bottom of the done in-tray and rescuing three long forgotten forms.

'Yes thank you, Lisa.'

The more Bill eyed up the *Sunshine Soft Drinks* folder the larger it seemed to get. He took it from the current in-tray and opened it. He heard Lisa talking to someone in the corridor.

'Good morning, Mr Carstairs.'

'Morning, Lisa. Is that Bill's, Mr Reeve's filing?'

'Yes, but there isn't much.'

'Do you mind if I have a quick look?'

'Help yourself.'

Bill listened to the pause as Carstairs rustled through the old forms. He heard him make a disappointed noise.

'Anything up, Mr Carstairs?'

'Oh no, Lisa, just a job that's a bit urgent that's all. Is Bill, Mr Reeves in yet?'

'Yes he's just there in his office.'

Bill closed the *Sunshine Soft Drinks* folder, opened a desk drawer and dropped it in just as Carstairs poked his head around the door.

'Morning, Bill.'

'Morning, Fred.' Everyone was suspiciously early for a Monday morning.

'That *Spiked* fire certificate, has it already gone for filing?' Carstairs peered around the room as though Bill might be hiding it somewhere.

Bill smiled broadly. 'No, I'm still working on it.'

'Don't delay. They're very keen to get everything in order so they can trade under their new name.'

'Well, I don't know about that, it seems to me that they're trading anyway,' Bill said. There was no evidence that *Spiked* was waiting for a fire safety certificate. *Spiked* wasn't waiting for anything, throwing big money in every direction.

'They're on my back, Bill,' Carstairs continued trying to sound important.

They were harassing Bill too. 'Are you saying you want me to push it through without due diligence?' Bill said, echoing Carstairs' self-importance.

'Of course not, Bill,' Carstairs became more pally. 'But there's no problem with the application of course. It's just a matter of procedure.' Carstairs' smile matched Bill's in its sincerity. Bill followed him to the door of his office and watched Carstairs' back as he ambled towards the lift.

'But there is a problem with the application,' Bill announced loudly.

Carstairs looked behind him worriedly and came back into Bill's office, shutting the door behind him.

'What do you mean there's a problem with the application?' Poor Carstairs' mouth was hanging open.

'Just that. There's a problem.' Bill wondered how he could elaborate his position to make it sound more convincing. 'A problem with procedure,' he said.

Carstairs wondered whether this warranted a sigh of relief on his part. 'Oh, well, if it's just procedure.' He said waving a grand arm over Bill's desk as though Bill's desk was covered in procedure.

'I don't mean a problem with my procedure.' Bill stood up tall so that he was on eye level with Carstairs. The broad shoulders suddenly looked extra powerful in the small office. 'I mean there's a problem with their procedure.'

It would be mildly interesting if Carstairs fainted, thought Bill as he ushered Carstairs towards the door again.

'But you're on to it,' said Carstairs weakly from the corridor, 'I mean you're dealing with it as a matter of urgency.'

'I'm on to it all right,' said Bill and he shut the door on Carstairs and went back to his desk.

A short while later Bill was standing at the window in his office eyeing up the Audi Sportback which had smoothed its way into a guest parking slot. A man, early middle aged, presented an immaculate dark leg to the world before the rest of him emerged out of the car. He was tall and lean. It might have been the same man who visited Carstairs last Friday. Bill wasn't sure. They all looked the same apart from the car and the lipstick.

After pondering the various exigencies of escape via the fire stairs, or locking his door, Bill returned to his desk. He opened the drawer where he'd hidden the *Sunshine Soft Drinks* file and took it out. The few meagre papers soon littered his desk but offered neither comfort nor enlightenment. He put the application form for fire safety certification on top and eyed his own signature distastefully. He could just take the wretched thing up to Carstairs now. Carstairs would sign it with pathetic eagerness and the man from *Spiked* now charming or threatening his way into Carstairs' confidence could no doubt sign on behalf of the company. It would all be over. Bill would remain an eccentric but reliable member of local government. He would probably also remain as East Wolds' Cricket Club wicket keeper until the day he chose to make a graceful retirement. Annie would sail into an American sunset waving a cheque worth tens of thousands of training opportunities.

His telephone started ringing. Bill delved into another desk drawer. He found an old inkpad. Somewhere were some rubber stamps. The telephone continued to ring. Bill could picture Carstairs sweating at the other end, his clammy hand clutching the receiver. He weakened and picked up the receiver. 'Chief Fire Officer's office,' he said.

Carstairs paused. 'Bill? There's someone here from -'

'I'm on my way up.' Bill cut him off decisively and put the receiver down.

He found two rubber stamps in the drawer. One with dates, one with the council offices' address. Delving even further into office supplies of the last century he caught his finger on a packet of refill staples and as he pulled his hand out of the drawer he found a third rubber stamp. He opened up the old tin of ink and pressed the rubber stamp into it several times. He then stamped the form in red ink with the words 'approval withheld' and a second time for good measure. He felt even more self-satisfied when he got the date stamp to work and added the date, also in red. He took a copy for his own file and stuffed the *Sunshine Soft Drinks* file into his drawer again. By this time the original application for fire safety certification was looking rather battered. Bill found a pristine looking plastic folder and slipped it into that. Then bracing his shoulders he marched out of his office, along the corridor and up the stairs to Carstairs. His whistling disturbed at least two Monday morning reviews.

Before Carstairs could emerge from the protection of his large and empty desk the sleek youngish man strode across to meet Bill at the door.

'We haven't met,' the man said smoothly. 'Mark Hammond.'

'William Reeves,' Bill said accepting the man's hand. It was difficult not to feel inadequately provincial and Bill's eye contact didn't get further than the man's black leather brogues.

'Bill,' said Carstairs.

'Fred,' said Bill putting them both in their place.

Bill came further into the room and wafted the plastic folder in front of him so that Mark Hammond had to step back a couple of paces. Gaining space to stretch out his own shoulders Bill put the plastic folder on Carstairs' desk.

'I presume it's this you'll be wanting,' he said to the desk.

The red stamp saying 'approval withheld' shone through the plastic. Carstairs remained standing but Mark Hammond quickly pulled up a chair. A big comfy chair.

'Now Mr Reeves, Bill, please sit down,' he said and sat down himself. 'Let's all talk about this. Man to man,' he looked from Carstairs to Bill.

Bill sat down and felt himself shrinking again. The chair was too soft. Carstairs also sat down and hid all the nervous twitching parts of himself behind the desk.

'I'm sorry, Bill, that we seemed to get off on the wrong foot last week. I think some of my colleagues behaved inappropriately towards you with regards to a document that they had lost. They're all keen, very keen.' Mark Hammond gleamed at Bill. Keen was good.

All very nervous more like, thought Bill. He was starting to feel like a teenager all slumped and grumpy in the soft chair. Bill roused himself. 'Will I be getting that in writing,' he said.

Carstairs twitched behind the desk.

Mark Hammond sharpened around the eyes then gleamed again. 'If that's what you want.'

Bill noted the sincerity slipping and made bold to meet Mark Hammond's gaze.

'We are a company dedicated to local development. Global outlook, local input, is our motto,' Mark Hammond waved a generous hand over East Wolds. 'Good relationships with all our local partners at all levels are an essential part of good company practice for us. As you know,' here Mark Hammond embraced Carstairs with his wave, 'we are already the main employer in your area and set to become a major employer for the region. In these difficult times no one who is willing and able need be without work.'

Carstairs glanced pleadingly at Bill and Bill felt a rush of blood spread across his cheeks.

'And, as you yourself know, Bill, it doesn't stop there. We are, through sponsorship, rejuvenating local sports facilities. Without us there won't be a cricket club.' Mark Hammond raised a hand as if Bill or Carstairs had been about to interrupt him. 'We also favour sponsorship of young outstanding sports men and women. Just think, Bill, what this could have meant to you in your day.'

Bill looked at him sharply. Had this man been reading Bill's thoughts as well as his e-mails?

Mark Hammond leant forward and tapped a finger on the plastic folder. His tone changed from beaming to serious and intense. Not threatening but still expansive and business like. 'If this doesn't go through we will close our production plant here in East Wolds.'

Mark Hammond caught a flash of triumph in Bill's eyes before he lowered them back to the desk.

Carstairs broke in feebly and he in turn tapped a finger at the plastic folder. 'But this surely isn't so important. I mean it's just a formality.'

Mark Hammond replied to Carstairs but looked straight at Bill. 'Fire safety certification is not just a formality as your chief fire officer well knows. In the first instance we can't get insurance and in the second instance your chief fire officer can have us shut down pending compliance with fire regulations.'

Carstairs also looked at Bill. He'd never considered Bill as important before.

'But we won't shut down, we'll just move and take all those jobs and sponsorship opportunities to another area.' He stood up and now looked down on the two aging local government employees. 'You sort this out between you. We're covered under the old agreement with *Sunshine Soft Drinks* until the end of the month but I want this sorting by next Monday.' He held out his hand and smiled at them both to disguise the threat. 'I'll come in person again, same time next Monday morning.' Then he strode out of the door leaving Bill slumping in the too soft chair and Carstairs twitching behind his desk.

Carstairs put out a hand and pulled the plastic folder towards him. 'I don't understand,' he said.

'I do,' said Bill.

'I mean I don't understand what's wrong with the application.' Carstairs ran a chubby finger over the red rubber stamping of non-approval. 'I thought this was all done and sorted last Friday.'

'There've been developments,' Bill said trying to sound important from the depths of the ridiculous chair.

'There can't be developments,' Carstairs continued. He was getting more confident again now that he only had Bill to face across his desk. And Bill looked much smaller than usual.

'The ingredients aren't right,' Bill said evasively.

Carstairs scoffed something dismissive from his great height on the other side of the desk.

'They are explosive,' Bill announced.

'Explosive. Don't be daft. It's just a soft drink for children.'

'It's not just a soft drink and it certainly isn't for children.'

'Now, Bill, let's not get this out of proportion. My grandchildren drink this new *Sprite* thing all the time.'

'It's not *Sprite*. It's *Spiked.*'

'Now look, Bill, you're behaving out of character. You've been working too hard. Spiked indeed. Of course it's not spiked it's just...'

'It's called *Spiked*,' shouted Bill.

'Oh I see. Sorry, Bill, I thought you were getting rather fanciful there. Well well, it's called *Spiked* then is it. No wonder my granddaughter kept correcting me yesterday. I thought you meant that it was spiked in some way sort of illegally,' Carstairs almost chuckled in his expansiveness.

'It is. It is spiked and it is illegal,' Bill said quietly. He pulled himself up on the edge of the chair and looked hard at Carstairs.

Carstairs looked alarmed. 'Bill, what the dickens are you talking about? Luckily it's just between the two of us so I will ignore your last comment. Now get that form validated, or else.' The or else hung in the air between them and Carstairs picked up the plastic folder and pushed it towards Bill.

Bill stood up and snatched the paper from Carstairs. 'Are you threatening me?' he said raising his voice.

'Now Bill,' Carstairs said for the forth time, trying not to cower back behind his desk.

'Now, Fred,' said Bill happier to be standing and stretching out those wicket keeping shoulders, 'I'm not happy about the ingredients that go into this new drink, *Spiked*. Which by the way is not a soft drink but an energy drink which even the regulatory authorities deem unfit for children under 16. I'm not happy and I'm going to consult a senior colleague at county level.'

Carstairs remained sitting despite the disadvantage it suddenly gave him. 'If you insist,' he said. He didn't look at Bill but at his telephone. 'But if you persist in this inexplicable nonsense I shall have to pursue the possibility that you are unfit for duty. I can as you know suspend you from any case where there is a conflict of interest.' Carstairs was warming to his theme, gaining inspiration from the telephone. 'And in this case there are two issues which could constitute a conflict of interest.'

Bill knew in a flash what was coming.

'There is the issue of sponsorship of the cricket club of which you are a long serving member and on the committee, and even closer to home the sponsorship of your granddaughter who is now recognised as an emerging tennis talent at national level. Both these sponsorships amount to considerable sums of money.'

'Look here,' Bill was also staring at the telephone on Carstairs' desk, 'this sponsorship nonsense would be all well and good if I was suppressing evidence to illegally grant fire safety certification so that I could get the money, but I don't want the money.'

'The money is not for you,' Carstairs said quietly as if this was all the confirmation he needed to suspend Bill from the case.

Bill waved the plastic folder impotently. His heart had given a huge lurch and knocked the words from his tongue. He retreated to the door. 'As I say, I'll contact my colleague at county level.' He turned in the doorway regaining some of his composure. 'You can't say that he has a conflict of interest, can you?' With which parting shot he slipped out of the door before Carstairs could issue any more threats.

Bill paused on the other side of the door to wait for his heart to normalise. A telephone rang. Bill waited straining to listen. 'No, no it won't be a problem, Mr Hammond,' Bill heard Carstairs say. Then his heart went into overdrive as a voice behind him said, 'Are you alright, Mr Reeves?' It was Lisa innocently going about her business which was more than she would now be thinking about Bill. So he reluctantly abandoned his eavesdropping and wandered back down the stairs.

Bill paused in the open doorway to his office. He was sure that he remembered shutting it. He moved cautiously into the room. All the in-trays were empty and the light on his computer screen was on. Bill dived for the drawer containing the *Sunshine Soft Drinks* file. It was still there. It didn't make any sense. None of it made any sense apart from the desire on *Spiked's* part to find their missing documents and to cover up illegal activities.

He had an old-fashioned address pop-up file which was still sitting untouched on a small cabinet in the corner. Bill pressed the C button and went through the numbers to the County Council. Adam Smythe, Regional Fire Officer extension 412. Bill dialled the number and hoped that it was still functional after all the up-dating and computerisation. The number worked but Bill was either becoming paranoid or someone else had clicked onto the call as he dialled the number.

10

Adam Smythe readily agreed to meet Bill at the *Spiked* offices early the following morning. 'I'll give them a ring,' he'd said. Bill had attempted to tell him not to ring. If he rang it would warn *Spiked* that an additional inspection was planned. Now Bill sat at his empty desk and wondered what to do in the meantime.

'I'll spy on them,' he announced to the bugged telephone. Probably to the whole council offices. He took the *Sunshine Soft Drinks* folder from his desk drawer and stuffed it into his briefcase. He decided to leave his computer switched onto screen saver, put some forms on his desk and scattered a few pencils about. Clutching his briefcase he checked the corridor, quietly shut his office door and crept out to the fire escape. From the fire escape exit there were the usual bushes which he optimistically decided would provide enough cover for him to reach the bicycle racks unnoticed. From then on he reckoned it was a matter of speed and he sailed through the car park and out onto the road in top gear.

He now had two problems. One he was hungry, two he hadn't a clue how to spy on anyone. He couldn't be out on a spying mission and leave a trail behind him. He had to act as anonymously as possible which meant not going into the newsagents to buy anything. There was a new Morrisons out of town so he put his head down and pedalled off there. A short while later he was cruising along the canal path eating an egg sandwich and washing it down with a bottle of Buxton Spring water. He spread his shoulders and sailed along the canal path whistling and chomping.

At this point it started to rain. Cricketers go in when it rains. Bill's windproof jacket was woefully inadequate and he noticed for the first time that he'd forgotten his helmet. The rain splashed onto his baldhead and ran into his eyes and down his neck. At least it made him stop whistling and at least no one was about when he hid his bicycle behind a large willow shrub between the canal path and *Spiked*. It was an overgrown willow not manicured into blunt fingerless hands so Bill knew that he wasn't trespassing. Yet.

He sheltered under the bush with his bicycle and finished his wet sandwich. Being a wicket keeper he could squat but neither the squatting nor the bush prevented him from getting wetter. He emerged from his shelter, or hiding place, he wasn't quite sure which, and surveyed the ordered winter grounds which now surrounded *Spiked* and its car park. The rain, which formerly would have spread into cracks in the tarmac surrounding the old *Sunshine Soft Drinks,* now ran neatly away from the buildings and puddled on the canal path making new rivulets into the murky water. He couldn't see anybody about so he decided to make a full reconnaissance of the whole site.

The Minis and Audis were neatly parked in the car park. The office buildings were wet but gleaming. So gleaming that Bill couldn't see anything through the big glass doors and windows. Bill dodged through the cars and splodged wetly through the landscaped grass. In contrast the older buildings were drab and the windows were small and unused. The warehouse doors were closed and three red lorries adorned with the black *Spiked* logo were parked by a loading bay.

The rain ran into Bill's ears. He went on further and came to a back entrance. Here was another car park less neatly parked with Hondas and Fords. One looked vaguely red and familiar.

Bill carried on. Nobody. Nothing. The perimeter was no longer landscaped and the grass was heavy and brown, sagging with docks and nettles. Bill dragged his way through it, soaking his shoes, socks and trousers. Behind the old buildings the land was flattened, marked and prepared with rough foundations. *Spiked* must be expanding. It looked as though a big expansion was planned. Had *Sunshine Soft Drinks* owned this much land? Bill had thought that they'd sold off land when they started to lose money a decade or so ago. As far as Bill could remember the council had bought it with ambitious plans to initiate a green belt scheme and a development of the canal site. Nothing had come of it. Could the council have rescinded the planning restrictions and sold it back to *Sunshine Soft Drinks*?

Bill was now coming back round the old buildings and approaching the refurbished office section. At this point the boundary came right up against the office building. Bill sludged along the wall of the building glad of the bit of shelter it gave him. Certain now that there was nobody or nothing to see he peered through the rained smeared windows which looked out from one of the long marble corridors. Except the last window. This window looked in on a smart office, furnished with black wood and steel, brightly lit and full of people. Bill's face was momentarily glued to the window as he locked eyes with a man he vaguely recognised, lipsticked woman, Mark Hammond, Fred Carstairs and Robin Dowling, the cricket club chairman.

Encouraging himself with the unlikely hope that he hadn't been recognised Bill ran off in the direction of the sheltering willow bush and his bicycle. His eyes were so full of rain that he struggled to see the code on his bicycle lock, and glasses were no help either. With an attempt at patience rather than panic the lock finally clicked open and Bill was pushing off down the canal path as fast as his getaway mounting technique allowed.

Large muddy puddles were now stretching across the canal path and the muddy water splashed up onto Bill's trousers as he raced along. It was too wet to make a coherent plan but if he had any plan at all it was to return to his office and sit at his desk as though he'd never left it. Explaining small details like the state his clothes were in seemed a minor irrelevance in the circumstances.

With this inadequate idea in mind Bill pulled onto the main road and headed off back to the council offices. A red car was lurking as if curb crawling along the main road. It roared into action as Bill turned off onto the side street which led to the council offices. It was so wet that Bill neither heard the roar nor saw the red car. He sailed into the council car park and was cruising to a standstill with one foot on a pedal when he saw the red car screech to a stop by the bicycle rack. Bill didn't know if this was a Honda or a Ford or if it was being driven by Shaun Bean but he could see that it was a red car. With impressive athleticism he spun the bicycle 180°, turned his dismount into a mounting operation and headed back out onto the street.

In its eagerness the red car had got entangled in the bicycle rack which gave Bill at least a minute's head start. There was an old council estate between the council offices and the main road and Bill swung into this, fairly confident that he would lose his pursuer in the maze of swings, cul-de-sacs and snickets. Bill went down a main street and the red car zoomed up behind him. Bill went down a cul-de-sac and the car followed, ready to block off his retreat. Bill dived into a snicket and the car appeared on the other side. When the car actually followed him down one of the snickets Bill decided that the driver was someone with special local expertise even beyond his own.

Traffic was building up and Bill surmised that it must be near school leaving time. The traffic slowed down his pursuer and gave Bill a chance to lay a few false trails. First, assuming that the driver knew where he lived, he let the driver of the red car believe he was heading homewards. He then cut down the short cut to the village green and almost whistled with success as he cycled down the snicket and along the edge of the cricket pitch. Bill, however, hadn't reckoned with the rain. It was hard work, muddy and slippery. With a final great squelch he left the sodden grass and turned into the new estate where his daughter and family lived. The red car was already there, waiting for him.

Bill was soaked, he was hungry and he was tired. He cycled round and round to no avail and in desperation decided to see if Carol was home from work yet. He bicycled at full speed towards the house. There was no car there. Will was standing under the porch looking wet and despondent. There was something akin to a shout of recognition from Will but Bill was filled with a sudden fear that this could all be dangerous, that it wasn't a game just for someone's amusement. That the person in the red car might want to hurt him. And if he/she/they wanted to hurt him they might also want to hurt Will. Bill put his head down and charged past Will who stood on his doorstep waving confusedly.

Bill decided that there was nothing for it but to go home. If he made a dash for it he could get himself in and the door barred before the red car managed to assault him in any way.

He risked the village green again. It was a much shorter way and the traffic on the main road would slow the red car down so that it might not manage to cut him off. The red car however had the same thought and as Bill pulled out on to the sodden outfield of the cricket pitch so too did the red car. The mud pulled and squelched at Bill's bicycle wheels and the red car, rally style, spun and whined behind him. There was a notoriously wet part of the outfield about half way around the perimeter. Bill decided it was time for desperate measures and headed suicidally for this part of the ground. If he got stuck it would be the end. A verbal threat? A good beating? His shoulders braced, his muscles clenched, his teeth gritted and he was through to the other side of the worst of the bog.

He risked a backwards glance. The driver behind was enjoying himself. Was it Shaun Bean? There was so much rain that Bill couldn't be sure. The car skidded and growled, now almost on a level with Bill. But then it skidded too far round to the left and in making too sharp a turn back to the right a front wheel started to spin. Bill watched as he himself approached firmer ground. The front wheel of the car was digging itself into the outfield. The driver tried reversing, tried turning back the other way. Both front wheels were spinning now and digging their way into the mud churning up around them.

The last thing Bill saw was the driver opening the car door. Someone shouted and it might have been Shaun Bean. Bill didn't look back again. He raced home.

Susan must have just got in as she was sitting at the table idly opening a newspaper and sipping a steaming mug of tea. Bill stood in the doorway dripping copious amounts of mud and water all over the kitchen. He tried smiling.

Amidst tuttings and exclamations and remonstrations to 'take those wet things off' Susan put the kettle back on to boil.

'And then you'd better explain yourself,' she said severely to Bill.

Bill returned to a mug of tea wearing his pyjama bottoms and an old sweatshirt. Susan opened a packet of chocolate digestives and Bill ate four and drank half his tea by which point he couldn't avoid Susan's hard gaze any longer.

'I've got a heart condition,' he announced.

Susan's mouth formed a big question mark.

'One of those irregular things. Like Tony Blair had. Didn't he?' Uncertain of Susan's response Bill ate another biscuit and finished his tea.

'You mean arrhythmia?' She sounded sceptical.

'That's the one, arrhythmia,' Bill almost sounded happy.

'Symptoms,' Susan demanded.

'Well my heart goes all bumpy as though it's bubbling over and then stops again.'

' "My heart goes bumdidy bumdidy bumdidy bumdidy",' Susan sang badly.

'It's not funny,' Bill exclaimed.

'No, I'm sorry, it's not funny, but you should see yourself. Those old pyjama bottoms and your hair sticking up on one side like a horn and mud spattered all over your bald head,' the description ended in a burst of laughter.

'I tell you I've got a heart condition and you laugh at me.' He just stopped himself from saying, it's not fair.

Susan tried to contain herself. 'It sounds more like palpitations,' she tried to carry on more seriously, 'if it is just short bursts of discomfort that then stop.'

'Well, yes,' said Bill reluctantly. 'Isn't that serious?'

'Not if that's all it is. You could go to the doctor and she might suggest that you have a ECG to check that it isn't anything more.'

'An ECG? Is that wires and things that you are plugged into all day?'

'That's the usual test, yes.'

'I don't want all that,' said Bill.

'Then don't make such a big song and dance about it,' responded Susan.

'I'm not making a big song and dance. You're the one who's singing,' Bill said crossly.

Susan started laughing again. 'It's probably just all that *Spiked* stuff you keep drinking,' she said.

'It's not *Spiked*,' Bill shouted, 'I'm not drinking *Spiked*. Nobody should drink *Spiked*.'

Susan got up and cleared the tea mugs off the table. 'There's no need to shout at me,' she said. 'If you're not drinking *Spiked* what are you doing with it then?'

'I'm investigating it.' It sounded implausible. 'They applied for a fire safety certificate and I'm not issuing it because of pending investigations.'

'To do with caffeine?'

'Yes, no, well.'

'Which strictly speaking has nothing to do with fire regulations?'

'I'm meeting the county fire officer at the *Spiked* offices tomorrow morning,' Bill said trying to sound important in his pyjama bottoms.

'Then he can sort it out and you can stop meddling. Because that's what it sounds like to me, Bill Reeves, it sounds as though you're meddling.'

'Someone's got to meddle,' he was almost shouting again.

'And all this sponsorship thing. Isn't that a good thing? It's going to be fantastic for Annie.'

'I'm going to tell Annie not to take it up.'

'Bill! You can't do that.'

There was an uneasy pause.

'And Melanie said something about the cricket club being sponsored and getting a new pavilion. Isn't that great? Haven't you spent years trying to raise money to revitalise that old cricket club of yours?'

'Yes, no, not like this, not.'

Susan waited. 'I don't approve of these energy drinks either but what can we do about it? We can't stop it so we might as well get some good out of it.'

'I can't explain,' Bill said tiredly, 'but would you just look at the file for me?'

'Left overs for tea,' Susan said, 'I'll make potato cakes out of the left over mash.' Bill liked potato cakes. 'Oh, get the file out and let me have a look at it then,' she finally conceded.

He wasn't sure how sympathetic Susan would be about whistle-blowing so he decided to show her the *Sunshine Soft Drinks* work folder which was in his briefcase first. His briefcase was still dripping in the corner of the kitchen where he'd dumped it when he came in. He pulled out the folder which was starting to glue itself to the leather inside. It was sodden. He put it on the kitchen table and opened it up. There wasn't much left. The only visible word left anywhere was *Spiked* and a lot of red ink was splodged all over inside a plastic folder.

'Oh dear,' said Susan, 'that looked important.'

Bill didn't say anything.

'Is it council property?'

Bill still didn't say anything. Was Susan laughing at him again? She was certainly busying herself making potato cakes. Bill thought of all the things he should or could be doing. Instead he sat down at the kitchen table again and watched Susan make potato cakes. After a while a reassuringly buttery smell emanated from the frying pan. Bill got up and set the table. The *Sunshine Soft Drinks* folder had left a wet stain on Susan's clean table. At least *Sunshine Soft Drinks* didn't exist anymore so perhaps it didn't matter. Although the certificate *Spiked* had was from *Sunshine Soft Drinks*. Therefore that certificate would be in the *Sunshine Soft Drinks* folder which had now dissolved in Bill's briefcase. Which meant that that certificate no longer existed.

When Bill sat down to enjoy left overs and potato cakes he was almost rubbing his hands.

'Someone called Shaun Bean tried to kill me. Twice,' he announced gleefully.

11

A strained tea had been followed by stony rejection on Susan's part of all Bill's attempts to help with the washing-up. Bill waved a tea towel about like a truce flag.

'You can leave it to dry,' was Susan's icy reception of the truce plea. Then, accompanied by the dangerous clunk of The Worlds Best Grandad knocking against the frying pan. 'Why do you always have to go too far?'

It wasn't an easy question to answer. There was the albeit unlikely possibility that Shaun Bean was trying to kill him. There was the much more likely scenario that Shaun Bean was trying to frighten him off.

'If you can't talk sense I'd rather you didn't talk at all,' said Susan as The Worlds Best Grandma risked a similar fate to The Worlds Best Grandad at the hands of the frying pan.

'I thought I might pop over to Carol's,' said Bill.

Susan turned from the washing-up to look at him. 'You're not going anywhere dressed like that,' she said waving the washing-up brush at Bill's pyjama bottoms. 'If I don't laugh I'll have to cry,' she said turning back to clean off the surfaces.

Bill put down his truce flag and whisked upstairs to get changed. He found a posh jumper that he didn't like, but Carol had given it to him for his birthday and she would both notice that he was wearing it and approve.

Susan was watching the regional news and knitting when Bill came back downstairs. He stood in the door of the front room still hoping if not for peace then at least for a cessation of hostilities. Susan's glasses slipped down her nose as she looked at him.

'I thought you didn't like that jumper,' she said.

Bill smiled broadly.

'If you think that you're going to soften Carol up by wearing that jumper - and if you're going to stir things up about Annie then -'

'Can I take the car?'

There was a sigh and a long pause.

'Yes, you can take the car because I don't think I can face a whole evening of you in those old pyjamas if you get wet through again going out on that wretched bicycle of yours.'

Bill wondered whether the truce was secure enough to allow for a marital exchange of affection. He smiled uncertainly in the doorway until Susan turned her attention back to her knitting and two amber flood warnings on the local weather forecast.

The rain had eased off, but it was dull and dark and the few streetlights up The Avenue looked desolate. Bill adjusted the seat in Susan's Honda and fiddled with the mirrors. Curtains were drawn in most of the front rooms, including his own. Nobody was about. The little Honda ventured bravely up the street and out onto the quiet main road. Even the main street in East Wolds was quiet. The Fish 'n' Chip shop didn't open on Mondays.

As he had the car Bill thought that he might as well cruise round for a bit, anonymously as it were. He snooped around the council estate but at least half of the cars looked red and bedraggled and how would it help him if he found a particularly muddy red car anyway? He headed off for Carol's posh estate. On the corner by the snicket to the village green he parked the car and, checking that all was quiet, slipped out of the driver's seat and crept up the snicket. There was a lot of mud in the snicket. There was more mud dragged up at the edge of the outfield of the village green. There was no red car but there was a grand old mess all over the dodgy bit of sodden outfield. Bill drove on to Ben and Carol's and parked the car in the drive behind their four wheeled SUVs and rang the door bell before opening the door and attempting to wipe his muddy shoes on Carol's welcome home doormat.

'Hey, Grandad.' Will came careering down the stairs. 'Mum, it's Grandad,' he shouted at Carol who had emerged from the large family room-cum-kitchen.

'Hi, Dad,' said Carol uncertainly. Then she noticed the jumper and smiled.

'I'll take my shoes off,' said Bill sensing an advantage.

'Hey Grandad,' repeated Will, 'why was that big man chasing you?'

Bill banged his head on the hall table and the picture of Annie receiving a tennis trophy fell over.

Carol groaned. 'Really William, don't start all that nonsense again. What would Grandad be doing outside our house on a Monday afternoon at half past three? I thought you had some reading to do?'

'But you were weren't you, Grandad? And the big man in the red car chased you down the snicket and onto the cricket pitch. Was it Danny's dad?'

Bill opened his mouth.

'Was it because you thrashed Danny's dad at the nets on Sunday?'

'William!'

Will retreated up the stairs, elaborating on his story, and Bill followed his daughter into the kitchen. Real coffee was percolating on the kitchen worktop and an aubergine melanzane was baking in the oven.

'Ben not home yet?' Bill asked casually.

'He's on his way,' said Carol glancing at the kitchen clock. She poured her father a cup of coffee and added a graceful splash of thin milk. Bill didn't really want coffee. He and his heart would be up all night.

'I need to talk to you about Annie,' said Bill, 'Annie and *Spiked*. There's something not right about it. About *Spiked*,' Bill continued into the pause while Carol poured herself a glass of wine and ascertained that Bill didn't want one.

There was another pause which meant go on then explain yourself.

'I mean what do we know about this *Spiked* company,' Bill said.

'According to William you seem to know rather a lot about *Spiked*,' Carol said dryly, sipping her wine.

'I had to do an inspection and, well,' Bill was blustering already and the conversation had hardly started. He should have planned this more. It was typical of him to charge off and not spend a few days thinking about it. At least that's what Susan would say. What could he say about *Spiked*? There were clauses in his employment contract about revealing things in his line of duty. Clearly he couldn't use information gained through his office for his personal gain. He couldn't for example sell the *Spiked* recipe to another company. Or to a newspaper. Or even give it away for that matter. Did that also apply to illegal recipes? Did it apply to stolen confidential documents? And he thought again how difficult it was to become a whistle blower. He looked at his daughter's face. It was calm, controlled, tight.

'I mean are you sure that *Spiked* is all that it seems to be?'

Carol looked at him with Susan's look, except it was sharper. 'What are you trying to say, Dad?'

'We don't know anything about this company. It could all just be a,' he fought for the word, 'a fraud.'

'We're not stupid, Dad,' Carol became if anything even calmer. 'Ben's making discrete enquiries. We don't want to sign Annie up to a sports college in The States which costs a fortune, find that the sponsor can't actually foot the bill and discover we've underwritten it and are therefore liable to a mortgage worth of fees.'

Ben was a lawyer.

'And what's he found out?' asked Bill.

'It's looking good, Dad.' The calmness lifted and a light shone in Carol's eyes. 'So far it's looking really good. *Spiked* has big, solvent backers. The guys taking over have a good track record in turning companies around and people are keen to invest in them. They have plans for expansion and their launch this summer has been the most successful since, since -'

'Sliced bread,' Bill put in.

'Oh, Dad, trust you,' but Carol was smiling. 'And locally they've already got a fantastic reputation.'

'Yes, but love,' he would have to stop her before it became completely impossible, 'have you thought about what *Spiked* actually is?'

'Yes, it's an energy drink. The in thing. You drank coke and the kids today drink energy drinks.'

'I drank beer.'

'Don't be awkward, you know what I mean. And as far as I can make out energy drinks are just glorified coke.'

'They are not just glorified coke. They are dangerous,' Bill tried not to shout.

'Now, Dad, you're really overreacting. I'll get you some more coffee.'

'No!' this time Bill did shout and realised in horror that he'd absentmindedly drunk his first cup. All that caffeine. He would have to make an attempt to keep calm. 'It's the caffeine, love. There's a lot more caffeine in these energy drinks, in *Spiked*, than there was, is in coke.'

'And you know this?' Carol said.

'Yes.'

'And you think that this is a problem?'

'Yes.'

'But nobody else does? Not the government. Not the food regulatory bodies.'

'Yes, I mean no. I mean that doesn't mean that it isn't a problem. There's a case in America.'

'There's always cases in America. Ben says it's a lawyer's dream to work in The States.' The wine was sipped a little more, the oven adjusted. Carol got up and started to set the table. 'I presume you've eaten,' she said to Bill.

'What if it is a problem. What if there's too much caffeine in a drink? What if it harms someone?'

'Mum warned me that you were getting into one of your little prejudices.'

'It's bad for children. Even Mum agrees with me about that.' Bill was getting too loud again.

'It's not for children,' Carol continued getting a wine glass down from the shelf for Ben.

'Then if it's not for children who is it for? Will can just walk into a shop and buy that stuff. No one stops him. No one says, oh you can't buy that you're too young, do they?'

'William wouldn't buy it. He knows he's not allowed.'

'Yes, but other children do.'

'And what do you want me to do about it?' Carol was getting agitated herself now.

'I don't think it's right that Annie accepts sponsorship from a company that sells something that harms children.'

'So that's what this is all about, is it? Annie's big chance. Probably the only chance she'll ever get to use her talent. Nothing, nothing, I say, is going to cheat her of that. You come here with your vague talk and start moralising. It's always the same, Dad. You're always moralising. Bikes not cars. Living within our means. Working all hours so that no one's home when William comes home from school. I've heard it all before. But not this time. This time I'm not listening to your nonsense anymore. Annie's got the chance of a lifetime and she's going to take it and not you, not anyone is going to take it away from me. Her.'

Someone coughed in the doorway. 'Don't mind me,' said Annie.

Annie slid into a seat at the kitchen table and pulled at the ragged too long sleeves of a hoodie. Carol fiddled with oil and vinegar for a salad. She didn't like the children to see when she was upset. Will had escaped from his reading and hovered in the doorway.

Bill looked sadly at his family. He hadn't a clue what to do or say.

Annie finally broke the silence. Annie like Bill, brave, solid, handsome. It had taken Bill a week to teach Will to ride a bicycle, but Annie sat on a bike and sailed down The Avenue without realising that it was meant to be difficult. She caught a ball one handed before she could walk. She had all Bill's talents, looks and more.

'I'm with you, Gramps,' she said tugging at the tatty sleeves. 'But.' And the but was Bill's eyes looking straight at Bill.

Bill waited. Carol kept out of it now but Bill could feel that she was holding her breath somewhere behind him near the sink.

'I'm not giving up my tennis.'

'I'm not talking about giving up tennis, love,' Bill said.

'Not taking sponsorship would be the same as giving up.'

Bill opened his mouth to protest and a tatty sleeved arm was raised to stop him.

'The others at my level will go to America and get better. Those lucky few of us with sponsorship will become the elite of British junior tennis. In a year I'll be playing at Wimbledon, Gramps, the junior championships.'

'But.'

'I'm with you, Gramps, but I agree with Mum. I'm not giving up this chance for anything or anyone.'

'There are other ways, Annie,' Bill sounded unconvincing.

'Such as?'

'Your coach is good,' Bill said already getting up to go home.

'Yes, but not good enough. I'm going to be the best.'

But it'll be at a price, Bill said, thought, wanted to say. He wasn't very good at arguing with the women in his life, not very good at standing up to them. Give him a fast bowler any day. Was it worth falling out with his granddaughter over a bunch of crooks making money immorally and possibly illegally?

Annie had had enough too. She turned to her mother. 'I have a condition training session tomorrow. I can get the bus there but can someone collect me afterwards?'

Carol went to check the calendar and Bill felt himself forgotten in the trivia of family arrangements with which Annie had deftly dampened the discussion. Bill ruffled Will's hair on the way out and Will followed him to the door, mute with sympathy. Bill put on his muddy shoes and Will leant down and hissed dramatically into his ear. 'I'll never, ever drink *Spiked*, Grandad,' he whispered.

The door opened, knocking Bill into the hall table again. Will picked up the picture of Annie and Ben walked in.

'It's you in the Honda, is it?' he said jovially to Bill while receiving a hug from his son. 'It's not often you're not on your bike.'

'No well, it got a bit wet earlier,' said Bill escaping out of the door. He heard Ben's voice as he shut the door. 'Hello, darling, your father looks a bit -' and Bill didn't hear any more. He'd done enough eaves-dropping during the past few days. He fell into the Honda and drove home.

Susan was still knitting. 'Carol's been on the phone,' she said when Bill walked in. 'If I'd thought you'd listen I could have told you not to go in and start telling them what to do. Like you usually do.'

Bill felt that Susan was being a bit harsh. 'I still think I'm right,' he said defensively, 'just because no one agrees with me doesn't mean I'm not right.'

'It's not about not being right,' continued Susan, still knitting, 'it's the way of being right.'

'That sounds like splitting hairs,' said Bill unable to keep a bitterness out of his voice. 'If something's right then it's right.'

'Sometimes wrong things have right things about them.' Susan knitted into her purple neck role.

'And I suppose all that is too sophisticated for me,' the bitterness continued.

'Now, don't start feeling sorry for yourself. You started all this. Yes, I'm sure you have a point. I'm sure that drinks like *Spiked* are not good, bad even. But did you listen, Bill, or did you just charge in with your own objective, as usual?' The 'as usual' was almost inaudible and managed to muffle itself up into the neck role.

There was a folder of documents in Bill's box room office which could mean the end of *Spiked* and the end of Annie's dreams. And so far, despite his best efforts, he had kept the whistle-blowing to himself. Perhaps he should just keep it that way.

12

Adam Smythe was already waiting for him when Bill arrived at *Spiked* the following morning. Bill didn't know him well and looked around hoping to see a friendly face but Miss Summers was not on reception. A young man in a tight suit was sitting behind the glossy wooden counter.

Adam Smythe looked comfortable. He was that sort of man. He waved a buff folder in Bill's face and suggested that they got on with it. Bill looked at the buff folder conjuring up all the possible documents it might contain.

'Picked up the file from Carstairs on my way in,' waved Adam Smythe.

'But,' said Bill. He sat down as Adam Smythe stood up. Bill held out his hand towards the buff folder being waved above him. 'Do you mind?' said Bill and took the folder from Adam Smythe.

Adam Smythe sat down again, reluctantly. Bill opened the folder and went through the documents. There were copies of various documents from the original file. There was a blank application form for certification replacing the one which Bill had stamped with approval withheld; the one which was now part of a papier-mâché sculpture on Bill's desk at home. Although Carstairs didn't know that. As far as Carstairs knew Bill's original file still existed.

'The previous certificate held by *Sunshine Soft Drinks* is missing,' Bill said mildly.

'Really?' A slight frown furrowed through Adam Smythe's comfort. He opened his palms expansively. 'That hardly matters now, does it? As a new certificate will have to be issued anyway.'

'However,' persisted Bill carefully putting the documents back together again, 'my understanding from Mark Hammond is that *Spiked* is currently operational under the authority of that original certificate.'

Adam Smythe retook possession of the buff folder. 'Well, now,' he said.

'And if that certificate is missing from the file then *Spiked* is operating without fire safety approval which in short means that it is operating illegally and should be shut down. Now. No valid insurance without that. No health and safety validity without that.' Bill just stopped himself from rubbing his hands together.

Adam Smythe stood up. 'Now, Bill.'

Bill stood up. 'Adam.'

'All credit to you, Bill, for declaring a conflict of interest. I'm sure it wouldn't have influenced your decision in the current assessment but in the unlikely event of something happening it is wise to be on the safe side.'

Adam Smythe was sturdy, confident but slow. Like a good policeman, but like a good civil servant he was now missing the point.

'Adam, what about the missing certificate? What about the fact that *Spiked* could be operating illegally without one?'

The words operating illegally rebounded off the glass and marble just as lipsticked woman appeared.

'Mr Smythe and Mr Reeves, sorry to keep you waiting.' The glossy lips vanished entirely as she greeted Bill. 'No problems I hope,' the glossy lips appeared again as she smiled at Adam Smythe.

'No, no problems at all,' said the comfortable Mr Smythe. 'I'm sorry for the inconvenience caused at our end. Mr Reeves, you understand, has declared a conflict of interest with regards to the issuing of your fire safety certificate.'

'I'm sure that wasn't necessary,' the gloss vanished again as lipsticked woman sucked in her cheeks at Bill, 'but we appreciate that things are done properly.'

'We always do things by the book in the fire department. No other way you understand. Isn't that right, Bill?' The folder waved expansively.

Bill opened his mouth in a futile gesture.

'Lead on, dear lady,' boomed the comfortable, dependable Adam Smythe. Lipsticked woman led them at a brisk pace down the marble corridor.

Bill scurried after them. Had Adam Smythe really said, dear lady? Forms were produced and lots of ticking and pleasant murmurings were exchanged as Adam Smythe applauded the new systems that *Spiked* had put in place. Lipsticked woman led them onwards at breakneck speed until she got so far ahead of herself that Adam and Bill got stuck on the wrong side of a door that needed a security code to go through. Adam used the pause to fill in a few sections of the form more expansively. Bill wondered idly if he could crack the security code and lipsticked woman reappeared. She was so annoyed that she padded in the wrong code three times and the door started bleeping. Bill sidled up behind her.

'774533,' he said. He put out a big wicket keeping finger to punch in the numbers but lipsticked woman came to her senses just in time and shooed him out of the way. Her alarm had creased the gloss all along her lower lip.

'Just trying to help,' said Bill, smiling.

Adam Smythe finished being expansive on the form and lipsticked woman furtively punched in Bill's code on the keypad by the bleeping door. When it worked she had no lips left at all. Bill walked blithely through and lipsticked woman waved Adam Smythe in front of her crossly as he was trying to be gentlemanly and hold the door open for her.

They had now reached the production rooms. Before lipsticked woman could hand them over to Shaun Bean Bill made some deferential noise and asked innocently if they would need to give another fire safety talk.

'Surely that can't be necessary.'

'It is only recommended policy,' expanded Adam Smythe.

'Not in East Wolds,' said Bill.

'But you've already given the wretched talk,' said lipsticked woman.

Bill and Adam turned to look at her.

'There surely can't be a conflict of interest in the giving of a talk.' Her exasperation crackled between them and Adam Smythe raised his big arm.

Bill said nothing because Shaun Bean was glaring at them on the other side of the door where they had all gathered. He looked Bill up and down with one scornful glance.

'Bloody hell,' he said. He took in the large presence of Adam Smythe. 'How many fire officers does it take to count fire extinguishers? One for you and one for me,' and he started to laugh, his joke spiced by Adam Smythe's obvious discomfort.

'And we'll need the recipe for what's actually going in those big vat things,' said Bill.

'Will we?' asked Adam Smythe, who after enjoying the ministrations of lipsticked woman was now quaking a little under the unaccommodating gaze of Shaun Bean.

'A list of ingredients, again.' Shaun Bean waved a bit of paper in the direction of Adam Smythe and his buff folder.

'Yes, I'm sure that's just the ticket,' said Adam trying to smile in the face of Shaun Bean's sneer which stretched from ear to ear.

'No, not a list of ingredients. We need the recipe. We need to know what is actually going into those vats,' said Bill.

Shaun Bean's sneer froze and his eyes flicked past Bill's and fixed on the wall behind him.

'Will we?' Adam Smythe repeated. He didn't like the thought that he was losing his authority. 'Bill, a word please,' he said.

Bill planted his feet firmly on the concrete floor of the production room ready to receive Shaun Bean's next bouncer. He'd already knocked Adam Smythe's weak off spin back up the pitch.

'We need the recipe, Adam,' he said firmly.

'Now look here,' said Shaun Bean.

'Bill, I really don't think this is helping,' said Adam Smythe.

'Are you into thieving trade secrets, or what?' said Shaun Bean.

Bill caught that particular bouncer awkwardly right in the stomach. 'Just doing my job,' he said defensively.

'Oh aye, your job or his job?' Shaun Bean jerked his head in the direction of Adam Smythe. The gesture wasn't very complimentary.

'Our job,' Bill said hastily. He needed Adam Smythe on side.

'But Bill,' Adam Smythe said puzzled. It had all been going so smoothly.

'We have to analyse the explosive risk of the contents of that vat,' Bill said grandly.

Adam Smythe looked alarmed.

'The what?' said Shaun Bean, 'explosive bloody risk? What a load of -'

'If you want that fire certificate I want that recipe,' said Bill quietly.

'Are you spying on us?' Shaun Bean came towards them menacingly. Adam moved behind Bill but there was more of Adam Smythe than there was of Bill. Bill stretched his shoulders out which made them both feel better.

'I'm not spying, don't be ridiculous, I'm just doing my job. It's standard procedure to check the explosive risk of large amounts of chemicals mixed together and then heated up,' Bill said wondering who he was bluffing.

'We're making a bloody soft drink not a Molotov Cocktail,' said Shaun Bean.

Bill took a deep breath and a big risk. Chemistry had never been his strongest asset when it came to fire fighting. 'In particular we need to check the combustible effects of mixing citric acid, sodium citrate, sodium chloride and hydrochloride.' He took a deep breath. 'With Caffeine,' he added. It sounded pretty impressive to Bill.

Shaun Bean went sulky. Bill hoped that this was a good sign. Adam Smythe looked embarrassed and hurt. This was his case now, not Bill's. It was a big glossy case with posh people from the south and expensive chairs to sit in while one filled out the forms.

'I'll need to consult someone,' Shaun Bean said.

Bill spread his hands out to show how reasonable he was being. 'We don't need to make a fuss,' he said, 'we could just have a copy of the recipe that you use. You are in charge of making up the vats, aren't you?'

Shaun Bean glared at Bill. Bill had wrong footed him and he knew that Bill knew. Bill tried smiling again. 'I'll have to ask someone,' Shaun Bean repeated and left them to go into his office.

Bill had wanted Shaun Bean's recipe. Now he was going to get an official version. He wished he was better at this espionage business. It might have been easier if he'd been blond and thirty and female.

Adam Smythe prodded him in the back. 'Can we get on with this?' he said. He looked at his watch and told Bill that he was in danger of missing an important meeting.

'I'm sorry. I could finish off here if you like,' Bill said quickly. His smile so broad that his lips were sticking to his gums.

'You're off the case because of a conflict of interest,' said Adam Smythe petulantly.

'Oh yes, that,' sighed Bill. 'Shall we get on with it then? You check the fire doors and I'll count the fire extinguishers.' Again, he thought.

'Maybe I should just take over and finish the job on my own,' Adam Smythe said.

'No, I'll stick around,' said Bill. He had nothing else to do. His desk had been cleared. And he wanted that recipe for what it would now be worth. Was Shaun Bean's discomfort evidence? Evidence of forged recipes, spiked recipes?

Shaun Bean was taking a long time. Adam Smythe filled in his forms and they moved onto the packing sheds.

'It all seems very orderly, I must say,' said Adam Smythe.

It was very orderly. No spillages and packages of chemicals or ingredients making a mess in the production room. No thermometers broken. Everything connected with heat had a thermostat and an emergency cut out. The packing room had boxes and pallets neatly stacked when not in use. There were no heaps of broken bits of cardboard or wood piled into forgotten corners gathering dust like fires waiting to happen. Bill had never seen such a neat factory floor and neither had Adam Smythe. Adam started to beam again. His boxes were all ticked and the result was looking very satisfactory. Bill was wondering whether to turn awkward again when Shaun Bean appeared. Shaun nodded at them dismissively, but Bill noticed that he could no longer look him in the eye.

'They'll have a copy of the recipe waiting at the front desk for you,' he said. 'You can collect it on the way out.'

'We're done then,' expanded Adam Smythe. He held out his hand towards Shaun Bean who looked as though he'd rather bite it than shake it. Bill tucked his hands in his pockets and let Adam lead them back to the front offices. The thin man in the tight suit exchanged forms and copies with Adam and then flourished a sheet of A4 paper in front of them.

'Here's the recipe you insisted on having. You understand that this recipe is to be treated in the strictest confidence,' he said busily.

Bill's arm shot out reaching for the catch before it carried to Adam Smythe at second slip.

'Thank you,' he said and thrust the recipe into his briefcase.

Adam Smythe made as if to contest the decision but was interrupted by the appearance of the smoothly familiar Mark Hammond. The man on reception almost genuflected.

'Good to see you again,' gushed Mark Hammond.

Bill tried to deflect the bonhomie with an equal amount of his own until he realised that Mark Hammond's hand was outstretched towards Adam Smythe not him.

Bloody hell, thought Bill. The vaguely familiar figure in the glass room seen through a myriad of raindrops yesterday. It had been Adam Smythe.

While Bill watched Adam Smythe and Mark Hammond sign forms he found himself leaning against the reception desk. The thin man in the tight suit hovered and worried about the broad crumpled shoulders that occupied his ergonomically designed space. If he'd had a dust pan and brush large enough he would have brushed Bill under the counter.

Bill got bored of the self-congratulatory signing of forms going on and turned to the thin man.

'Just filling in today are you?' he asked.

The thin man looked alarmed. 'No, I assure you -'

'I'd have thought you'd normally be in one of those new posh offices,' Bill said, although his attempt at flattery sounded more like criticism.

'I've just started,' the man said defensively.

'Oh? Have they promoted that Miss Summers, then?'

'Miss Summers?' The thin man had obviously never heard of a Miss Summers.

'She was a good lass. Used her initiative,' Bill said. He pulled himself off the counter, goading the lackey was bad manners. The effusions front of desk continued.

'We'll be all signed and sealed by Monday,' Adam Smythe was saying. 'I must say it's been a pleasure to inspect the premises, Mark, Mr Hammond.' Adam noticed that Bill had now joined them. 'Good tight ship isn't it, Bill,' he continued sending large waves of comfort washing over them all.

'You'll be issuing the fire safety certificate on Monday then will you?' Bill asked.

'Yes indeed,' glowed Adam Smythe.

'And in the meantime?' Bill continued innocently.

'In the meantime?' Mark Hammond butted in, his voice sharp.

'In the meantime, Mr Hammond, where's your current certificate?'

'It's in the file,' Mark Hammond continued, his voice getting thin and his nose going razor sharp.

'It wasn't in the file this morning was it, Adam? I, we checked.'

'I, well, did we?' said the helpless Adam Smythe.

'We did. No certificate no operation. Without a valid certificate, Mr Hammond, I'm afraid we'll have to ask for a temporary closure of your enterprise. You can't be too careful with fire risk, can you, Adam. And the insurance companies won't like it, not to mention the unions if you're operating without all the proper licences in place.' Bill smiled, nicely, professionally.

Mark Hammond swung round and put himself in front of Bill and facing Adam Smythe. 'I thought that file -'

Adam looked at him blankly.

That file, Bill thought smugly, is papier-mâché.

Mark Hammond was pointing a finger. 'You fix it, Smythe, you fix it pretty damn quick.' Then he swung round just in time to catch the smug expression on Bill's face. 'And you keep off this case, or else.' His anger formed a tick under his right eye.

'Are you threatening me, Mr Hammond?' Bill asked quietly.

The anger was sucked in and the teeth ungritted. 'Whatever would give you that impression, Mr Reeves,' he said. He stepped back and opened his arms out towards both fire officers. 'I appreciate you stepping in Mr Smythe at the last minute. It can't have been easy. It would have been better all round if Mr Reeves had declared his conflict of interest right at the start. As it is we're all having to chase our tails and push things through at the last minute. That is not my problem, that is yours. If Mr Reeves had given up the case immediately a fire safety certificate would have already been issued, wouldn't it Mr Smythe?'

Mr Smythe nodded.

'Therefore, in the circumstances, it seems unreasonable to penalise us for your failure to do your job.'

Mr Smythe nodded again. Bill waited.

'If you push this farce any further and demand a closure we'll have every lawyer in London on your backs and a claim for loss of earnings mounting to millions.'

'So you are threatening us,' Bill said softly.

Adam Smythe was backing towards the sliding glass doors, his eyes pleading with Bill. Bill stood in the centre of the marble floor for a good half minute, his broad shoulders expanding in a stubborn line. But Mark Hammond had prodded another finger towards the unhappy bulk of Adam Smythe and walked away to some smooth executive office. The thin man with the tight suit genuflected again and stood on one leg wondering how he could sweep Bill out into the rain. Because it was raining again and it was cold.

The glass doors opened and a few dead leaves blew across the marble floor. Bill followed Adam Smythe out into the car park.

'I suppose you're just going to approve that form, aren't you?' Bill said, jabbing his own finger at Adam Smythe. The big man was hunched miserably against the cold.

'I'm getting wet,' he said. He clicked the locks open on his car and while he put the buff folder on the back seat Bill nipped round and got in on the passenger side. Adam lowered himself into the driver's seat. When seated his tummy folded over like a thick sauce. 'Do you want a lift back to the office?' he asked Bill.

'No, I've got my bike.'

'I can give you a lift anyway. You won't want to be riding your bike in this weather.'

'I don't want a lift,' Bill tried to tone his voice down. Perhaps he could emulate Mark Hammond's icy coolness. 'Adam, there are issues with this application and you know it.'

Adam looked at him in genuine surprise.

'Look, I don't want to get personal but you, Fred Carstairs and God knows who else, you're all hobnobbing with these fellows here and it's not right.'

'Hobnobbing?' Adam Smythe still sounded innocent or ignorant, either way Bill was finding it hard not to start shouting.

'You were all here, yesterday, I saw you. In that posh meeting room.'

'Oh,' the alarm rose and faded across Adam's dimpled cheeks, 'that. That was a meeting to get this application moving again. You're the one who's got money on the table here, Bill, not me, or Fred for that matter. I understand that your granddaughter stands to gain by a large amount through her sponsorship with *Spiked*. And we're talking tens of thousands here, Bill, not peanuts.'

Bill opened his mouth to speak then gave up. He opened the car door instead. The wind sped up his trouser leg and a rivulet of rainwater ran off the door onto his knee. 'I'm not giving up,' he said, but the wind sent his defiance swirling up into the skies and Adam Smythe started backing out of the parking space before Bill had even slammed the car door closed.

13

Bill put his head down against the rain and battled along the canal path. The mud was spattering up on his trousers again and it was hard not to feel beaten by the wind. The bitter north-easterly and the winds of change.

He headed off towards the council offices then changed his mind and pedalled in a vaguely homewards direction via the village green. The cricket pitch was a sorry site in the winter gale and Bill sploshed on his bicycle to the cricket pavilion which was an even sorrier sight. Sorry sights all round; water logged pitch, rotten timber boarding with peeling green paint, muddy bicycle, and bedraggled soaked over-aged wicket keeper. The over-aged wicket keeper dragged his bicycle into the shelter of the pavilion veranda and sat down on the bench which leant against the pavilion wall. The bench was propped up at one end by an old cricket bat and wobbled dramatically when Bill sat down on it.

Bill fished his mobile out of a wet jacket pocket and clicked on the message icon.

'Hi,' he typed in, found Carol's number and pressed the send option.

'Hi,' the answer jingled back.

'Are you on lunch break?'

'Noo. It's past two. Writing up reports for discharge papers.' Carol worked as a physiotherapist at a local hospital. 'What do you want?'

'Sorry about yesterday.' Bill waited for a moment then continued. 'I didn't mean to upset anyone.'

'But?' Carol's answer jingled back aggressively.

'You know these energy drinks can be v. harmful.'

No response.

'I think *Spiked* is,' Bill paused with his finger poised over the keypad on the mobile. Bad? Wrong? Immoral? Illegal? He typed in 'bad' and pressed the send option.

'You think. Maybe I don't.'

'I think,' typed out Bill then deleted the letters. 'What if it is harmful?' He deleted harmful, 'dangerous?' was that overdoing it? He deleted dangerous and wrote, 'bad for children?' and pressed the send option.

'I'm busy.'

Pause, this time in Bill's texting.

'Annie isn't drinking *Spiked*. She's getting lots of money from them,' was Carol's next message.

'But other kids are.'

'Not mine.'

Another pause at Bill's end.

'That's not our problem. If we don't take the sponsor money someone else will. Kids will drink *Spiked* whatever we do.'

Carol was right of course. Although in this particular case Bill could do something about it. He looked out at the sodden cricket ground and saw a sunny pitch, Headingley, about forty years ago. Bill's trial with Yorkshire. They'd asked him back for a second trial. One of a few of the older players already in their twenties to get a chance like that. But Susan was pregnant with Carol and they'd just bought their semi in The Avenue and Bill already had a job as a fireman. If it hadn't been for the money he'd have gone for that second trial.

He fiddled with his mobile again. 'Is Annie training tonight?' he typed and sent to Carol again.

'Yes. Condition training at York.'

'At the Uni?'

'Yes.'

'Can I collect her?'

Then Bill's mobile rang.

'Dad, look I don't know why you're not working, but this had better be quick,' said Carol.

'I'll collect Annie from training tonight,' Bill said.

'Dad, you are not to say anything to Annie. Right? Do you understand?'

'Of course I won't say anything to her. I just want to collect her.'

'Are you sure that Mum doesn't need the car tonight? When does she do her knitting thing?'

'I don't think that's tonight.'

Bill could feel Carol juggling all the pros and cons.

'Okay, it would be quite helpful actually because I have to pick William up from some kid's party. Dad, I really have to go but ring when Mum gets home so I'm sure that you can do it. It will save Ben a long drive around from Leeds.' She hung up.

Bill put the mobile back in his soggy pocket and shivered. He was out of the wind on the rickety bench but it was still cold and wet. He pushed his bicycle back into the rain and cycled home.

Susan was still at work. Bill put the kettle on and optimistically got two mugs down from the shelf but she still hadn't appeared by the time the kettle had boiled so he made his own mug of tea and dripped his way up the stairs. He rescued the *Spiked* recipe which was sticking to the inside of his briefcase and while his computer got itself going he changed his trousers.

He had an e-mail from the cricket club which was a reminder about the extraordinary general meeting on Saturday. He'd never had the original mail, in fact he hadn't had any mails for a few days, but now they were coming through again. Had *Spiked* given up hacking into his mail account? He was now out of play, no longer a threat, clean bowled and dropped from the team. So much for his big plans of standing up to the evils of unscrupulous business, guiding his community and family into the truth and light of fair play. They'd all just over-ruled and sidestepped him. The has-been who should retire.

He slurped his tea and a droplet escaped from his mouth and dribbled down his chin. He wiped it away and typed in 'retirement schemes' on the *Google* search bar.

'I think I might put my name down for an allotment,' Bill announced as Susan came through the door. He beat her to the kettle and waved a mug with a teabag in it at her.

'Why aren't you at work?' Susan said.

'Oh,' Bill wafted a hand evasively and bent over the kettle. 'You're later than usual aren't you?' he said to Susan.

'Carol rang.'

'Oh?'

'Yes, oh. She didn't think that you were at work and it sounded as though a storm was raging in the background.'

'Oh.'

'And she said you sounded very odd.'

The kettle boiled and Bill poured water onto the teabag in The World's Best Grandma mug and topped up The World's best Grandad.

'So why this sudden enthusiasm to collect Annie from training?'

Bill shrugged. 'I used to go quite regularly.'

He slumped onto a chair at the kitchen table. Susan rescued her mug which Bill had abandoned by the kettle and fished the teabag out. She bustled about finding milk and pulled the biscuit tin down from the shelf. Bill absentmindedly took the last chocolate digestive and Susan eyed up a ginger nut with less enthusiasm.

'So it is alright if I use the car tonight? You don't have your knitting thing?' Bill asked.

'My knitting thing as you so glamorously call it is on Thursdays as you must surely know by now.' A piece of ginger nut fell into Susan's tea. She got up crossly and poured the whole lot into the sink.

'So I can take the car then? This evening, to collect Annie?'

'Yes, for God's sake.'

'Is something the matter, love?' Bill looked up from the crumbs of his biscuit and took a big slurp of tea. Susan was crashing about in the vegetable cupboard. 'Did someone bother you at work?' continued Bill.

'No, it's not work. No one's bothering me. It's you, Bill, that's bothering me.'

'Oh, I, but - I came home early so's we could just sit down and have a quiet cup of tea together, just the two of us. It's been a busy weekend what with one thing and another.'

'Yes, you've had a busy weekend. God knows what you've been doing, charging around on that wretched bike of yours, getting William into trouble and then upsetting Carol. And if you think that you're going to collect Annie just for some stupid reason of your own then you can think again.'

'I just wanted to help out,' Bill said.

'When was the last time that you just wanted to help out?'

'I always help, love. I don't think that's fair, I mean I do the washing up.'

'So because you occasionally do the washing up you think that that counts for always helping?'

'Come on, love, I don't want to argue.'

'Maybe I do.'

'I can help now if you like. I could make the tea. I don't have to leave to collect Annie until six thirty-ish.'

'Just leave me in peace can't you. Go and fiddle on that computer of yours. As long as you don't come menacing me about whatever it is that you think you've found out this time.'

Bill hovered by the door for a bit but as Susan was ignoring him he obediently headed up the stairs to his little office. She got like this sometimes, all upset about nothing much then by teatime she'd be back to normal. Bill looked sorrowfully at the blank screen then switched the computer back on. It whirred into life and after another few minutes Bill checked his e-mails again. He wasn't really expecting anything as he'd already gone through them less than an hour ago but a little icon popped up saying you have new mail. He didn't recognise the address but it could have been something to do with the cricket club so he opened it. 'Keep your nose out Bill or else,' it said.

'I thought they'd done with me,' he said out loud to the computer. He was sad rather than worried about the clumsy threat. Bill was sure that *Spiked* had so successfully got everyone else into their pockets that he had become a minor, irrelevant nuisance.

There was the small detail of the highly confidential memo and the *Spiked* recipe. Bill put the recipe he'd snaffled that morning onto his key board. It was almost dry. The amounts were of course all legal now. He looked closely at the font in case the size was out of sync with the rest of the figures. It wasn't. In the old days there might have been tell-tale Tipex brush strokes on a zeroxed document but not anymore. A little handy knowledge of computers and one could probably forge anything.

Bill's computer had gone onto screen saver and Bill watched dotted patterns come and go across the darkened screen. Miss Summers had accessed the actual ingredients being put into Shaun Bean's vats. Could Miss Summers have any more innocent little forays into *Spiked* files? Perhaps Bill should look up her grandfather, have a chat over a pint at The Cricketers Arms. Miss Summers could be his mole.

There was nothing better than a bit of ill-timed bullying to revive the spirits like a spell of ill-timed fast bowling; you got your bat to it and the fours rolled up on the scoreboard.

'You'd better come and have some tea if you're eating before you collect Annie.' It was Susan calling up from the kitchen.

Bill bounced down the stairs. Susan looked at him sourly and plonked a plate of pasta down at his place at the table.

'Have you found an allotment then?' she asked.

'A what?'

'You said you were going to try and get an allotment.'

'Did I?'

'Oh, it's worse than dealing with a brick wall, I don't know why I bother.' Susan attacked her pasta.

'Why would I want an allotment?'

'To keep you out of trouble,' Susan said darkly, still not looking at Bill.

'Oh, I'm not in any trouble,' said Bill, but he was smiling.

14

It was a new gym at the university especially designed for condition training. Bill slid in through the swing doors and stood against the wall. A man, presumably the trainer, noticed him and came over at once. He walked on his toes and a tattoo snaked its way across a bare shoulder.

'Can I help you,' he said.

Bill tried to look as un-perverted as possible given that he was male, sixty something and wearing an anorak. 'Just collecting one of the kids,' he said, but as he raised an arm to take in all the kids he realised that there weren't any. Just Annie.

A muscle twitched on the trainer's forearm.

'I mean I've just come to collect my granddaughter, Annie Whitby Jones.'

Both men looked over to where Annie was doing controlled weight training. Luckily she reached the end of a count and looked up. She looked pleased, surprised. 'Hi Gramps.' Then she frowned. What was he doing here? The question was so visible as it played across her features that Bill thought the trainer must have picked it up too.

Bill opened his mouth to say something reassuring to the trainer but he'd already turned his attention back to Annie.

'Okay, we'll do the beep test to finish.'

'Great, my favourite,' Annie said twisting her mouth into an exaggerated sarcastic grimace.

Bill said something innocuously in the background like, do you mind if I watch? If they heard him they ignored him. The focus here was Annie. At a distance, the tattoo out of sight and the muscles less threatening, Bill could see that the trainer knew what he was doing. He set up the beep test and Annie started jogging. The first round he let her build up speed then he started to push, then he pushed her hard until the time ran out. Annie collapsed onto an exercise mat breathing heavily and laughing with the sheer joy of it.

'Not bad,' said the trainer obviously pleased. 'Stretching routine please then shower.'

'Yes, sir,' said Annie, the sarcasm glinting again, but it was friendly sarcasm. No one was overstepping the limits here.

The trainer came back to where Bill was standing. 'Impressive,' said Bill.

'Yes, she is impressive,' said the trainer.

'I meant the set up here,' said Bill. Could he catch a slight antipodean lilt in the man's vowel inflections? 'Have the other's gone home then?' he asked.

Annie walked past them giving a little girly wave as she pushed through the swing doors. 'With you in a mo, Gramps.' She turned round and pushed on through the door backwards. 'Have we another session this week? Lynn thought I should maybe do two sessions now in preparation for the new season.'

'It's already in the book,' said the trainer, 'see you Thursday?' The sentence dipped up into a question. Australian perhaps.

'Great thanks, Simon, see you then,' and Annie hopped off to change.

Simon switched his attention back to Bill. 'The others?' he said to Bill with the same rising inflection.

'The other kids, have they gone home already?' Bill repeated.

'I'm a personal trainer for high performance athletes. I don't do gym club for kids.' The tattoo rippled.

Bill's mouth formed an oh and he said 'But,' quietly and ineffectually.

'She's a talented kid. Your granddaughter you say?' Bill could feel Simon eyeing him up. He squared his shoulders and stopped leaning against the wall. 'I can see where she gets it from,' Simon continued.

Bill gleamed. 'I was a cricketer. I still am, but just a local club now.'

'There you go then,' lilted Simon.

'How long has Annie been coming here? I mean how long has she had personal training sessions?'

'We just started that today. She's been coming regularly for the group sessions on Saturdays but now we've geared up so she can have individual training.'

'Is it necessary?' Bill couldn't stop himself from saying.

Simon started to clear up bits of equipment while he talked. 'Depends what you regard as necessary. It's a lot better for her. She gets tailor made routines so we can expect to see a 50% improvement in performance.'

Bill's mouth dropped into another oh.

'And there is much less risk of injury. In fact I think with the right personal training you can actually protect an athlete from injury. I'm doing a PhD on just that very subject. That's why I'm here.' Simon chatted on, then paused to roll up the exercise mat. He flung it over one shoulder and went through to a storage room at the back of the gym.

'It sounds very expensive,' said Bill when Simon emerged from the storage room.

'Believe you me, mate, it is.'

Another oh.

'They'd all have individual sessions if they could afford it. Annie's one of the lucky ones. You get a sponsorship deal like she's got and the sky's the limit. She puts in the work and it's straight to the top.'

'Surely,' Bill struggled to find the words, 'surely you can get to the top without having to get sponsorship. I mean she's just a kid.'

'Not any more. The competition out there is shit hot. I don't know when you played your cricket at prof level but you'd have to do a hell of a lot more than catch a few balls these days. No offence, mate.'

'So,' said Bill.

'She's lucky, but she knows it. She works hard and as long as she does that then I think she's worth it. She's given up her whole childhood to becoming a tennis star?'

It was almost a question again. Bill nodded.

'With sponsorship she has a chance to make it. Without,' Simon made an expressive gesture and manoeuvred Bill out of the swing doors so that he could lock the gym.

Annie appeared swinging a kit bag and grinning with that special satisfaction one grins with after a good training session. Bill knew all about that, the endorphins and the satisfaction. There was nothing to beat it.

They waved goodbye to Simon and headed off to the car park. Annie was wearing a red hoodie and as Bill moved behind her to open up the car boot he caught the black provocative letters emblazoned across her back. *Spiked.*

Annie plugged into an iPod, or telephone or whatever gadget she had these days and Bill occasionally caught the faint tinny beat above the engine noise from Susan's Honda. He hoped it was a companionable silence and not an easy way to ignore him after Monday evening's debacle. She looked happy enough. Bill moved off the ring road roundabout onto the Hull road and settled into a comfortable cruising speed.

Annie pulled an earplug out. 'Did Granny let you have the car then?'

'Yes,' Bill said wondering why he had to sound guilty. He could feel Annie's eyes assessing him. On a bicycle he could speed up or slow down to give himself more thinking time when beset with questioning grandchildren.

'Gramps?'

Bill said yes again reluctantly.

'You'd have done the same, right?'

Bill pretended not to understand.

'When you were my age, if someone had waved a magic wand and said you could play for Yorkshire, you'd have leapt at the chance, wouldn't you?'

'Well,' Bill said inadequately.

He tried to concentrate on the road ahead, but Annie still looked at him with her earplug dangling down on her chest.

'I don't think there's anything magic about *Spiked*,' he said. He sounded bitter and he hadn't meant to.

'I don't care about *Spiked*, Gramps. But they want to give me money to play tennis and as far as I'm concerned they might just as well have waved a magic wand.'

'They're not giving you money,' Bill felt his voice rising. He paused. 'They're not *giving* you money they're sponsoring you.'

'So?' Annie shrugged and started fingering the dangling earplug.

If the so called serious and experienced members of the cricket club couldn't see the difference between sponsorship and gifting then how could he expect Annie to? Although people usually only understood what suited them, especially when it came to money. Bill sighed. The earplug popped back into position, but Annie wrenched it out again.

'You would have done the same, wouldn't you, when you were my age?' she persisted.

Bill opened his mouth. The honest answer was yes. He turned his guilty gaze back to watching where he was going and Annie popped the earplug back into position. She had all the answer she needed.

A tinny drumbeat trailed the modern world between them and Bill turned off the main road and headed towards East Wolds' High Street. When they pulled up outside Annie's home they sat for about half a minute looking in front of them. Not wanting to fall out but not able to agree. Annie opened the car door first.

'Are you coming in?' she asked.

'I don't think so.'

She grinned suddenly. 'I don't blame you. Mum's seriously got it in for you just now, Gramps.'

'Oh,' there really wasn't anything Bill could say to that. He got out of the car to get Annie's things out of the boot.

Annie swung her bag onto her shoulder and walked up the garden path. She turned round to wave goodbye while Bill stood and watched her. 'At least you're keeping her off my back for a change,' Annie said still grinning as she turned and walked into her mother who was waiting by the front door.

Bill waved goodbye to Annie and then waved guiltily at Carol. Was he supposed to smile? He heard Carol saying, 'Thanks, Dad,' as she ushered Annie into the house. Then he heard the beginnings of questions and instructions as the door closed. It was perhaps Annie's first individual training session as a professional athlete. He had heard the excitement buzzing in Carol's voice and he'd excluded himself from it. He was the one member of the family who really understood what it meant to Annie. Not what it meant to get money but what it meant to be an athlete and taken seriously. The little twist of anger propelled him back into the car and he drove off quickly and rebelliously in the direction of The Cricketer's Arms.

A coal fire glowed in a Victorian fireplace and Tuesday night drinkers lurked in corners made dark with nicotine from an era before cigarettes were banned. A couple were bravely eating a pub meal version of scampi and chips. Bill leant against the bar and ordered a pint. The landlord slowly drew out a pint of best bitter.

'Now then, Bill,' he said, carefully building up a good head on the beer. 'We haven't seen you around for a while.'

'You know how it is,' Bill said.

'Too much to do and not enough time to do it.' The beer was now placed on a small towel on the bar as a creamy spillage made its way down the side of the glass. 'That'll be £2.95 please, Bill.'

Bill took a handful of change out of his pocket and jangled it about until three pound coins fell onto the bar next to his glass of beer. 'By heck, three pounds for a pint of beer. It's daylight robbery.'

'It is indeed,' agreed the landlord as he dropped the three pounds into his till and gave Bill his change. 'It's even worse in the south,' he continued.

'Really?' Bill pocketed the five pence piece and took a long slurp of beer.

'Aye, it costs over three pounds for a pint in the south.'

Bill took another slurp of beer. 'You're kidding,' he said wiping a large creamy smear from his mouth with his sleeve.

'It's no joke. Some posh chap in a suit.'

'From London,' Bill butted in.

'Aye from London, some posh chap decides that us poor hard working blokes up North have to pay three pounds for a pint just so's he can drive around in some fancy car.'

'Audi Sportback,' Bill butted in again between another long slurp.

'Oh, aye, it'll be an Audi Sportback all right,' piped up a third voice as someone else joined them at the bar.

'An Audi Sportback,' continued the landlord, 'and before you know it the rest of us is out of business and poor blokes like you have no where to go to get an honest pint.'

'No, by heck, we'd have to go to some fancy wine bar in York,' said Bill and a vague vestige of conscience that Susan might actually like it if he occasionally took her to a fancy wine bar in York was easily drowned as he drained the last creamy drops from his pint.

'Same again, Geoff?' The landlord took the other man's outstretched glass.

'And you can fill mine up while you're at it,' said Bill. He turned to acknowledge the second man at the bar. 'Well I'll be - if it isn't himself, One Shot Summers. How are you doing? How are you doing, Geoff?'

'Not so bad, not so bad. And how's yourself, Bill?' One Shot Summers asked mournfully.

More pound coins changed hands and Bill had to pull his wallet out of another pocket and dig out a ten-pound note. Then due reverence had to be paid to the first long slurp from the refreshed glasses.

'What a coincidence,' continued Bill after another wiping mouth ritual was completed, 'I was talking about you just the other day. I met your granddaughter. She's a grand lass.'

'Aye, she said,' One Shot Summers said sorrowfully eyeing a pint which would soon be half empty.

The landlord had moved away to clear some glasses from a table and ask the brave eating couple if they were enjoying their meal.

'She's working up at that new place, *Spiked*,' Bill said casually, trying to cock a clever eye in One Shot Summers' direction.

'Not any more she isn't.'

'Oh?' Bill looked up sharply.

'Gave her the ruddy push, didn't they.'

Bill swallowed nervously and hid his face behind another slurp at his pint. One Shot joined him and both men looked down at their glasses as they put them back on the bar.

'I am sorry to hear that,' Bill managed to say, but his cheeks were burning with the memory of getting her to send him confidential documents to his private e-mail account. 'Did she say why, I mean did they say why she got the elbow,' Bill continued nervously.

'Not posh enough, that's what she reckons.'

Bill disguised his relief by taking another mouthful of beer.

'They're all posh suits and posh cars. I think she's well shot of them,' One Shot Summers said resignedly.

'She is indeed,' said Bill a little too eagerly, and then anxiously added, 'but has she got something else lined up?'

'She's staying with her cousin in York doing some waitressing and seeing if she can enrol for a course at York College.'

'That was quick,' Bill exclaimed.

'They don't hang about, kids, these days,' said One Shot knowledgeably.

'But,' said Bill then stalled not wanting to incriminate himself, 'I only just spoke to her on Saturday.'

'They gave her the push on Monday, first thing, told her to pack up her things and go. Just like that.'

'That's terrible,' said Bill guiltily.

'She said they knew where they could put their job and got a bus to York the same morning and had herself a waitressing job by lunchtime today.'

'Aye, as I said, she's a grand lass that granddaughter of yours. Have another drink, Geoff.'

'As you're asking I don't mind if I do.'

Bill caught the landlord's attention and put in the order for two further pints. He turned back to One Shot Summers but as no further comment was forthcoming they both watched their glasses emerge from the tap. Bill jiggled change onto the bar and joined One Shot Summers in a silent exchange of thanks involving eyebrows as they both raised their glasses.

'I don't hold with this *Spiked* whatnots,' One Shot Summers announced.

Bill nearly choked on his beer. He wondered if he could get One Shot to speak those honeyed words again.

'What was that you said, Geoff?' he asked.

'You know this *Spiked* thingumajig.'

Bill waited. He did know. He nodded encouragingly.

One Shot leant in towards him and Bill got a whiff of beery breath.

'I don't hold with them,' One Shot repeated nodding sagely.

Bill continued his own nodding. 'What makes you say that, One Shot Geoff?'

'I just don't,' One Shot said aggrieved, his face after its brief animation returning to its melancholy resignation.

'Well,' said Bill leaning in towards One Shot Summers with his own beery breath, 'I'll tell you summat and that's neither do I.'

'You don't?' One Shot looked suspicious. No one usually agreed with him.

'And I'll tell you why,' Bill said. He took a dramatic pause and a long slurp of his beer. 'There are goings on at that *Spiked* set up and it's not right.'

One Shot started nodding again and a couple of other people gathered round the bar.

'Now they say,' Bill stood up, shoulders spread and finger vaguely pointing, 'they say that they're going to put lots of money into the local community.'

'And jobs,' One Shot Summers broke in almost excitedly, 'they said that local people would be given priority on job applications but that's not true, is it? They give our Sadie the sack and who do they replace her with that's what I'd like to know?'

It was a long interruption from One Shot but Bill wasn't to be distracted from his own theme. 'But where is this money?'

'A posh bloke in a tight suit, that's what our Sadie says. A posh bloke from London. That's not giving jobs to locals now, is it?'

'It's all just promises,' Bill said emptying his glass.

'All talk and no trousers,' One Shot said also viewing his own empty glass with tragic intensity. 'What the heck, Bill, let's have another.'

'I don't mind if I do, thank you One Shot.'

Both men held out their glasses and the landlord filled an expectant pause by providing further inspiration in the form of full glasses. The replenished glasses had to be tasted before Bill gathered his thoughts and continued.

'The council's bending over backwards giving them permissions like there's no tomorrow.'

Another person casually sauntered towards the bar and stayed there.

'And this money they're supposedly handing out, they're not giving it away. It's all sponsorship. And you know what sponsorship is don't you, Geoff?'

One Shot nodded as if he did.

'It's advertising. Clever advertising that's what it is.' Encouraged by One Shot's resigned nodding Bill wetted his throat with another mouthful of beer and carried on. 'When you see a sports centre with *Spiked* written all over it you don't think advertising you think isn't that nice *Spiked* have given the school or the council or whatever it is lots of money so they can build a sports centre for the kids. And then they think that *Spiked* must be good and generous. So they associate,' associate was rather a difficult word to say and Bill got momentarily tangled up in it before he could carry on. 'They associate *Spiked* with something good so that when they see it in the shop they don't think there's that horrible caffeine drink that's too sweet with the silly advert on telly, no they don't think that, they think there's that drink that sporty people drink, that must be good. I'll try that.'

One Shot Summers had got as far as 'associate' but the large crowd that had now gathered around the bar was less intoxicated. One of them now joined in the discussion. 'Sponsorship is still money, isn't it,' he said.

Bill moved in even closer to One Shot. 'Sponsorship,' he said, 'is selling your soul to the devil to get to heaven. And Geoff One Shot there's things I know. Things that will have to come out.' Bill interrupted himself by burping loudly and wondered how he'd managed to drink so much beer in so short a time.

One Shot Summers was suffering the same sorrowful reaction. 'I think I'd better be getting home,' he said.

'Things, Geoff, that will have to be said.'

One Shot had finished his beer and was making an attempt to leave the bar but for some reason the gathered crowd did not part and Bill, carefully adjusting his gaze, found himself looking up at the bulk of Shaun Bean. One Shot pressed in behind Bill's elbow and Bill shook himself enough space to put his anorak on.

'Now then, Shaun,' he said unsteadily.

'Bill,' said Shaun Bean with a full and impressive display of Shaun Bean menace. 'Who's your friend?'

One Shot moved even further behind Bill's shoulders.

'Oh,' Bill desperately tried to get his brain to communicate with his mouth, 'just an old, One Shot Sum - Geoff, cricketing ass - ass - ociate.'

'Member of the cricket club then is he?'

'I don't rightly -'

'You can tell your friend from me that we don't want any trouble at Saturday's meeting. All pals together eh, Geoff,' said Shaun Bean looking over Bill's shoulder.

One Shot's permanent melancholy fused into alarm. A gratifying sight for Shaun Bean who now magnanimously moved out of their way to follow them out towards the door. He put a reassuring hand on both their shoulders. 'We don't want any trouble now do we, lads?' He gave One Shot a helpful push towards the door but his other arm was still gripping Bill's shoulder. He leant in towards Bill. 'You get my meaning, Bill, don't you? No trouble. We don't want anyone getting hurt, do we. Now go and look after your dead-end friend.' He pushed Bill so hard out of the door that Bill fell into One Shot.

'Who the heck?' said One Shot.

'That's *Spiked*,' said Bill, 'that's *Spiked* for you.'

Both men crossed the car park and walked a few yards along the footpath towards the High Street.

'Now where on earth can I have left my bike?' said Bill.

15

'Where's my car, Bill Reeves?' Susan was leaning over the bed and dangling a set of car keys over Bill's nose. 'These were in your trouser pocket but there's no car outside.'

Bill squinted cautiously at the dull trickle of light which came in through the window. But the window was on the wrong side of the bedroom.

'Where the -' he was about to ask, then he remembered. He was in the spare room. After a few attempts at amorous assaults on Susan the night before he had been banished to the spare room. He smiled. Guiltily. And wished that Susan would stop waving her car keys in front of his nose. It made him feel queasy.

'You're not suggesting someone's stolen it are you?' Susan said crossly.

'Stolen what?'

'My car.'

Bill wondered if it would be politic to ask Susan to keep her voice down. He tried to pull himself together. 'Has someone stolen your car?'

'That's what I'm asking you as the person last seen with my car was you and you are, or were, still in possession of my car keys until about two minutes ago when I found them in your trouser pocket. Your trousers which, by the way, were left in a horrible heap in the bathroom.'

'Susan, love, can we just take things a bit more slowly and quietly.'

'No we can't. I have a clinic starting in twenty minutes. And don't love me.'

'Oh,' Bill fell back into the pillows. He had a horrible feeling that he knew exactly where the car was. 'The car,' he began.

'My car.'

'Your car is in the car park of The Cricketers Arms,' he mumbled into the pillows.

Susan looked as though she might explode and Bill dived for cover under the duvet.

'I'm taking your bike, but you'd better get my car back to me before 12.30 as my first home visit is at one o'clock. And,' she hovered in the doorway still speaking as loudly as it was possible to speak without actually shouting, 'how you square that with your job is up to you.'

Bill hoped that he heard footsteps retreating down the stairs.

'And if I come back to a big mess here -'

Bill heard a door bang loudly enough to knock a dent in his head. He groaned, rolled over and went back to sleep.

At a quarter to twelve Bill woke up. He was desperate for a cup of tea but otherwise felt much better. He pushed the duvet off him. Susan's car keys fell on the floor and he picked them up and put them on the bedside table. Bill was a bit puzzled as to why he was naked. He went to the bathroom and went through a slow bathroom routine ending with a shower. The shower felt good. His clothes were already conveniently on the bathroom floor so he put them on and went down to the kitchen and put the kettle on. He stretched out. Yes, he felt almost human again. He supposed he ought to make some pretence at going to work. He could bicycle over there after lunch, or brunch. He smiled. It was quite satisfying to have a night out with the lads and drink too much and shirk. Really quite satisfying.

'Bloody hell,' and he suddenly remembered what it was he was supposed to be doing by twelve thirty that morning. Tea and kettle and muesli went all over the kitchen. 'Susan's bloody car. Bloody hell.'

The kitchen clock said eight minutes past twelve. There were no socks, no shoes, no car keys. Upstairs, downstairs, an old pair of trainers found in the cupboard under the stairs, car keys retrieved from the bedside table, out of the door and on to his bicycle. Which wasn't there.

'Oh no, she's taken my bloody bike.' Another bloody hell routine ensued as Bill started cantering up The Avenue.

Twenty paces walk, twenty paces run. Scouts march or something. Twenty paces - his heart was turning inside out. Run - Walk - He daren't look at his watch. The Cricketers Arms finally came into view. The church clock struck a chime or two. Quarter past twelve? Half past? Worse? Bill's heart was completely out of control. No time, no time, he muttered, thought. In the car. Yes. On my way, he thought, muttered. And at twenty-two minutes to one he skidded into the only free parking lot at the health centre. It was right by the door and it had a sign saying 'Head of Practice' by

103

it. But Bill didn't see that. He fumbled with the keys but failed to lock the car and charged through the door into reception. An old lady struggling with a walking stick wobbled dangerously and Bill heaved himself over the counter of the reception.

'I think I'm having a heart attack,' he said.

The receptionist looked suitably alarmed and sympathetic and Bill certainly looked wild and dishevelled enough to be having some kind of attack.

Susan appeared. 'My oh my, you were cutting it fine,' she said icily. She stretched out her hand. 'Keys. Thank you. And you'll find that wretched bike of yours in the bicycle racks on the other side of the car park. I suppose you know that the back brake is defect?'

Susan swung out through the door, steadying the wobbling old lady on her way and Bill leant over the reception counter clutching his heart and grabbing for the receptionist's hand. 'Feel here,' he said, 'it won't stop pumping.'

The receptionist backed off uncertainly then shook herself into professional action. 'Mr Reeves, please take a seat and I'll see if Dr Adams can fit you in before she has her lunch.'

'Now,' Bill asked retreating a little.

'As soon as she is able.'

'You don't have a -' Bill stopped himself from saying 'a male doctor' just in time.

'I suppose she's only going to listen to my chest,' Bill thought quietly to himself. Although he can't have thought it that quietly because the old lady wobbled a bit more and a teenage girl discreetly moved to the other side of the waiting area. Bill picked up the local newspaper and resigned himself to a long wait. His heart was still hopping about here and there and all in all he was grateful just to sit somewhere quietly. If only he'd had time for that cup of tea.

The back page of the *East Wolds' Gazette* was given over entirely to an announcement from the cricket club. Although it looked more like an advertisement. All members, non members, would be members of all shapes and sizes were encouraged, no exhorted to attend Saturday's extraordinary general meeting. This meeting would decide the future of East Wolds' cricket club. This meeting would decide whether East Wolds' cricket club *had* a future. As a full turn out was expected everyone should please note that the meeting would take place not in the cricket pavilion (which anyway had been served with a demolition order) but in the East Wolds' School new *Spiked* sports hall. The meeting would begin at 7pm precisely.

There was something of an article which followed in smaller print. Bill scanned the paragraph quickly. He picked up a few pertinent phrases; disruptive elements, reactionary backward thinking, past their prime, hindering progress, time for new blood.

'William Reeves?' A tall dark-haired woman, younger than Carol, was standing by reception and surveying the occupants of the waiting area. It didn't take her long to deduce that the only male patient waiting must be William Reeves.

Bill rolled the newspaper up and thrust it under his arm. Dr Adams stretched out a cool un-manicured hand. An attractive hand. 'Jenny Adams,' she said.

Bill was a bit taken aback. He put out his own hand. 'Bill Reeves,' he said, but in the middle of saying this he had to make a diving catch to his right to retrieve the newspaper before it hit the floor.

He thought he also heard the words, 'the infamous Bill,' as he followed Dr Adams to a consulting room at the back of the health centre.

'Please sit down,' continued the doctor, pointing to a chair by her desk. Her desk was occupied entirely by an old computer only marginally more up-to-date than Bill's one at home. 'I've heard so much about you from Susan.'

Bill clutched the newspaper to his chest and wondered what to say. It was a bit difficult to launch into symptoms when the offer of a cup of tea seemed more appropriate. He cleared his throat and started fidgeting with the newspaper.

Dr Adams smiled. 'So how can I help you?' she asked.

'I -' his voice sounded strangled and as he opened his mouth even he caught the whiff of stale beer as it escaped into the room.

Dr Adams typed something onto her computer and waited.

'I,' Bill put the newspaper down on the floor and tapped his chest, 'I keep getting problems with my heart.'

'Ah, let's begin with today. What specifically made you request an emergency appointment today?'

'It wouldn't stop. It usually stops.'

Dr Adams looked interested but unenlightened.

'My heart. It sometimes hops about for a bit then stops. Today it just hopped about and got worse and I thought it wasn't going to stop.'

'Is it still 'hopping about'?'

'No, not really, I don't think so.'

'You're not sure?'

'No, I mean yes I'm not sure.'

'Do you have any pain?'

'No not really, it's not really painful as such it's just -'

'So it's more of a palpitation?'

'Palpitation? Yes of course, that's what it is.'

'Now can you tell me when it began today?'

'At seventeen minutes past twelve.'

Dr Adams started typing up notes onto her computer. Bill didn't notice her guarded smile. 'Did it start gradually or was it sudden?'

'Oh, it was sudden alright, but I couldn't stop running because I was late you see. Susan needed the car and I didn't even get to drink my tea.'

'And it got worse or better?'

'I don't rightly know. I mean it got better once I got here.'

'So you were driving and in a rush -'

'No, I was running then driving.'

'And you came straight here because you were worried about your heart?'

'No, I came here because Susan needed her car.'

'But you did have palpitations and you did come here and request an emergency consultation?'

'Yes.'

Dr Adams sighed. 'Did you feel anything else?'

'No, it's always just my heart hopping about.'

'So this has happened before?'

'Yes.'

'But you've never sought medical guidance about these palpitations before?'

'No.'

'Is that because it was particularly acute today?'

'Well no, I just happened to be here.'

Dr Adams' sigh was more perceptible this time. 'As you are here, even though it seems by accident, we might as well check you over.'

'I'm not here by accident.'

'If you can just take your shirt off and lie down on the couch.'

This was the bit that Bill didn't like, the bit that required man-to-man treatment not probing by a woman with beautiful hands who was young enough to be his daughter.

The stethoscope was cold, but in fact it was quite nice to lie down again. Bill's stomach rumbled.

'Have you eaten today?' The question was sharp, a Susan kind of tone.

Bill shook his head and tried to smile.

'You seem otherwise very fit.'

Bill wondered what the otherwise meant.

'Do you train regularly?'

'No, not really, I don't hold with these here training places.'

'Perhaps you should consider it. It's a good idea for a man of your age to keep himself fit.'

'I keep myself fit enough. I bicycle everywhere and in the summer there's cricket.'

'Cricket?'

'I still wicket keep for East Wolds, you know.'

Dr Adams tucked the stethoscope away into the pocket of her white coat. 'I really don't think that there's anything to worry about but I'll send in a referral for a specialist, as at your age one should be careful.'

This didn't sound as reassuring as it was meant to. Bill stood up and buttoned up his shirt. Was he meant to go now? Dr Adams was typing onto her computer again.

'Mr Reeves, Bill?' She stopped him as he put his hand on the door handle. 'Are there any personal problems at home or at work that might be causing undue stress at the moment?'

Bill came and sat down again. He didn't know where to begin.

'Perhaps some issues at work?'

'Yes.'

'I don't want to give you anything but I wonder if in the circumstances you should take a few days off work. Are you able to do that?'

In the circumstances sounded alarming. Bill looked at Dr Adams anxiously.

'Is it very busy at work just now?'

'No, in fact just now my desk is completely empty.'

'Well that's it then. I'll give you a sick note for the rest of the week and you can take it easy and give your body a chance to settle back down to normal.'

There was a pause. Bill retrieved the newspaper off the floor and stood up again. The room was stifling with the smell of stale beer.

But Bill had something else on his mind. 'These energy drinks, you know, like *Spiked*, could they cause Palpitations?'

'Yes, undoubtedly. Is that what you've been taking? Energy drinks to give you more energy? Because you know it's a complete fallacy don't you? No real athlete would even smell them let alone drink them.'

'But they are sponsored by them,' Bill added.

'Yes and people like me have to pick up the pieces when people like you come in with palpitations. Energy drinks, Mr Reeves, are strictly off the menu.'

'Would you like to come to the East Wolds' cricket club extraordinary general meeting on Saturday? The secondary school sports hall at 7pm?' said Bill.

16

One Shot Summers lived in a cul-de-sac off the maze of council houses where Shaun Bean lived. Over the years the council tenants in One Shot's cul-de-sac had bought their houses off the council and the once modest crescent of semi-detached houses now sported a riot of extensions, stuccoed finishes and porches. One Shot's claim to home ownership had limited itself to a bright blue door and new double glazed windows.

Bill glided elegantly onto One Shot's drive, stopping neatly by the blue Escort parked there. One Shot was outside looking at the winter mess of his garden.

'Now then, Geoff,' said Bill.

'Oh it's you,' said One Shot. He jerked his head backwards towards the house. 'She wasn't too pleased last night.'

Bill pulled the *East Wolds' Gazette* out from the luggage rack on the back of his bicycle, 'Have you seen this?' he said waving the back page somewhere in the vicinity of One Shot's nose.

'Happen,' said One Shot.

'Had you heard anything about it before?'

'No.'

'Because I hadn't.'

One Shot looked sorrowfully at his wind battered garden.

'You are still a member of the cricket club aren't you, Geoff?'

'Yes.' Another silence. 'Although.'

'Although?' Bill questioned.

'She,' another jerk towards the house, 'thinks it's daft. Just a waste of money, especially now I'm retired.'

'But you're a fully paid up member? Hang on a minute One Shot, if you're retired you should get pensioner's rate.'

One Shot made another evasive answer. 'Are you coming in for a cup of tea?' he said resignedly.

Janet Summers was in the kitchen and filled up the kettle as they trooped in.

'How are you doing, Janet?' Bill asked politely.

'Not so bad, and how's yourself?'

Janet Summers was an attractive woman somewhat younger than her husband and when he and Geoff were ushered into the living room and then served with tea and custard creams Bill wondered enviously what One Shot had done to deserve her. If Janet Summers had been cross with her husband earlier it certainly didn't show now. Bill stirred four spoonfuls of sugar into his mug and drank it down in one go. He'd needed that and he gave his heart a little friendly pat as it settled down comfortably into a deep armchair with him.

'Can I get you another mug?' Janet Summers asked.

'Well, if it's no bother I don't mind if I do,' Bill said.

One Shot was chewing silently on a custard cream. Bill ate three while he waited for Janet to come back with another mug of tea.

Janet stood over them. 'Is there anything else before I go?'

'You're leaving a bit early aren't you, love,' One Shot said sadly.

'Just popping into Morrison's on my way to work. You won't forget to switch the oven on at six will you, Geoff.' This last was accompanied by a meaningful look at Bill.

'Odd time to go out to work,' said Bill helping himself to another custard cream.

A hand hovered over her hip. 'Some of us work when there's work to be done.'

'Janet cleans at *Spiked*. Mornings seven 'til nine and evenings five 'til seven,' One Shot explained.

'At *Spiked*?' Bill sat up in the deep chair and dropped several biscuit crumbs on the carpet.

'That's right, same place as our Sadie,' One Shot continued.

'Same place as our Sadie used to work.' A sour twist disturbed Janet's usual genial expression. 'I don't think they've twigged though.'

Bill looked puzzled.

'I reckon if they'd twigged we was the same family they'd have sent me packing an all.'

'You don't know that, love.'

'So you're off to *Spiked* now to clean?' Bill said waving a fifth biscuit dangerously over the carpet.

'Doesn't your wife feed you?' Janet asked.

Bill was not to be distracted. 'So you empty bins and the like. In the offices?'

'That's what they seem to expect of a cleaner, yes. You never told me Bill was into worker's rights,' she said to One Shot. 'We could have done with him when you were made to take early retirement.'

'Janet, these bins you empty, can you empty them into a bin bag and give it to me?'

Janet looked alarmed. 'All the bins? What on earth?'

Bill thought carefully. 'Not all the bins just the paper. Do they have separate bins for paper like we do at the council?'

'Well, yes. You want me to -'

'Put all the paper rubbish into a bin bag and give it to me.'

'But how on earth? I can't carry a big black bin bag and put it in my car. What if someone saw?'

Bill saw a suspicious cloud begin to settle over Janet.

'You normally put it in the company's rubbish bins I presume?' Bill said quickly.

Janet nodded.

'So instead of putting it into the bin you could just leave a big black bin bag next to the bin. As if the bin was too full.' Bill felt inspired and smiled expansively.

'It's only Wednesday, the bins won't be full today.'

'But who else knows that, Janet, apart from you?'

'So you want me to put, or rather not to put the paper rubbish in the bin but leave it next to the bin in a bin liner?'

Bill nodded. He was rubbing his hands together, not good for either biscuit or carpet.

'And then?' Janet said hovering in the doorway.

'And then?' Bill asked.

'And then what?'

'Well then,' he hadn't actually thought the next stage out yet, 'then I'll collect it.'

Janet shrugged. 'I'm late enough already,' she said and left One Shot and Bill sorrowfully eyeing empty tea mugs and an empty plate of biscuits.

In the meantime Bill had a demolition order to investigate. One Shot Summers almost smiled when Bill stood up and said he'd better be going. He followed Bill to the door and looked bemusedly at a copy of the *East Wolds' Gazette* which fluttered damply by his front door. On closer inspection it was adorned with a large stamp saying: East Wolds' Health Centre. Not To Be Removed. One Shot gathered up the fluttering pages anxiously but no one was watching him as he stuffed the remains into a recycling bin. Bill was already several hundred yards away dashing through a snicket which led to a short cut to the council offices.

Bill had several uncomfortable moments as he approached the council offices' car park. He'd now been shirking for most of the day. He patted his heart reassuringly and marched into the reception area clutching Dr Adams' sick note.

'Morning, Sally Anne,' he said.

'Good afternoon you mean.' It was twenty five past four and Sally Anne was clock watching and planning what to have for tea. 'There's a message for you.'

'Me?'

'From Mr Carstairs.'

'Oh lord.'

'He wanted to see you before ten.'

'That's a bit late isn't it?'

'This morning.'

'I had to go to the doctor's.' Bill waved the sick note which was starting to look as crumpled as he did. It now occurred to him that he didn't actually know what to do with a sick note. Bill was never off sick. 'Sally Anne, who do I give this to?'

'Mrs Groves,' said Sally Anne.

'Really?' said Bill, 'well I never.'

'But she left early,' Sally Anne continued.

Bill was at a loss.

'Here, give it to me. I'll put it in an envelope and give it to her in the morning.'

Bill wondered how many rules and procedures he would break if he kissed her, so decided that he'd better not.

'How long are you off for?' Sally Anne asked sealing the evidence into a white envelope now addressed to Mrs A Groves.

'I don't know,' Bill said as he set off towards the stairs leading into the interior of the council building and the offices. He hadn't actually read the sick note. He thought he heard Sally Anne saying, 'But I thought you were -' just as he went out of earshot.

Out of habit he had a cautious look into his own office. The in-trays were still empty and his computer was still flashing on

112

screen save. He went to switch it off then stopped himself. A large yellow sticker was placed next to his telephone. 'My office before 10, Carstairs,' it said. That wasn't very friendly. He heard a familiar shuffle in the corridor, Lisa with her files. He hid behind the door. When he ventured into the corridor he saw Lisa waiting for the lift wearing her coat and clutching a handbag. 'That's a bit of luck,' he said. Lisa looked round to see if the voice was addressing her but luckily the lift arrived just in time to save Bill from exposure.

He went back into his office and sat at his desk. He was trying to remember council procedure on demolition orders. Of course fire safety was often an issue with demolition orders but he just did an assessment and sent it off to the appropriate department. Did he send it internally or did it go to county council level? Perhaps both? The planning department. He couldn't go wrong there.

The planning department was in the basement. Bill did a few James Bond moves down the corridor and sidled onto the stairs. He heard an office door close and the distant sound of voices making going home noises. He looked at his watch but in his desperation to reach Susan at lunchtime he'd forgotten to put his watch on. He'd also forgotten to pick up his mobile. Although it must be reasonable to suppose that it was now past five o'clock.

The stairs were empty and when he got to it the planning department was in darkness. Bill clicked all the lights on and stood in the middle of the illuminated space wondering where to begin. And then he found it; a whole filing cabinet devoted to *Spiked*.

Sunshine Soft Drinks' planning application was extensive. Bill picked out a folder at random. In it there was an expensive drawing of *Spiked* with glass doors and landscaped trees, a neat car park with cars dutifully parked and carefully coloured in muted tones of red and blue. There was even an aspidistra showing on the other side of the glass doors. The surrounding area was all designated as 'brown site' and therefore appeared to be perfect for the regeneration of industry in East Wolds.

He dropped the folder back into the filing cabinet and picked out another one. An overview of land acquisitions made by *Spiked.* There was a big map of East Wolds and Bill had to spread it out on the floor to see it all, but the details were beyond him without his glasses and they of course were wherever all his other usual belongings had got to.

Bill stood up from the large map and had a rummage around the planning officer's desk where he found a pair of glasses which worked even better than his own. Bill went back to the map.

Spiked acquisitions were marked in blue. The school playing fields, the large rough area at the back of the council offices, several buildings along the High Street including The Cricketers Arms, the whole of the area on the east side of the canal including the footpath and the conservation area to the southwest of the original *Sunshine Soft Drinks* property, the land to the north of the town which had originally belonged to some Oxford college, the Rectory, or Old Rectory as it was now, the four acres of original glebe land and the village green. 'The what?' Bill leapt to his feet, except he didn't leap to his feet because he'd got cramp in his left leg and he had to roll over on his back instead and pull at his foot to stretch the cramp out. He was making so much noise that if there was anyone left in the building they were bound to get suspicious.

Bill resisted the urge to scrumple the land acquisitions map up into a big ball and drop it into the bin. He folded it carelessly and stuffed it back into its folder as a slight sop to his anger.

There was another map. Bill pulled it out and spread it out on the floor. It wasn't really a map, it was another expensive architect's drawing of East Wolds Utopia. East Wolds Utopia had an expanded *Spiked* which now occupied the whole of the conservation area to the southwest of the original property and extended along the canal footpath with walk ways and recreational areas with *Spiked* employees eating picnics and feeding stylised ducks which had miraculously started to nest along the old canal banks. The land at the back of the council offices was designated as a new housing development and about fifty houses identical to the kind that Carol and family lived in were carefully drawn in with SUVs and children riding bicycles along safe cul-de-sacs. The High Street properties had become modern service and recreational buildings housing quaint teashops and wine bars. The land to the north of East Wolds was now a shopping centre with cinema, landscaped lake and bus stops. The Old Rectory had become a day centre for the elderly with a large residential home attached to it. The school playing fields were more-or-less intact except for the new *Spiked* sports hall which had already been built. Bill was carefully avoiding looking at the big green splodge designating the village green. Even so it was impossible not to get a rough idea of a large new multipurpose clubhouse occupying the site of the old cricket pavilion.

Finally Bill remembered his original purpose which had been to find the demolition order. He went back to the filing cabinet but as he opened another drawer a burglar alarm starting hooting. Bill was confused. Surely the filing cabinet couldn't be alarmed? He closed it but the alarm had now settled into full screech.

'Bloody hell, bloody bloody,' Bill shouted. Someone had put the council's alarm on. He tried to fold the big architect's drawing up but it was all twisted and sweaty from his hands. He hopped and swore and sort of threw it in the direction of the *Spiked* filing cabinet and pushed the drawer closed. He stuffed the glasses in his pocket and charged to the door. He switched the lights off and was subsumed in thick basement darkness. He groped his way to the bottom of the stairs where he hoped to find a fire exit. There seemed to be so many doors and knobs and things propped up against walls. He felt his way around the stairs, saw the dull glow of an emergency exit sign and hurled himself at what he hoped was the green bar of the fire door. A rush of cool damp air hit his face. He slid out of the building and did a running squat towards the usual cover of the few shrubs at the back of the building.

Outside wasn't the stifling darkness of the basement but it was too gloomy to read the code on his bicycle lock. Somewhere from the vicinity of the town centre a police siren started blaring. Then Bill found the glasses in his pocket and within seconds he made his elegant gliding escape out of the car park via a dark grassy area to avoid the road just as the local police car came blazing into the car park making so much noise and commotion that it missed Bill. Safely out of sight Bill pedalled at top gear in the direction of *Spiked* whistling a tune closely resembling *I love to go a wandering.*

It was a murky dusk and not ideal conditions for bicycling at top speed along a canal path. The path oozed with mud from the previous days of rain and the overcast evening made anything that wasn't muddy slimy with damp.

Bill however arrived safely at *Spiked*. He guessed by the light, or rather lack of light, that it must be some time after seven.

Spiked though wasn't encompassed in the same end of day darkness as the council offices. There were two cars in the car park and a soft light shining behind a light grey curtain. The curtain was drawn and the office was on the first floor so even if Bill had wanted to have a little spy he wasn't able to. Bill however did not want to go anywhere near the offices. He hoped that the rubbish bins would be well out of sight of the dark glass frontage and rode his bicycle in a wide arc well out of sight of the discreetly lit first floor. The bins, as expected, were at the back of the original *Sunshine Soft Drinks* warehouses. There were no cars parked here and no lights. Janet Summers had obviously packed up and gone home.

Bill rode his bicycle over a rough verge at some distance from the bins and the back entrance. Once upon a time there had been gates but these had been removed. They would be too narrow for modern transport lorries and were unnecessary with all the new technological methods of security available to a company like *Spiked*. Surveillance cameras perhaps? Bill hadn't thought of that.

He left his bicycle a good few yards away from the entrance. A bicycle might be recognisable but a shadowy figure hovering around bins would be less distinct. He then had the brainwave of rustling up on all fours in the hope of being mistaken in the gloom for a dog or even a fox. So within sight of any possible CCTV cameras he dropped down onto hands and feet and with a high bottom bearing closer resemblance to an ape than any canine creature he hunkered along to the bins.

Janet, bless her, had left a large black bin bag next to a big green wheelie bin. Bill hunkered on to his prey, sniffed it convincingly, raised a leg in doggy salute then grabbed the bag with an unusually agile paw and dragged it away out of the sights of any lurking camera.

This was all gratifyingly easy. Attaching the bin bag to his bicycle however was not. It was too big for the luggage rack over his back wheel. He experimented dangling it down from one handlebar but it was too big for that too.

He pushed his bicycle back up the rough verge towards the main entrance to *Spiked* and then on the flat terrain by the car park he finally managed a successful manoeuvre which involved holding the bin bag along the handlebar and gripping it with both hands. It wasn't possible to change gears and neither could he brake but as the back brake didn't work that well anyway it didn't really matter. The gears were more of a problem because Bill had set them rather high, so getting himself launched at slow speed was a wobbly affair which involved getting closer to the darkly glossy glass entrance to *Spiked* than was desirable.

He just got himself turned in the right direction when about thirty security lights suddenly flashed on and there was Bill, now turned into a rabbit staring at headlights, in full illuminated view as a grey curtain on the first floor twitched aside. But the bicycle was now moving forwards, and at some speed, such that Bill couldn't have stopped it even if he'd wanted to.

Bill tried to assess the risks of a first floor office phone call being made to Shaun Bean. However after only a few squelchy turns along the canal path it was clear to Bill that the canal was far more dangerous than Shaun Bean and, after being thoroughly shaken by a plopping splash of water only inches from his left ankle, Bill decided to complete his dash for home via the main road.

The High Street was quiet and the few youths hanging around in the centre weren't interested in an old bloke on an old bicycle carrying a black bin bag. Bill got his Bicycle safely tucked away in the shed and himself into the kitchen clutching his swag bag of paper waste before seeing any signs of red Fords, Audis or Minis.

Susan was sitting at the kitchen table. Her eyes were red at the edges and her mobile phone was on the table next to Bill's. They looked at each other startled. Bill smiled over his bin bag and Susan's mouth hung open for almost a minute before she managed to speak.

'Your dinner's cold,' she finally said.

'Oh, that's alright, love,' Bill said, sidling towards the door and attempting to keep the bin bag out of sight of Susan.

'And you forgot this,' she continued, pointing to Bill's bicycle helmet which was also on the table.

'Oh.' Bill had one foot out of the door.

'I left it at reception for you.' Susan's teeth were starting to grind.

'Oh,' repeated Bill inching a shoulder and the bin bag out into the hall.

'And look at the state of you.'

Bill looked at the state of himself. The crumpled clothes he'd begun the day with were now spattered with mud and the knee of one trouser leg was ripped.

'Not to mention the state of the house when I got home.'

'Oh.'

'There were six pairs of odd shoes all over the hall and the kitchen was covered in muesli. And I mean covered.'

'Oh, well,' Bill looked around the kitchen then longingly out into the hall. 'It doesn't look too bad,' he said.

'It doesn't look too bad. Of course it doesn't look too bad because I've spend all evening cleaning up after you.' Susan scraped the kitchen chair back dangerously.

Bill got a second foot into the hall.

'You can at least tell me where you've been all this time. There's been police sirens howling and goodness knows what going on in town. I was worried sick.'

'Oh,' Bill carried on trying to look nonchalant and wondered what sort of expression would denote innocence. Where should he say he'd been? He didn't think that prowling around *Spiked* would be a very good answer. 'I've been at One Shot Summers,' he said.

'Geoff Summers?' Susan said surprised. 'But you can't have seen him for years.'

'Well you know, catching up. I just happened to run into him in the pub last night.'

'Oh, you did, did you? And since when did Geoff Summers become a big drinker? I thought that wife of his kept him well in order.'

'Who Janet? Oh no, Janet's alright.'

'She is, is she?'

'I mean she's, well, she's alright with One Shot.'

'And don't call him that ridiculous name. So give me one good reason why you should suddenly be hanging out with One Sh... Geoff Summers.'

Bill squared his shoulders in the doorway. 'Cricketing business,' he said.

Susan made a dismissive grunt. She stood up and started fiddling with the kettle and a tea mug.

'I'm rallying support for the meeting on Saturday.'

'Oh that,' Susan said to the kettle. 'You know that the whole town's talking about that wretched meeting, don't you?'

'Are they?'

'It would seem that every able bodied person in East Wolds has suddenly become devoted to the cricket club.'

Bill turned back into the doorway. 'Everyone? You mean that lots of people are joining the cricket club?'

'I don't know what they're doing but everyone's talking about it.'

'But lots of new members?'

'I thought you wanted lots of new members? I thought it was one of life's tragedies that no one takes any interest in cricket any more?'

'But new members? New *Spiked* members?'

Susan turned back from the kettle and looked at him sharply. 'Were you at work today by the way?'

'I'm off sick,' Bill said, 'I went to see Dr Adams and she gave me a sick note.'

'I know, except she couldn't really tell me anything. So she gave you sick leave did she? How long for?'

'I don't know.'

'You don't know? What did she say, Bill?' Susan sat at the table again, 'are you really ill?'

'I don't rightly know. She said something about specialists and then something about stress.' In fact he wasn't interested in what she'd said. The only thing he could remember about the conversation was that Dr Adams was against energy drinks. Passionately against them. In fact, if he remembered aright, he'd also invited her to attend the meeting on Saturday. But such a lot had happened that day that he was struggling to remember where it had begun.

'But you must know,' Susan exclaimed. 'You arrive at the health centre in a terrible state, dressed like I don't know what. You tell the receptionist that you are having a heart attack.'

'I never.'

'And demand to see a doctor. You then vanish into thin air. No one has seen you for seven hours or so and you arrive home looking like you've had some sort of a fit and rolled under a hedge.'

Bill tried ineffectually to assuage Susan's worries.

'I'm going to ring Carol and tell her you're home and apparently more or less okay. Just your usual bloody self.' Susan picked her mobile up off the kitchen table and left the room. She was blinking back tears and Bill heard an angry growl as she fell over the bin bag and crashed into the sitting room

Bill followed Susan into the hall and watched her from the sitting room door as she punched in numbers to ring Carol.

'You know what?' he said swinging his arms awkwardly in the doorway, 'I think I must be better. I haven't had a palpitation all day since I saw that Dr Adams. She's grand, isn't she, that Dr Adams of yours.'

17

The classification of paper rubbish in the bin bag now emptied out on Bill's office floor was an interesting affair. He picked up an empty sandwich case and dropped it back into the bin bag. He picked up a less empty sandwich case and dropped that into the bin bag as well. There were three cans of *Extra Spiked*, four more sandwich cases, six wrappers from energy bars, a miniature box of orange juice with a picture of Molly the Rat or Hilly the Hare or to be honest some picture book hero that Bill didn't know about, nine used teabags, one unused teabag, three broken biros, a pencil stub (pencil shavings from which were already half ingrained into Bill's carpet), four wrappers off chocolate bars, a cartridge of printer ink 'and a partridge in a pear tree,' sang Bill as he was now left more-or-less with paper rubbish.

There were lots of different coloured post-it notes, floating sheets of A4 paper, magazines and newspapers. Bill dropped three copies of *The Times* and two copies of *The Mail* into the bin bag. The magazines were mostly advertising leaflets and there was one copy of *Top Gear*. Bill dropped these in the bin bag together with ten travel brochures.

Now for the A4 sheets. Nine sheets of unused headed paper from the *Sunshine Soft Drinks* era, twenty-one blank sheets, one scrumpled up picture of a dog and nineteen sheets with ends or beginnings of print runs with not much more than page numbers on them.

Bill put it all in the bin bag, yawned dramatically and surveyed the remaining heap of post-it notes. He wasn't feeling very inspired. He heard the chimes of *Big Ben* hailing the beginning of the ten o'clock news. If he'd felt a bit less tired he would have rallied himself and gone downstairs to watch the news with Susan. As it was it was too much bother to pick himself up off the floor so he started colour coding post-it notes instead.

There were thirty yellow post-it notes, eighteen blue ones and nine pink ones. Two of the pink ones were blank, three were crumpled up and three had numbers on them. The last one said 'OK'. As 'OK' at least made sense Bill put it on one side and opened up the three crumpled ones. One was a doodle around the letters DL, one was rather a good cartoon drawing of an exploding bomb and the third one was just a big ink splodge.

The blue post-it notes volunteered a list of dates, a hand-drawn map including an A road clearly demarcated as A19, a four digit number and 'YES' written in capital letters and surrounded by exclamation marks.

The Yellow post-it notes yielded 'later', 'BR', lists from a twenty-four hour clock denoting bus times or train times, another list of percentages, a London telephone number, a mobile telephone number, a cryptic note saying 'try SB' and another cryptic note saying 'need more caffeine' which was also accompanied by four exclamation marks.

When Susan came up the stairs to go to bed and to tell Bill that he needn't bother waking her up in the middle of the night again she found Bill asleep on his office floor snoring loudly, his head resting on a bin bag and a pink post-it note stuck to his forehead. A blank yellow post-it note attached itself to Susan's slipper. She picked it up, found a pencil on Bill's desk and wrote 'If you wake up DON'T wake me – sleep in the spare room'. And then with forty years of wifely compunction behind her she checked his pulse, listened to his heartbeat and tucked him in with the blanket she kept at the end of their bed.

Bill snuggled into the bin bag and smiled. 'Good night, love,' he said, and carried on snoring.

At some point in the middle of the night Bill woke up and went to the bathroom. His face was all sticky and plasticy and his back groaned. He stripped off his dirty clothes and tiptoed into his bedroom. In a noble gesture not to disturb Susan's gentle breathing he abandoned any thoughts of trying to put pyjamas on and slipped into the clean warm sheets next to her and fell sound asleep.

Susan was dressed and ready for work when she leant over him with a mug of tea. 'I presume you're still off sick this morning?' she asked.

'Oh yes, I should think so,' Bill said. He propped himself up on all the pillows and took the tea from Susan, savouring its bitter milky smell.

Susan puckered her mouth but Bill didn't notice. 'You wouldn't mind bringing up the radio would you, love?' he asked.

Susan's mouth now drew out into a long thin line.

Bill slurped the tea and made a loud satisfied noise. 'I must've slept like a log,' he said.

Susan turned to go. 'And will you be in this evening or will I have to watch the clock all evening again wondering when it's appropriate to call the police?'

'Call the police?'

If Susan hadn't already been half way down the stairs she might have wondered at Bill's guilty alarm.

'Oh, love, I was wondering if I could borrow the car again this evening?' he called out after her.

The footsteps paused somewhere near the bottom step of the stairs. 'Well you can just go on wondering,' the voice called back and somewhere at the back of the house a door slammed shut.

'Did that mean yes or no?' Bill asked the empty house.

Thoughts of police, cars and half made plans disturbed his little piece of morning bliss. He got out of bed and put his pyjamas on. The bathroom smelt of wet dog so he put his dirty clothes in the wash basket and, for want of anything better to do, he went downstairs and put the kettle on. A pale watery patch of sunlight filtered through the kitchen window and cobwebby dew glistening on the grass outside in the garden suggested an early frost.

Bill wondered where his slippers were and went back upstairs. His office was a horrid mess and smelt of compost. Bill retrieved the bin bag, sealed it tightly and took it downstairs. It could go straight into the wheelie bin. The concrete outside the back door felt damp and cold to his bare feet and in an attempt to keep warm he ran along on tiptoes to where the wheelie bin resided by their front gate.

It felt good to see the incriminating evidence vanish into the depths of the black wheelie bin and Bill ran back towards the house, but just as his right foot met the warm linoleum of the kitchen floor Bill noticed that the shed door was hanging open. Had he forgotten to shut it the night before? On closer inspection the shed door wasn't just hanging open it was lolling, maimed, on one hinge. Bill's mouth formed a big round, oh. He tenderly eased the shed door open and peered into the gloom. He felt for the light switch and scraped his pyjamaed knee against something sprawled over the floor. It was his bicycle. It was up-ended on the floor and its tyres had been mutilated.

123

Shock gripped Bill so tightly that he didn't hear the gate click, not did he hear the tread of boots up the garden path. A heavy purposeful tread. The first Bill knew of it was when a large hand rested on his shoulder. Bill swung round and a reflex fist powered by those broad shoulders was within two inches of knocking out the local bobby.

'Mr Reeves?' said the policeman.

'Someone's broken into my shed,' said Bill, 'and destroyed my bicycle.'

Bill and the policeman looked uncertainly at the bicycle.

'Perhaps we should go inside, sir?' the policeman suggested, steering Bill away from the carnage and into the warmth of the kitchen. 'I'll make some tea, shall I?' he asked.

Bill nodded and flopped down onto a kitchen chair. His thoughts were all over the place and unwanted images of illegal swag recently abandoned in the wheelie bin, not to mention sirens the previous evening, getaway bicycles, CCTV and security lights at *Spiked,* kept popping up and confusing him.

The policeman was remarkably proficient at producing tea in unfamiliar surroundings. He even presented Bill with the sugar. After four spoonfuls were carefully stirred into Bill's second steaming mug of the morning Bill managed to look the policeman in the eye.

'How come you knew about my shed?' he asked.

'I don't know anything about your shed,' said the policeman.

'But my shed's been broken into and my bike's been vandalised and you're here,' said Bill.

The policeman got his notebook out and cleared his throat. He was trying to work out the procedure for investigating a crime before it was reported. Bill slurped a few mouthfuls of tea and stood up. He needed a bit of time to sort his thoughts out.

'Do you mind if I put some clothes on?' he said. 'It's a bit chilly in my pyjamas.'

The policeman readily agreed with this request. 'Perhaps I should investigate the crime scene while you're changing?'

'Yes,' said Bill, 'excellent.'

Bill rushed upstairs. The post-it notes were still scattered all over his office floor. He picked them up randomly and stuck them in various places on his desk with a couple of inspired lists of numbers on his computer screen for added effect.

Bill had a quick anxious look out of the window. The police car was parked outside the gate and the policeman was ambling slowly up the path.

'Oh heck, can't he just stick to the crime scene, or at least stay put in the kitchen?' Bill said to window.

His breath made a little patch of condensation on the glass pane and the policeman looked up. Bill dived out of view and went to his bedroom to find some clothes. Clothes were not all that forthcoming, what with being soaked and muddied and torn at the knees. He found an old pair of corderoys at the bottom of a drawer. They were in quite good nick except the zip was broken. Then he found a long baggy jumper which almost covered the zip and galloped back down the stairs.

The policeman had beaten him to it and was sitting at the kitchen table calmly drinking a second mug of tea. He motioned his head in the direction of the kettle but Bill declined. His bladder was already filling up painfully. He pulled the jumper over the broken zip and sat down.

The policeman opened his notebook and cleared his throat for a second time.

'Time 09.35,' he said.

Bill glanced at the kitchen clock and agreed with him.

'And when did you first notice the damage, Mr Reeves?'

'I don't know, just before you came,' said Bill.

'I arrived on the scene at 09.04,' said the policeman.

'Well then, then,' said Bill.

'So you hadn't noticed anything suspicious before?'

'No,' said Bill.

'And when did you last notice that there was nothing wrong with your shed?'

'Er?'

'When did you last use your bicycle, Mr Reeves?' the Policeman asked.

'Yesterday,' said Bill promptly.

'So you used your bicycle yesterday and it was in full working order?'

'Yes.' Bill hesitated slightly. Was it illegal to ride a bicycle with faulty back brakes?

'And when you returned home yesterday with your bicycle you locked it in the shed?'

'Yes,' said Bill confidently.

'At what time would that have been, Mr Reeves?'

'That would have been at,' Bill stopped. He looked at the clock. He looked at his half drunk cold mug of over sweet tea. He looked at the policeman. 'At tea time,' he said.

'And what time is teatime?' the policeman asked patiently.

'Teatime is usually at about six,' said Bill carefully telling the truth.

'So at about six o'clock last night your bicycle was undamaged and your shed was securely locked?'

Bill listened very carefully to the policeman's words. He nodded. 'Yes.'

'And you didn't hear anything suspicious after that time?'

Bill shook his head, although it was a bit unnerving to think that someone, probably Shaun Bean, had been lurking around in the night.

'Because they must have made a bit of noise forcing the shed door open.'

Bill looked unhappy. 'I slept like a log,' he said lamely.

'I wonder if you wouldn't mind coming outside and checking over the damage again. We also need to ascertain if anything else has been damaged or taken.'

'Yes of course, officer,' said Bill. 'I'll just find some shoes if you don't mind.'

One morning trip outside with bare feet was quite enough. There was an issue about finding shoes but somehow with a goodnight's sleep behind him it was so much easier and his shoes were where they always were; on the front doormat.

Bill joined the policeman outside. They inspected the shed door first and both agreed that the splintered wood both above and below the lock indicated that the door had been forced open with some force, perhaps with a crowbar.

'Do you need to take a picture of the damage for insurance purposes?' asked the policeman.

Bill looked blank. The thought hadn't occurred to him. In fact he'd already worked out what he needed to do to fix the damage. 'No, I don't think so,' he said.

'And your bicycle was in full working order when you left it last night?'

They both looked at Bill's bicycle sprawled all over the shed floor.

'Shall we take it out?' said Bill.

The policeman agreed and they lifted the bicycle out of the shed. Once the right way up the damage looked less dramatic.

'It's just the tyres,' said Bill. He almost sounded happy. 'It doesn't look as though he's managed to do much else.'

'He?'

'Them. Whoever did it,' said Bill quickly. He pushed the bicycle around on its flapping tyres just to confirm his diagnosis.

'Is there anything else?' the policeman asked, peering into the shed and sounding distinctly less sympathetic.

Bill gave the shed a cursory glance. 'I don't think so,' he said, wheeling his bicycle around and checking the wheel spokes.

'I feel I should warn you, Mr Reeves, that a small criminal offence such as this will not be given very high priority.'

'Oh,' said Bill.

'And in the unlikely event of the perpetrator being apprehended would you be willing to press charges?'

'Oh,' repeated Bill, 'I don't rightly -'

'Because it would be a waste of police resources wouldn't it if we were to spend time looking for the offender if you didn't intend to press charges?'

Bill nodded and shook his head not knowing how to respond to the policeman's logic. He anyway had two old tyres in the shed, assuming they'd not been found and mutilated as well, and if they didn't fit then there was John from the committee who batted at number four and fixed up bicycles in his spare time.

The policeman shut his notebook and Bill looked up hopefully, expecting to escort him to the gate.

'There's a large black bin bag in your wheelie bin containing headed paper from *Sunshine Soft drinks*. Can you explain how it might come to be there, Mr Reeves?' said the policeman.

'Well now,' said Bill looking innocent, anxious, perturbed and confused all at once.

'It's just that there were a number of incidents yesterday evening linking you with *Sunshine Soft Drinks*.'

'*Spiked*,' corrected Bill.

'That's right,' agreed the policeman, '*Spiked*.'

'And these incidents were reported last night?'

'No, they were reported this morning at,' the policeman opened his notebook again, 'at 08.07.'

'By whom?' asked Bill.

'By whom?' asked the policeman.

'Yes, who reported these so called incidents?' continued Bill.

'Well now,' said the policeman looking innocent, anxious, perturbed and confused.

'Am I not allowed to ask that?' asked Bill.

The policeman consulted his notebook then looked up at Bill. 'I believe I'm not at liberty to divulge my source at present.'

'Source or sources?' asked Bill.

The policeman opened his mouth to speak then paused. 'As I say I'm not at liberty to divulge any source or sources at this moment in time.'

'I presume you can however divulge the nature of the incident or incidents?'

The policeman looked happier and turned back to his notebook. 'There are two incidents reported from yesterday evening and independent witnesses place you at both incident scenes.'

'So you have two sources,' said Bill.

The policeman looked up crossly. Bill decided to smile, helpfully.

'The first one was a report of a break-in at the council offices at around 18.30 yesterday evening. At around 16.30 you were reported as entering the council building but no one could report having seen you leave.'

'I work for the council,' said Bill.

'You do?'

'Yes.'

'You're not at work today.'

'I'm on sick leave.'

'Oh?'

'I went to the doctor's yesterday with an acute heart condition. You can check if you like. I had an appointment with Dr Adams at some time after 13.00.'

'A heart condition,' the policeman nodded. He felt much more comfortable with heart conditions than incidents and secret sources.

'So I went on to work, at the council offices, and delivered in my sick note.'

'Indeed,' said the policeman in an agreeing sort of way.

'It is quite possible that the receptionist, Sally Anne, didn't notice me leaving the premises. It was after all near leaving time for everyone,' Bill said carefully.

'Well,' said the policeman.

'What exactly was the incident at the council offices?'

The policeman looked up from his notebook again looking less innocent and more anxious this time.

'I suppose you can't divulge that either,' Bill said.

The policeman didn't say anything, although there was obviously something else troubling him in his notebook.

'And there was another incident?' prompted Bill.

'Indeed. There were two incidents at *Sunshine Soft Drinks.*'

'*Spiked.*'

The Policeman looked at Bill suspiciously.

Bill half shrugged and tried smiling again.

'One at 19.37 and a second incident reported at 19.48.'

'Reported at 19.48? I thought that the incidents had been reported at 08.07 this morning?' said Bill. He reckoned he was getting quite good at this interrogation lark.

'This is a serious matter, Mr Reeves, you are caught on CCTV footage at the back entrance to *Sunshine Spiked* and further more were seen by the front entrance to *Spiked* carrying a large, heavy parcel on the front of your bicycle.'

'I was caught on CCTV footage?' questioned Bill. He leant over and tried to read the tag on the policeman's chest. 'Sergeant?'

'Smith,' supplied the policeman.

'Are you saying that I have been positively identified?'

'Well.'

The policeman blustered and Bill slowly and quietly let out a sigh of relief.

'Someone was caught on CCTV footage at *Sunshine Spiked Drinks* and someone was then seen riding a bicycle on the forecourt at *Sun Spiked*.'

'And that someone is supposed to be me?' Bill sounded suitably indignant.

'There are certain points of identity which link the person seen with you.'

'Am I allowed to ask what?' asked Bill.

'Apparently you are often seen around *Spiked Soft Drinks* riding a bicycle.'

'But, Sergeant Smith, you've already reported a further incident which links my bicycle with a break-in and act of vandalism which could have occurred anytime after six o'clock.'

The policeman consulted the last page in his notebook. He had indeed written the words, 'shed and bicycle last seen intact by the victim at about 18.00 the previous evening.'

'I wonder if that is all now?' pressed Bill. 'My doctor did most seriously recommend rest for the next few days.'

'Of course, Mr Reeves, it does seem unlikely that a man in your state of health would be out on a bicycle so far away from home and so late in the evening.'

Bill decided not to disagree with the policeman.

'There is however the issue of the bin bag containing papers from *Sunshine Soft Drinks*,' said the policeman unhappily.

'Unused headed paper,' said Bill a little too promptly.

And the policeman looked up a little too quickly.

'I was tidying up my home office last night,' said Bill his smile getting a bit thin. 'I had a job at *Sunshine Soft Drinks* or *Spiked* as it is now. I'm the local fire officer. I must have picked up some headed paper by accident when I gave a talk there last week.'

'So you won't mind if I have a quick look in your, office while I'm here?' Sergeant Smith stood up purposefully.

'No, I don't suppose I will,' said Bill.

The policeman followed Bill up the stairs and squeezed through Bill's office door. What with Bill's broadness and the policeman's bigness there wasn't much office left to look at. The policeman looked closely round the small room. The computer was old and anyway switched off, most of the books were about cricket, a briefcase which was hanging open rested against the desk chair, a buff folder labelled East Wolds CCC was pushed to one side on the desk and the desk was littered with an array of different coloured post-it notes. There was a yellow post-it note with a particularly clear message written on it. Both men bent over the desk to read it.

The post-it note said 'If you wake up DON'T wake me – sleep in the spare room'. Bill looked at the note puzzled. He reached for a rather fine pair of reading glasses which were conveniently placed next to his keyboard. He was still puzzled. He hadn't seen that message the previous evening.

The policeman coughed and looked embarrassed. 'I don't think I need to take up any more of your time, Mr Reeves, I'll be getting along now. And thank you for your assistance with our enquiries,' he added uncertainly.

18

Bill didn't like the thought that it was Susan who had written the command on the post-it note. And of course Susan had written it. Even Bill could recognise Susan's handwriting. He put it to one side. It wasn't going to help with his investigation. The remaining post-it notes he put in a heap and jumbled them up and then turned them all the right way up as if he was playing Memory.

Bill looked at the various figures first. The four digit number was probably a pin code. The dates and timetable he put together just because dates and timetables go well together. The dates were days only so that Bill couldn't guess whether they denoted a current plan or a future plan. The timetable would of course be a scheduled route. The times were spaced at more-or-less regular half hourly intervals. Did the local buses go that frequently? Did trains from York to Hull go every half hour? It didn't seem likely. And if they did they would go regularly at the same time. Bill switched his computer on and while it took its five minutes to warm up he picked up the telephone numbers and went downstairs to find a telephone. His mobile was still on the kitchen table so he picked it up and punched in the London number. Only after it started ringing did Bill realise that with modern phones the person at the other end would see his number, their telephone would no doubt store his number and if they so desired they would easily be able to trace him. He pressed the red button on his mobile and decided to leave the phone numbers for later. He would have to do something clever like use a phone box or borrow someone else's phone. It might be best not to use Susan's though. Susan was a bit off him just now which he didn't think was entirely fair.

He put the kettle on. Forgot that he'd put the kettle on and went back upstairs. For a moment he was confused by the buzzing of the computer then he remembered his planned detective work with regards to the timetable. He searched National Rail, found York station and clicked on live departures. Trains going to London were identical to his list of times. 'Yes,' he shouted and the blue post-it note saying 'Yes' surrounded by exclamation marks seemed to shout back at him.

At this point, stimulated by his success, his brain went into overdrive. Goodness knows what would have happened to his heart rate if the wonderful Dr Adams hadn't administered such an effective placebo.

He pulled himself back to the numbers. He still hadn't analysed the percentages, but the last time he had looked at percentages it was to do with amounts of caffeine in *Spiked*. And indeed there it was in blue and yellow, 'need more caffeine!!!!' As he paired them off and moved them out of the way he found himself looking at the letters, or initials 'BR' and it was hard for his hand not to shake and his heart not to jump because BR was him, Bill Reeves.

Bill Reeves, an exploding bomb to be got rid of 'later'. By whom? 'Try SB'. 'Shaun Bean,' Bill said hoarsely. 'DL' okayed it. Someone else was very happy about the conclusion and the map denoted where they were to dump the body. Somewhere up north on the A19 well away from East Wolds.

'Now if I can find out who this DL person is -' Bill muttered to himself. He typed in *spiked.com* and waited for his computer to download all the pictures which came up on the *Spiked* home page. He then clicked on the link which said, 'Our management team, always here to help you'. There was a beaming photograph of Mark Hammond listing all his qualifications and a few satisfied quotes about how clever he was and about how clever *Spiked* was. There was one other picture, this one of a woman Bill had never seen who was apparently based in London. There were no more actual photos, so when Bill found the name Dagny Lamb half way down the list he had no idea who it was. Whether it was anyone he'd met at *Spiked* nor even whether Dagny denoted a man or a woman.

There was, however, a DL who worked at *Spiked*, listed in the management team and therefore having authority over Shaun Bean and over the fate of Bill Reeves.

Bill's eye caught the message 'need more caffeine' and remembered that a long time ago he'd put the kettle on and that an even longer time ago he'd forgotten to eat any breakfast.

After a large breakfast which included five slices of toast and marmalade Bill went outside to fix his getaway vehicle. It had turned into a reasonably dry day and although the watery sunlight didn't warm it had dried up small patches of concrete outside Bill's back door. The mutilated bicycle was up-ended in the remains of a puddle but Bill found a dry patch and a gardening knee protector and when the first torn wheel popped off Bill whistled a bright refrain from *Carmen*.

Of course a newly repaired bicycle needed a test run so with a quick glance at the kitchen clock which claimed that it was already nearly twenty minutes past two Bill grabbed the yellow post-it notes with the two phone numbers on them, his bicycle helmet to appease Susan and locked the door behind him. It was only when he gracefully alighted his bicycle out on The Avenue that Bill realised that he'd carefully locked the door but forgotten to take his key. But the bicycle purred along and Bill decided to see if John Bailey, the number four batsman who repaired bicycles, was at home. Vision impaired by his bicycle helmet and concentration impaired by the realisation that his new back tyre had a slow puncture Bill didn't notice the white van which pulled out of The Avenue and followed him onto the main road.

To the north of the High Street was another post war development of three bedroomed semis similar to The Avenue. It was somewhere here that the number four batsman lived. This development had been more ambitious than The Avenue so that instead of one long simple cul-de-sac there were three cul-de-sacs, a crescent and two through roads. Bill bicycled around optimistically looking for signs of open garages housing bicycle repair kits. Then less optimistically as his back tyre degenerated to a critical level of air pressure he bicycled around looking for any signs of bicycles around the houses. He passed a white van twice and thought of asking them but every time he looked through the window the driver bent over as if he was tying his shoelace which was an odd thing to do while driving a van and the passenger, a gawping youth, didn't look as if he knew anything.

At last Bill spotted an elderly woman dragging a shopping bag on wheels behind her. Bill attempted to raise his bicycle helmet.

'Mrs Herrington, and how are you today?' he asked dismounting his bicycle and walking along beside her.

'It's you is it,' Mrs Herrington said. 'You can tell that wife of yours to tell that new doctor that them pills don't work and that my old ones were much better.'

'I'm sorry to hear that Mrs Herrington,' Bill said.

The white van seemed to be doing some sort of adventurous manoeuvre in the middle of the road. Bill and Mrs Herrington watched it curiously.

'Mrs Herrington I wonder if you can help me?' Bill asked still keeping a bright and courteous tone.

Mrs Herrington turned back to the footpath and the dragging along of her shopping bag.

'I'm looking for the man who bats at number four.'

'The man who bats at number 4? There isn't a man as bats at number 4. That's that old Fothergill chap and he doesn't bat nor nothing. Never has.'

One of the wheels on Mrs Herrington's shopping bag needed some oil.

'I don't mean he lives at number 4, I mean I don't know where he lives and I wondered if you did.'

'If I did what?'

'If you know where the man that bats at number four for the cricket club lives.'

Mrs Herrington paused and looked at Bill appraisingly. 'Still play cricket then do you?' she asked.

The broad shoulders stretched proudly. 'I do an' all.'

'There's another one daft as a brush about cricket. Lives at number 11 on The Crescent.'

'Yes of course,' announced Bill.

'If you say so,' said Mrs Herrington. 'Is that it then? Can I be getting on?'

Bill realised that he'd stepped onto the path and was blocking Mrs Herrington's way. 'Yes of course, very nice to see you Mrs Herrington and looking so well.'

Bill was already sailing off back down the street past the waiting white van so he didn't hear Mrs Herrington's last words. She paused and watched him and took a half-minute to rest and watch the white van perform a further operation as it turned around yet again. Bill missed all this and arrived at number 11, The Crescent just as the front door opened to reveal John Bailey.

Fellow committee member John Bailey was a big man who either hit 3 sixes or was out for a duck, but the 3 sixes when they came were invariably match winners. He was in his forties and Bill wasn't sure but he thought he did some sort of shift work out towards Hull way. Anyway he was home now.

'John, how's things?'

'Not bad, not bad at all. Grand day isn't it.'

'Do you still do the odd bicycle repair?'

'Oh aye, but you surely don't need my help, Bill, I thought you were the bicycle expert.'

Bill pointed to the flat back tyre.

'But that'll get you home, won't it?'

'I suppose so, but I wondered if you had a spare set of tyres?'

'Don't you?'

'I did.'

'Oh aye?'

Bill decided to say nothing.

'I'm sure I can fix you up with something. I was just going to do a repair myself so you might as well fix yours up while you're here.'

'Thank you,' said Bill.

John Bailey opened his garage door and they both gazed in admiration at the array of bicycle parts and tools. As John turned to usher Bill into his garage he noticed a white van pulling up onto the curb. The driver of the white van caught his eye and then looked away.

'Now what's a white van doing outside number 7?' said John.

Bill went out of John's garage to have a look but the driver was tying up his shoelace again.

John didn't wait for an answer. He walked out into the road towards the white van. Not aggressively. But when a big man walks purposefully towards a target it is hard for him to look entirely friendly. Bill watched with growing concern. He'd been about to tell John that he'd never seen the white van before but even as the words faded on his lips he realised that he had seen it before. He had seen it several times hovering around wherever he, Bill, seemed to be. Bill backed into the garage and consoled himself with a whole wall of bicycle parts and a workbench that was as big as Bill's entire shed.

John returned to find Bill appropriating a fine set of spare tyres. 'They're grand them, aren't they,' John said as he came up behind Bill. 'Trouble is,' continued John, 'no one buys them type any more.'

'They're just right for my bike,' said Bill.

'They would be. They're a tyre for a connoisseur, they are,' said John savouring the word connoisseur. 'You can have them for a tenner,' said John.

'A tenner? Really?' Bill scrabbled around in his pocket and found lots of change. The change was really destined for the anonymous phone calls he planned to make from a phone box to the telephone numbers on the yellow post-it notes. He counted it out. It came to £10.21. 'I'll have to give you all this change,' Bill said sorrowfully.

'That's no problem. Come in handy for parking that will.'

'I'm sure it will but I was going to use it to make a phone call,' Bill continued handing over the heap of change.

John jiggled the coins in a big hand. 'That's not a problem, you can ring from our phone.'

Bill, wondering if John was capable of suspicion, said casually. 'That van, was it anything?'

'Oh no,' said John, 'that was just that Shaun Bean chap who's joined the cricket club. Said he had some business this way.'

Bill clutched the tyres and waited for his heart to complain. It didn't. 'But he,' he said in a squeaky voice, 'he,' he continued in a deep important voice, 'he works for *Spiked.*'

'Does he?' said John. He couldn't be more unconcerned. He whipped Bill's bicycle upside down and levered off the back tyre before Bill had time to worry what business Shaun Bean might have outside John Bailey's house if it didn't concern Bill.

The slow puncture was pleasurably difficult to find and both men had gone through several cricket matches, an unfair leg-before-wicket given to John after a particularly in-form bit of batting working up to the statutory 3 sixes and a eulogy from John which Bill enjoyed about how he'd never seen a wicket keeper quite like Bill nor for the matter of it a finer spin bowler.

'We'd be lost without you, Bill,' he finished as the repaired tyre slipped back onto the back wheel.

'I'm getting on a bit now you know,' Bill said.

'Nonsense,' John said finding an oily rag to wipe his hands on.

'Are you going to the meeting on Saturday?' Bill asked.

'What meeting?'

This stalled Bill for a minute while he righted his bicycle. 'You know, the meeting on Saturday.'

'No, I don't know anything about a meeting,' said John.

'The extraordinary general meeting about the cricket club,' said Bill.

'It doesn't matter how extraordinary it is I haven't heard of it,' said John.

'It's,' said Bill, 'it's about *Spiked* sponsoring the cricket club.'

John jingled the coins in his pocket and turned to start work on another bicycle.

'*Spiked* are going to build a new pavilion,' Bill said loudly.

'A new pavilion,' said John dreamily. 'How grand is that then. I thought that had all been decided on at the committee meeting.'

'No, but,' Bill said, then stopped. 'John?' he said.

John made a muffled noise. He had up-ended another bicycle and his mouth was full of tools.

'This meeting is very important. It decides the whole future of the cricket club.' Bill wasn't sure but he thought that John might be whistling between his teeth and the tools sticking out of his mouth. 'We might get money to build a new pavilion.'

John nodded his approval.

'But it will have consequences. It will mean that we are bound to a sponsorship from *Spiked* for ever.' Bill paused before using the word ever wondering if it was too dramatic.

A frown creased across John's sizeable brow.

It wasn't too dramatic. Bill felt encouraged. 'Imagine our first game of the season this year not in whites but in red shirts with big black writing all over them.'

'Red shirts,' exclaimed John amidst a shower of tools.

'It's not right is it?' said Bill.

John was picking up tools but a bolt was missing. He clutched his chest and gave a large belch which tasted distinctly metallic. 'I'm not wearing a red shirt,' he said.

'But if we accept sponsorship from *Spiked* then we'll have to accept red shirts or anything else that *Spiked* decide we'll have to do.'

John stood up slowly and put the tools on his workbench. 'So it's new pavilion as against red shirts?' he said.

'Yes,' agreed Bill, 'if *Spiked* fund a new pavilion -'

'We'll get a new pavilion,' broke in John.

'Yes, but it will be a sponsorship deal so we'll have to do what ever *Spiked* says.'

'Sponsorship like the big clubs have?' asked John. He sounded impressed. 'A new clubhouse would be grand now wouldn't it, Bill,' he said.

Bill realised miserably that all he'd managed to do was mobilise John's memory of last Thursday's committee meeting and he wondered how he'd managed to lose the argument so conclusively yet again. 'I'd better be going I suppose,' he said.

John was taking the chain off the up-ended bicycle.

'Can I use your phone then?' Bill asked.

'Oh aye, help yourself,' said John concentrating on a long length of chain and a bent cog on one of the gear changes.

When Bill slipped in through John Bailey's front door he noticed that the white van was still in position. He took a deep breath. First things first. He found John's phone, punched in the London number and walked into John's front room while the number registered then started to ring. The curtains in John's front room window afforded enough camouflage for Bill to peer around them and watch the progress of the white van. In the meantime a woman's voice said 'Hello,' on the other end of the phone line. After about five hellos Bill couldn't think of anything else to say so he said hello back.

'Who is this, please?' the woman said. She had a deep voice and sounded efficient and professional. Her voice was neither posh nor regional and had a slight lilt in its tone as though she had lived abroad.

'Have I reached *Spiked* offices?' said Bill.

'Can you tell me who is calling please,' the woman continued and Bill could imagine her shoulders rising and her mouth puckering into indignation.

'It's just that I'd like to ask *Spiked* some questions,' Bill said.

'What sort of questions?'

She didn't deny the assumed connection with *Spiked*.

'Questions about *Spiked*.' This was no good. Bill braced his own shoulders. 'I'd like to ask some questions about *Spiked's* position, er, policy in the North East.'

'Who is this?' the woman repeated.

'A representative from a local cricket club,' Bill blundered on.

'All local issues are dealt with regionally. If you go to our web page, *www.spiked.com*, you will find a regional help line under *contact us*.' She paused. 'Can I ask who gave you my direct line?'

'Oh well,' Bill started to bluster and wished too late that he'd copied the woman's presence of mind and taken a pause long enough to think. But he hadn't. 'I'm ringing from the local press,' he said, and the woman put the phone down.

About 30 seconds later she picked it up again because the same voice answered the mobile number that Bill rang straight away afterwards.

'It's me again,' said Bill and then listened to the click of the phone being disconnected.

What did he do now? The white van was still parked outside. Bill couldn't stay at John Bailey's all night and what about John's wife? What would she say if she came home from work and found Bill lurking behind the curtains? He put the phone down and surveyed the back of the house. John's garden was separated by a low fence from another row of houses backing onto The Crescent on a street which curved around The Crescent and ended up adjoining Mrs Herrington's street.

Bill popped back outside. John was whirring the back wheel of the bicycle he'd just repaired and clicking the gears up and down.

'Isn't it a grand thing a bicycle, Bill? Did you find everything you needed?' he added.

Bill agreed with both questions. 'How do you get into your back garden, John?' he said.

'Out the back?'

Bill nodded.

'It depends. If I'm mowing the lawn I go through there,' John said.

There was a door at the back of the garage. 'And that door leads into your back garden?' asked Bill. He took his bicycle and pushed it to the door at the back of John's garage with the new spare tyres hanging off the handlebars. 'Thank you, John, you take care,' said Bill. He pushed the door open and bashed his way through with his bicycle. 'And don't forget that meeting on Saturday now will you. Seven o'clock in the new school hall gym thing.'

John had followed Bill to the door but Bill didn't look back; he skirted round some old raspberry canes, had a battle with a rose against the low fence then hauled his bicycle into someone else's spring bulb border. Moments later Bill was speeding down Mrs Herrington's road towards the High Street.

Bill's first thought was to go home but broken sheds and mutilated bicycles were not indicative of a save haven. His second thought was more appealing. He would pursue his pursuers. He cycled back round to The Crescent and rode up the street far enough to ascertain that the white van was still in position. He then retreated a bit. He needed to lurk.

Bill looked around. All he needed was an untidy garden with no sign of anyone at home. There was one untidy garden, it was overgrown with a scruffy Leylandii hedge. Getting to it meant a few seconds' exposure as he crossed the road in partial view of the white van. Once he'd successfully traversed the open stretch of road Bill was able to snuggle in behind the hedge with his bicycle, new spare tyres still swinging on the handlebars. Bill pushed his head through a gap in the bushes and had, as John Bailey would have said, a grand view. With a little manoeuvring he could see both the white van and John, concentrating over another up-ended bicycle.

What Bill didn't see was an old man in a dressing gown standing in the window behind Bill waiting and watching as well. Neither of them had to wait long for some action as Shaun Bean was just getting out of the van.

Shaun Bean stretched himself and flexed a few muscles. It was a long time for a big man to sit in a small space. Shaun then leant back to look into the van. He said something to the youth and gesticulated a lot. Bill couldn't hear what he said properly. 'I'm going to get him', or 'I'm going to see what's going on'. It definitely involved I'm going to do something or other.

141

Shaun Bean then marched up to John Bailey. John came out of his garage and Bill watched the exchange keenly. The old man at his upstairs window had an even better view.

Bill watched John, appearing to be unaware of either Shaun Bean's size or menace, make a friendly gesture with his oily rag. This resulted in a more friendly exchange than the one Shaun Bean had anticipated and John hit his on-form 3 sixes with an imaginary bat. There was then a distinct change in tone. Bill could see John shake his head but he couldn't make out the expression on John's face and all he could see of Shaun Bean was his back. John pointed into his garage and Shaun Bean stepped forward eagerly and then Bill's view was completely blocked because a silver Polo pulled up outside John's house and started to reverse into John's driveway. It was obviously Barbara Bailey coming home from work. The old man saw what Bill could no longer see; Shaun Bean peering through the door at the back of John's garage and getting very excited. What Bill did see was Shaun Bean come running out of John's driveway and Barbara Bailey emerging from her Polo looking indignant.

Bill ducked into the Leylandii hedge and heard rather than saw the door slamming shut on the white van. The engine started up and a lot of revving ensued as the van turned around.

Bill scrabbled onto his bicycle needing to be ready to follow Shaun Bean's speedy exit from The Crescent. The white van sped past and Bill was just launching himself in its wake when a croaky voice called from the driveway of the scruffy garden.

'Hey, you,' it said.

Bill paused mid-mount and turned round to face his new assailant.

'You forgot this,' the assailant said as he came at a hobbling run towards Bill his flapping dressing gown revealing striped pyjamas. The old man was waving Bill's bicycle helmet and clutching at a breathless chest.

'Thank you,' said Bill as the white van became a distant shrieking of tyres and hooting of horns.

The old man leant in conspiratorially as he passed over Bill's helmet. 'Go get 'em,' he said.

Bill pushed the helmet onto his head and launched off again in the direction of the white van.

The old man cupped his hands round his mouth. 'Those six catches at the cup final, best thing I ever saw. Good luck, son,' he shouted after Bill.

The streets were busy now and a small queue was gathering at the end of the road waiting to turn onto the High Street. The white van was sandwiched between a blue Golf and a grey Honda. Bill tucked in behind the grey Honda. Bill could see that the white van was not indicating to turn left onto the High Street so that if it was indicating at all it was indicating to turn right, which meant that Shaun Bean's plan, if he had a plan, was to head in the direction of Bill's Avenue.

After five more minutes of revving and hooting the white van made a right turn onto the High Street and Bill, pulling in front of the grey Honda, followed it.

At this point several things seemed to happen at once. It got dark, which meant that it must be later than Bill had thought, and the white van suddenly slowed down. Bill almost ran into the back of it but with sudden perspicacity Bill realised that if he was right up against the back curb side panel of the van he was out of sight of the van's occupants. The gawping youth or Shaun Bean could use the off-side mirror but Bill kept his bicycle lights off and decided it was worth taking the risk. Bill was now close enough to the van to hear a mobile phone ringing inside it. Someone answered the phone but Bill couldn't hear what they said until Shaun Bean started shouting.

'I've said I'll get him haven't I,' he shouted, 'just leave it with me can't you.'

Bill wobbled nervously and the white van shot off again. Bill put his head down and raced after it.

By the turning to The Avenue the van screeched to a halt and wrenched its way into a turn and roared down The Avenue towards Bill's house.

Bill followed them at a safe distance. A car further down The Avenue hooted indignantly and then came into view, its lights spot-lighting Bill as he crept up The Avenue trying to surround himself in shadow. The driver of the car gave Bill a very hard stare and Bill found himself briefly looking into Susan's eyes. It was possible that she was even angrier than Shaun Bean.

Meanwhile the white van had done a U-turn and was racing back up The Avenue. Susan drove sedately onto the main road and

Bill dived into a random driveway before following the van at full speed. By the time the van reached the High Street it was doing about sixty miles per hour and Bill might have been approaching forty when his friend, Sergeant Smith, pulled out of a parking lot by the Fish 'n' Chip shop. Bill couldn't stop as he'd still not fixed his back brake. Shaun Bean however did and the policeman and Shaun Bean were at the beginning of a fulsome negotiation as Bill raced past, the spare tyres flapping up from the handlebars into his face. It was possible that Bill heard the gawping youth cry out. 'It's him, look!'

Just past the village green Bill slowed down sufficiently to use his brakes effectively and came to a stop by the road where Carol and family lived. Bill decided that this was a good place to hide so he found a wheelie bin to loiter behind and waited for the white van to follow him up the street.

A while later the van came docilely up the High Street and as it was now cold and clear it seemed like a long while to Bill waiting by the wheelie bin. Bill made ready to chase after it but it didn't carry on down the High Street, instead it turned into the street where Bill was. Bill cowered down and launched himself after the van as it pulled up outside Carol's house.

Bill froze. Was this a new tactic? Threatening Bill's family? Perhaps they were going to take a hostage. Bill found another wheelie bin and watched helplessly as Shaun Bean marched purposefully up to Carol's front door and rang the bell. Bill craned his neck to see. Carol answered the door and he heard the high chirp of her voice which meant that she was being polite but was annoyed. Shaun Bean's voice sounded gruff, even apologetic.

Will's head emerged from behind Carol and just as Bill was about to shout out something to warn them Danny Bean also appeared from behind Carol. Danny Bean was duly collected and marched into the white van.

Bill was standing half on the road staring at the van as it turned around yet again and set off home. The occupants of the van turned and stared in equal bemusement at Bill.

'Dad, what on earth?' came Carol's shrill voice from the doorway.

'Grandad, Gramps' shouted Will and ran out into the road.

'Well now then,' said Bill feeling far too cold and dishevelled to face his daughter, 'I'd better be getting off home before Grandma wonders where I am.'

He was half way home when he remembered that Susan had been on her way out and that he didn't have a key.

19

Bill carried on towards home until he managed to apply his thoughts to Susan in a sufficiently organised way to remember that she went to her knitting group on Thursdays at Melanie Andrews'. The Andrews lived in a very done-up cottage on the main road out of town not so very far from The Avenue. For want of anything better to do Bill set off there.

Reassured by the sight of Susan's car Bill leant his bicycle against a large terracotta pot housing a bay tree and went for a prowl around the house. A lounge at the back which had a terrace leading into the garden was ablaze with light. Bill went up to a big veranda door and pressed his nose to the glass. It was a pretty room. A log fire burned in a modern hearth set with Italian stone and six women looked in alarm at the helmeted intruder. A seventh looked shocked, embarrassed then cross.

Bill waved apologetically at Susan. 'I forgot my key,' he mouthed through the window. His breath made a ring of condensation on the glass and when he wiped it off with his sleeve he left a big black mark in its place.

The veranda door opened and Melanie Andrews stood there showing a lot of ironic shock horror and a lot of bust in a tight fitting cream jumper. 'Bill Reeves, well isn't this an honour, we girls never get to see you these days.'

Bill took his bicycle helmet off and tried to do something gallant with his grubby arm.

'We'd better let you in I suppose. We thought you were a tramp,' Melanie laughed into the warm room.

'You can just as well leave him out in the cold,' Susan muttered from the depths of a discreetly orange armchair.

Bill was ushered into the room and at least three women started fussing around him. A chair was pulled up to the fire and a rug was hastily snatched up off the floor by the veranda door and put on the chair before Bill managed to sit down on it. The rug smelt of dog. Bill smelt, mainly, of oil. He looked anxiously at Susan then clutched his heart in a bid for sympathy. It wasn't behaving normally, his eyes said to Susan as she joined the women surrounding him.

She leant over him. 'It's you who's not behaving normally,' she hissed at him.

Melanie Andrews clutched at her ample chest. 'What with all these goings on we thought you must be the prowler,' she exclaimed excitedly.

'The prowler?' Bill asked weakly, wishing Susan would retreat back to her orange chair.

'And there was a break-in at the council offices,' piped up another knitter.

'Yes, but that was just a false alarm,' said another more stolid knitter who had abandoned neither chair nor knitting.

'No it wasn't,' continued the alarmist, 'one of the councillors lost a valuable pair of reading glasses.'

An alarmed look flickered in Bill's eyes just long enough for Susan to notice it. Luckily she was distracted as the alarmist clutched at her sleeve. 'And there was a police car down your Avenue, Susan, this morning.'

'Yes,' broke in another, 'and did you see Sergeant Smith had to pull in a white van for speeding? I saw it all on my way here. It must have been doing over 90 miles an hour and in the High Street.'

'But the prowler,' said Melanie breaking in calmly, 'was caught on CCTV at *Spiked.*'

A hushed silence greeted the entrance of Jonathan Andrews, or Jon as he insisted on being spelt, who appeared in the doorway.

'Bill, how are you doing old chap,' he said genially in a voice that had got considerably posher since he'd sold his business. To the rest of them he said. 'Indeed, Melanie's right. I know because I was at *Spiked* this morning and they told me all about it. They even showed me the CCTV clips,' he added importantly.

Bill looked at him through the sea of nail varnish that still surrounded him and managed to have three sensible thoughts. One, that it was a long time since Jonathan Andrews had shown any particular friendship towards him, two, that it would seem that money made recently in this town was a function of *Spiked* and three, Jonathan Andrews was drunk.

Bill stood up and held out his hand, man to man, to Jonathan Andrews. 'I'm not so bad, Jon, not so bad,' he said.

'Come and have a drink, old chap,' said Jon.

He shook Bill's hand and led him via the handshake into a clinically modern kitchen. The feminine concern retreated and Bill was invited to perch himself on a high uncomfortable stool at what Carol would have called a breakfast bar. The breakfast bar was topped in cold black stone and the floor beneath Bill's battered trainers was cold white stone flecked to look like marble. Or perhaps it was marble.

A warm smell of hot drinks and cake emanated from the lounge and Bill failed to hide his disappointment when Jon presented him with a large tumbler of whisky.

'Bottoms up,' said Jon.

'Cheers,' said Bill miserably. He took a careful sip of the fiery liquid. He didn't much like whisky and he certainly didn't want to have to face Susan again in another drunken stupor.

'So, Jon,' Bill said innocently, trying not to let the vapour from the whisky knock him out, 'what were you doing up at *Spiked* this morning?'

Jon tapped his forefinger on the side of his nose, not very accurately. 'You know how it is when you have money,' he said.

'No, not really,' said Bill sniffing at his whisky.

'Well, Bill,' continued Jon leaning over the breakfast bar to wave both a finger and a tumbler of whisky in Bill's face, 'money breeds money.'

Bill didn't see what this had to do with it. 'So what were you doing at *Spiked* this morning,' he repeated.

'Talking money of course,' said Jon, slurping in a large mouthful of whisky.

'Oh?' said Bill trying to sound casual.

'Good chap that Mark Harwell,' said Jon.

'Mark Hammond,' corrected Bill, 'he's called Mark Hammond.'

'Mark Hammond, that's what I said. Mark Hammond and I understand each other.'

'Oh,' said Bill unhappily, as Jonathan Andrews had once been quite a good friend and a decent fielder at short leg.

'I've been invited, invited mind, to invest in *Spiked*,' said Jon. He reached for the bottle, replenished his own glass and poured more into Bill's. 'We haven't gone public yet so you won't say anything, will you?'

Bill tried not to look alarmed.

'And the little woman doesn't know of course, so mums the word, Bill.'

'Um,' Bill didn't know whether to say anything or not. But why on earth would *Spiked* be interested in a small investor like Jonathan Andrews? 'I suppose you know what you're doing,' Bill said lamely and with all the wrong emphasis.

'Indeed I do, Bill, indeed I do.' Another dram of whisky vanished from Jon's glass.

'Because, Jon, well *Spiked*, Jon, well we don't really know anything about them now do we. I mean -'

'You of course may not, indeed can't possibly know what I know about *Spiked*, Bill. Besides I have a nose for these sorts of things. Made a nice few little investments on the way. You don't think all this,' Jon waved expansively at the glittering black stone surfaces and the floor which might have been marble, 'that all this would have been possible with the sale of the business. Oh no, that was just the beginning, just enough money to get us going.'

Of course if Jon really was overflowing with large amounts of cash then it wouldn't matter whether he invested in *Spiked* or not. But Bill was miserably aware not of what he didn't know about *Spiked* but that there was very little that he didn't know about *Spiked*.

'What if *Spiked* was found to be breaking trade regulations,' Bill said vaguely.

'Trading regulations?' Jon seemed to think that this was extremely funny.

Bill tried another angle of attack more likely to get Jon to listen to him. 'What if *Spiked* has solvency issues?'

'Solvent, Bill! *Spiked* is huge.'

Bill pretended to drink some more whisky.

'You see, Bill,' continued Jon, '*Spiked* likes to be seen as a local company and therefore gives preference to local investors.'

'Do you still own that plot of land on the other side of the canal?' asked Bill.

For the first time Jon woke up beneath the haze of whisky and looked sharply at Bill. '*Spiked*,' he said, 'and I won't deny it, are interested in my local connections.'

'Oh,' said Bill sadly.

'Which is why they showed me the CCTV footage of the prowler.'

Bill looked up and locked eyes with Jon, the one alarmed and the other smug.

'And of course it wasn't a prowler. That's just the women talking,' said Jon.

'If it wasn't a prowler what was it?' Bill risked asking.

'Just some animal. In fact it looked like a cow.'

'A cow?' Bill rashly took a large gulp of whisky and then couldn't swallow it because a big bubble of laughter was trying to choke him.

Fortunately Jon decided it was funny too. 'Can you imagine, a cow, and the whole town is getting hysterical about prowlers,' said Jon, also taking a large slug of whisky.

Bill, who had heard various feminine goodbyes taking place in the hallway decided that it was time to go. He stood up and extended his hand to Jon who opted to stay on the barstool.

'Good to see you again, Jon,' Bill said. They shook hands and Bill found his own way out. There was no sign of Melanie but a small dog met him by the door and looked at him longingly. 'Do you want to go out?' said Bill to the dog and he let both the dog and himself out into the freezing night.

When Bill arrived home cold and hungry the only heartening news that welcomed him was that Susan had left the kitchen door on the latch. Susan herself was crashing about in the sitting room. Bill tried to say hello in the most endearing way possible and Susan appeared in the kitchen doorway.

'Are you having an affair?' she said.

'A what?' said Bill literarily frozen to the spot.

'An affair.'

Bill noted that Susan looked cross rather than tearful and tried not to feel disappointed. 'Of course I'm not,' he tried to say.

'How do you explain this, then?' said Susan. She waved his mobile over the kitchen table at him and let it drop from a sufficient height to demonstrate an intent to cause damage.

Bill looked suitably bemused.

'You have seven missed calls and three messages from a woman called Julia,' announced Susan.

Bill looked at the mobile where it had skidded over the table to land at arms reach from him. Did he pick it up as if he was interested in this woman called Julia or did he ignore it? He'd never been in this situation before. Women tended to make a fuss of him but Susan normally just laughed and said something scathing about it.

'Do you mind if I have a cup of tea and something to eat?' he said, trying to slip around to the kettle and ignore the phone.

Susan's indignant snort was cut short because the phone started buzzing.

'A forth message,' said Susan.

Bill turned from the kettle and picked the phone up, he clicked a button and read 'Please confirm that you can meet tomorrow.' Bill turned the phone around and showed it to Susan. 'I think it says she wants to meet me tomorrow,' Bill said. Susan handed her glasses over to Bill wordlessly. Bill sat down and read a series of messages which began, 'We need to meet.' 'We should talk this through with Mark.' 'Did you try to ring earlier?' Susan had obviously already read them.

Bill turned back to the kettle and put it on. He then found a plate of cold pie, peas and potatoes. The gravy was congealed but Bill didn't care, he found a fork and shovelled the food in while the kettle came to the boil.

'Do you want some tea, love?' he asked Susan.

Susan stood her ground. 'I don't want tea,' she said, 'I want an explanation.'

'Julia must work for *Spiked*, I think she must be a London based boss,' said Bill.

'I don't need to know what she does I just want to know why she's so desperate to talk to you,' said Susan.

'She wants to kidnap me,' said Bill.

'Of all the, now, Bill Reeves, I'm sure men pass affairs off as many things and find all manner of excuses but kidnapping is just going too far.'

'I don't mean Julia is trying to kidnap me. *Spiked* is trying to kidnap me.' Bill calmly made a cup of tea and loaded it with sugar.

'Am I missing something here,' Susan said sourly.

Bill scalded himself on a long slurp of tea, but it was worth it. He was starting to feel human again. 'You know *Spiked*,' Bill began.

'No. But I do know that you're up to something.'

'Would it help you to know that I'm not having an affair but that I'm working on a sort of investigation to expose *Spiked*?'

Susan looked longingly at the kettle, which was still steaming. 'No,' she said.

Bill noticed the longing look at the kettle and made Susan a cup of tea. If not enough to forgive it was enough to thaw the sourness.

'You see,' said Bill, 'I've found out all sorts of things about *Spiked* and I think that they're up to no good.'

Bill handed Susan her mug of tea.

'I know things and *Spiked* wants to stop me.'

'What can you possibly know about *Spiked*, and why would *Spiked* be remotely interested in you?' Susan said. 'Bill, you're just the local fire officer, you're not Jeremy Paxman.'

'It's all to do with the cricket club,' Bill began.

'I might have guessed we'd get to cricket sooner or later.'

'You see *Spiked* wants to sponsor the cricket club.'

'The whole town knows that and by the way is enthusiastic about it.'

'I don't think it's right.'

'You can think what you like, Bill, but the town will go against you just like Carol has. They want their new pavilion and new sports halls and goodness knows what other benefits just as much as Annie wants to become a professional tennis player.'

'You see I know things about *Spiked* and that's why they want to kidnap me.'

'This Julia woman wants to meet you, Bill, not put you in a darkened room with a blindfold on and punch you occasionally.'

'I'll show you something,' said Bill and led Susan up the stairs to his office.

The post-it notes were arrayed all over his desk. Bill picked up the smart reading glasses he'd conveniently acquired and Susan repossessed her own. She scanned the post-it notes carefully and then pointed an accusing finger at Bill.

'Now, Bill, give me a straight answer. Were you prowling around the bins at *Spiked* last night and did you by any chance pick up some paper rubbish there.'

Her astuteness was disconcerting. Bill nodded.

'And don't tell me, you broke into the council offices as well, didn't you?'

'I didn't break in,' Bill said indignantly, 'I got locked in after hours.'

Susan pointed a dangerous finger at Bill's shiny new glasses and Bill whisked them off his nose and stuffed them into a scruffy old spectacle case. Susan turned her attention back to the post-it notes.

Bill explained their significance excitedly. 'You see there, my initials and the initials of someone else who isn't very nice and a map showing some place where a body can be dumped off the A19. And the not very nice man has been chasing me all day in a white van.'

Susan looked at Bill then she looked back at the post-it notes and then she started to laugh. 'I don't know what's wrong with your head, Bill Reeves, but there's nothing wrong with your imagination,' she said. 'And I don't see how you can have had time to start an affair with all the other things you seem to believe are going on in your life. But someone is,' she finished.

Bill looked at her blankly. 'Someone is what?'

'Someone is having an affair. Look at the notes. Exploding bombs, which means one of them is probably married. *Yes* with lots of exclamation marks denoting success, possible dates and even a map showing the assignation place.'

Bill looked open mouthed at Susan. He would like to have contradicted her but he had a niggling memory of a first floor office curtain twitching after hours in the darkened *Spiked* offices.

'What about the BR and the SB,' he said weakly.

'British Rail,' said Susan scathingly. Bill was going to point out that no one called it British Rail anymore, at least no one who worked at *Spiked,* but Susan carried on. 'SB could mean Santander Bank and those percentages could mean something financial.'

Bill looked at his wife admiringly. 'Shall I agree to meet this Julia woman tomorrow?' he said.

Susan shrugged.

Bill had just one more thing to do that day. If Shaun Bean was patrolling the Avenue in a white van rather than turning up for normal duties at *Spiked* then Bill should assume that the target was as likely to be his whistle-blowing documents as it was Bill himself. Scanning documents from his printer onto his computer was a laborious affair but after a long half hour of keeping Susan up with noisy exclamations Bill finally managed to attach five documents to an email which he sent to his son-in-law. Despite having had the further presence of mind to take another obvious precaution and change the password for his email account he deleted both the mail in his outbox and the scanned documents on his computer.

20

'What if you're wrong?' Bill asked Susan the next morning. He was wearing a newly ironed shirt and his Yorkshire Cricket Club tie. Susan was trying to get off to work.

'If I'm wrong and they are about to kidnap you I'll know where to find you, won't I?'

Bill looked unconvinced.

'I'll just follow the directions on the post-it notes.'

'Yes, but I'm just saying what if,' said Bill.

'Can I just go to work please?'

Bill scraped back his chair and they exchanged a chaste kiss which was a reassuring step towards a return to marital harmony. Bill was almost happy.

He was brushing his teeth when he heard a car come down The Avenue. The black Audi Sportback pulled up outside Bill's house, the engine purring quietly. Mark Hammond himself got out, aimed a key at the car to lock it and hesitated by Bill's gate. The hesitation was good. It gave Bill time to register that locking a car meant that there was no one else in there. No hidden and menacing Shaun Bean squashed into the back seat. It also gave Bill time to grab the buff folder marked East Wolds CCC, hurl himself downstairs, think long enough to grab his house keys and mobile and get out of the house in time to intercept Mark Hammond on his way up the path.

Bill's broad shoulders spanned the width of the path in a manly statement which could be taken as aggression if need be and Mark Hammond held out his hand. Mark was wearing a casual suit with a black jumper underneath, clothes that Carol would have explained were expensive Italian and cashmere. Bill was wearing his suit; his best suit as opposed to his funeral suit.

It was a pretty fancy car. Bill leant back on a pale grey leather seat. Even Jonathan Andrews didn't have a car like this. Mark Hammond set the engine purring again and did a neat reverse into someone's drive and off they went.

A further exchange of text messages the evening before had established that Julia was in Leeds for the day and that Mark would collect Bill and take him to Leeds to meet with Julia. They called it RHQ and Bill had let Susan interpret this as Regional Head Quarters.

As they pulled out of town driving smoothly past the Andrews' cottage Bill caught an image of Jonathan standing by his gate rubbing a sore head. Bill twisted in his seat and waved. It was the first thing to get a reaction from Mark Hammond.

Bill smiled. 'Good pal of mine, Jonathan Andrews,' he said, 'in fact I was there last night and he was telling me all about his proposed investment in *Spiked*.'

Mark Hammond was too clever to talk much. He pulled onto the main road and the car eased up to ninety miles an hour without even the sniff of a gear change.

'I must admit that I was a bit surprised that a company like *Spiked* should be interested in a small investor like Jon.'

The car slowed to cruise round a bend.

'I suppose you like to have a local profile,' Bill carried on innocently.

Mark's fingers tapped to an imaginary beat on the leather steering wheel. 'Do you mind?' he said pointing to a screen on the central dashboard. Bill looked at the display and Mark put some music on. This was an inadvertently good move on Mark's part because the space age electronics distracted Bill from his *Spiked* baiting.

'I've never seen anything like this,' Bill said.

A slight smile curled one end of Mark's mouth.

Bill reached out a hand to touch the gadget and Mark smiled. 'Go ahead,' he said.

Bill found a navigation button and played with the touch screen for several minutes. 'You'd think the car could almost drive itself,' he said.

'Almost,' said Mark.

The rest of the journey was completed in a resolute silence.

Spiked's RHQ was small but not modest. It was in a newly renovated part of Leeds abundant with glass and chrome. Bill was led through a small reception office into a large space fitted out as a meeting room where a sharp looking woman was waiting for them. The three of them gathered at one end of a polished wooden table where coffee, croissants and satsumas made a colourful display. There were also three glasses of water and three cans of *Extra Spiked*.

Julia was young, not glamorous but attractive in a fashionable, sporty way. Bill liked sporty. He wondered if he recognised her from the picture on the *Spiked* website but he wasn't sure.

'Bill,' Julia began once she had them all seated and obediently drinking coffee, 'you are obviously a great campaigner for local issues. A man of ideals and principles.'

Bill tried to remain aloof but it was hard not to enjoy the compliments. He put his buff folder down on the polished surface. It looked scruffy and out-dated like him.

'I think, and Mark agrees, that you should be spearheading *Spiked's* role in your local community not campaigning against it.' She held up a hand. Bill was expected neither to interrupt nor comment. '*Spiked* is about people like you, Bill, people who are idealists and sportsmen. What most concerns people like you in a local community? It is sports facilities, fitness and sports training in schools and the proper nurturing of local talent.'

Bill sat up in his chair, shoulders set, trying to live up to this image of himself.

'East Wolds, Bill, is chosen as our signature regional partnership enterprise. It is to be a model for all future developments. East Wolds is to have a new cricket club, a *Spiked* Academy, a local sports fitness and training centre and all the benefits of a retail boom.' Julia paused to take breath. 'Your granddaughter, Bill, has been one of the first to benefit. She has been picked out to be part of our national team to promote young talent and that she represents East Wolds is central to our aim of regional promotion and renewal.'

Bill gave in and took a big slug of coffee. His jacket fell open revealing his Yorkshire Cricket Club tie.

'You see, Bill, you know exactly what I'm talking about,' Julia said confidently, her gaze levelled at Bill's brief but memorable exposure to cricket at county level. 'We want you, Bill, to be our local representative in East Wolds. We want you to campaign for sports in East Wolds and the wider region.'

A hand stopped Bill from doing more than open his mouth to speak.

'You will have a generous budget, a car and a ticket for the members' enclosure at Headingley.'

157

The Mini Susan said she wanted. Watching the next test match at Headingley in style.

Julia looked at her watch, stood up and smoothed her jumper over close fitting black trousers. She extended a hand out to Bill which meant that he also had to stand up. 'I have so looked forward to meeting you, Bill. I hope that this is the beginning of a partnership beneficial to all.' She led him towards the door. 'I am sure that you and Mark will now be able to work together appropriately.' This was the first inclusion of Mark who had spent the whole meeting peeling satsumas and looking stonily at the wooden table. She paused at the door to let Bill out. 'Mark and I just have some business to discuss so I'm sure you'll excuse us. Mark will, of course, take you home when we've finished and you can go through the details of our offer with him,' Julia laughed confidently. Mark along with everyone else would do just as she told them. 'We won't be long,' she added as she turned to shut herself in the meeting room.

Bill finally managed to speak just as the door was closing. 'Unfortunately there's a problem,' he said. The door paused and Bill stood filling out the frame. 'These,' he continued and pulled a wad of documents out of the buff folder. Each incriminating document was shielded by cricket club minutes which confused Julia long enough for Bill to gather his thoughts.

'Perhaps you want them back, Mark?' Bill continued looking carefully at Julia. 'I don't know how far up the organisation this cheating goes.' Cheating sounded old fashioned but as far as Bill could understand it it was cheating and cheating seemed less libellous than accusing them of illegal activities.

The tick under Mark's left eye pulsed making him blink. Julia looked over the five pages giving herself time to assimilate the information. 'Have you talked to anyone else about this?' she finally asked. Her emotions were so controlled that it was impossible for Bill to tell whether she knew about the spiking of *Spiked* or whether it was something that Mark Hammond had instigated to bolster his own success at the East Wolds' production unit.

'No, not yet,' Bill said.

A stress line shifted along Julia's shoulders. 'I, we really appreciate it, Bill. That you have talked to us about this first.'

158

She didn't try to pretend that it was a misunderstanding. 'And I certainly appreciate it that you have brought this issue to me, Bill. I am also assuming that as you have come to me with these documents that you trust me to clear these issues up and that you don't intend to go public.'

Bill would have gone public as she put it if he'd found a way but he hadn't as yet found anyone who would listen to him unless one could count a drunken encounter with One Shot.

'And, Bill, we are genuine in our endeavour to improve local communities and I can only assume that as you have returned these documents that you will support us. As I said as our local representative you will have access to generous funds to facilitate sports in East Wolds.'

'I have copies,' Bill said.

Mark broke in. 'What do you want,' he demanded.

Julia immediately shut him up. 'Bill doesn't want anything. He just wants what's best for his local community.'

Bill found it difficult to say anything.

'Then I can count on your support at tomorrow's meeting?' Mark said. He wasn't toning down the aggression.

'You can count on me making my views clear, yes,' said Bill. 'Perhaps you'll stop spiking *Spiked*?' he paused as if waiting for confirmation of this but none came. 'But even if you do it will still be a cynically marketed product that harms children.'

At which point all three of them intervened at once. Mark began with an un-cool threat, Julia restrained him and Bill said tiredly. 'I don't wish to trouble you any more. I'll make my own way home.'

He wandered out into the newly renovated bit of Leeds, fished his mobile out of his pocket and rang his son-in-law.

'You're looking very smart,' Ben said, when they met up outside his chambers.

'I've been at a meeting,' said Bill.

'Carol said you were on sick leave and that you had a stress related heart condition.' Ben looked suitably concerned.

'Oh,' said Bill waving an arm, 'that's just palpitations.'

'Is that where you've been now, seeing a specialist? I can understand if you don't want to tell the girls.' By the girls he meant

Carol and Susan. 'But I hope you feel that you can talk to me, Bill?' Ben continued looking concerned and sympathetic.

'No, really,' said Bill, 'I'm fine.'

'But you're on sick leave?' Ben persisted.

'Technically,' Bill said unhelpfully.

'So you weren't at a heart specialist?' Ben asked again.

'No, I was at a meeting with *Spiked*.'

'*Spiked*?'

'You know, about their aggressive takeover of East Wolds.'

'You mean the cricket club,' Ben tried to sound jovial.

'No, not just the cricket club, I mean East Wolds in its entirety,' including me, Bill thought but didn't say.

Ben laughed in a way that suggested Carol had been getting at him.

'They're not one of your clients are they?' Bill suddenly demanded.

Ben looked distracted and shook his head vaguely. 'Look, Bill, I was actually going home early today. I finished a big case yesterday so thought I deserved a short day. How about a spot of lunch on the way home?'

They retrieved Ben's SUV from a car park and Ben found the motorway heading eastwards out of Leeds well ahead of the Friday afternoon rush hour. Bill finally broke the embarrassed silence which followed the two men into the car and out on to the motorway. 'Did you get my mail?' he asked.

'Yes I did get your mail, Bill.'

'Did you read it? Did you read the attachments.'

'Yes.' Ben's success was founded on succinct arguments and not long impassioned speeches.

'So what do you think I should do? What would you do, Ben?'

Ben switched the radio on and they listened to *The World at One* until Ben pulled into a pub car park. He'd obviously been there before because the publican knew him by name. It was a pub with waxed wood, an open fire, discrete couples eating prawns and cloth napkins. They both ordered something to do with lamb and Bill had a pint of beer from a micro brewery. At least the beer felt good and Bill took a large slice of bread from the basket which had appeared on their table. Ben drank a tomato juice and resisted the bread.

Bill tried to think of a more neutral way into the argument. 'So, Ben, what do you think of this *Spiked* business?' he asked.

'Can you be more specific?'

'I don't think I need to be specific, I mean it seems to be involved in everything,' Bill said taking another gulp of beer.

Ben cleared his throat. 'Shall we start with the cricket pavilion?' he asked.

'The cricket pavilion is only the half of it,' said Bill.

'You mean Annie?'

'I mean they're not giving anyone any money, are they? They're just buying us all out.'

'You have to be realistic, Bill. Of course Carol and Annie, and for that matter the cricket club, are excited about the offer of sponsorship. For them all it's money which enables them to do something they couldn't otherwise dream of.'

Bill looked at his son-in-law as large plates of lamb something were placed in front of them followed by separate dishes of vegetables and potatoes. 'So assuming that we have to accept sponsorship couldn't Annie get sponsorship from someone else?'

'So you don't disapprove of sponsorship per say?' Ben asked taking *Spiked* out of the discussion.

'No,' Bill said wondering whether he did approve of sponsorship in general or not. He approved of Yorkshire Country Cricket Club and they had sponsors. He decided to stop talking and eat for a while.

'But you know, Bill, it's not that easy to line up sponsors, especially in the current economic climate,' Ben finally responded.

'Then why can *Spiked* manage it if no one else can?'

Ben tried to distract him with a pudding menu.

'What about one of your clients, Ben, don't they do sponsorship? Couldn't they sponsor Annie?'

Ben looked uncomfortable. 'It would hardly be appropriate would it?' he said trying to persuade Bill to have apple pie.

'So, for example, who's one of your clients?' Bill persisted whilst agreeing to the apple pie.

'I suppose my main client is Yorkshire Water,' Ben said reluctantly.

'Yorkshire Water,' Bill said suddenly and loudly, 'what about them then?'

But Ben didn't get a chance to demur because Bill stood up and spilt the remains of Ben's tomato juice into Ben's lap in one excited gesture.

'Yorkshire Water. Can't you just see it, Ben, Annie can be sponsored by Yorkshire Water? You know, not drink *Spiked* but *Drink Water*! Because, Ben, now we know that *Spiked* is a cynically marketed possibly poisonous product we can't go on pretending that it's alright can we, just because it's convenient.'

Ben was trying to wipe the tomato juice off his trousers. 'Why are you dragging me into this, Bill?' he asked tiredly.

'Well because, for goodness sake,' Bill said inadequately.

'I wish you hadn't,' Ben said and cut the conversation dead by going to the bar to pay the bill.

When they arrived at Ben's home it seemed as though he almost deliberately led Bill into the kitchen so that he could understand the hopelessness of trying to instigate change into a jaded domestic arena bolstered by the whiff of success.

Carol, Annie and Will were all in the kitchen. Carol was making home made pasta and Will was trying to extract a coke from the fridge. 'But it's Friday, Mum,' he was saying, 'Danny has coke every day. He's even allowed *Spiked*.'

'Danny's different from us,' Carol said negotiating a fat lump of pasta dough through a new pasta roller attachment she'd just bought for her Kitchen Aid.

'Mum that's so gross,' interjected Annie.

'Why is it gross?' asked Will interestedly.

'I don't know what Annie means,' interrupted Carol.

'It means,' said Annie getting up from the kitchen table pointedly, 'that Danny's parents live in a council house and therefore eat junk food whereas we live in a posh house on the new estate and eat home made pasta and drink bottled water. Hi Gramps.'

'Dad, I wasn't expecting you,' said Carol hoping that her daughter would go and be a teenager in another room.

'What's with the posh dude stuff?' asked Annie.

'You can't call your grandfather a dude,' burst out Carol as a big skein of pasta plastered itself around the outside of the rolling gadget.

'Hey Grand…Gramps,' said Will, 'Can I come over to your place?'

'No you can't,' snapped Carol, 'why can't children talk normally any more. Everything's so Americanised.'

'Well if Annie's going to America,' said Bill.

Annie sat back down at the table and Bill noticed her hold her breath. Discussing her future must have become a frequent family occupation.

'I think it's all the television,' said Ben appearing behind Bill.

Carol gave Ben a nasty look and pulled all the pasta off the new rolling attachment.

'Shall we just have a frozen pizza, like Danny's family?' suggested Annie.

'I thought you had the afternoon off today,' Carol said to Ben.

'Oh, we had lunch,' said Bill as if that explained everything.

'I'll take Bill home. He just wanted to pop in and say hello,' Ben said as Bill confusedly tried to work out whether he was meant to be coming or going.

'Are you sure that Annie wants to go to America?' Bill asked as they got back into Ben's car.

Ben didn't reply at once and Bill decided to let him think. His son-in-law was a natural deliberator. 'I'm sure that she wants to be a tennis player,' Ben said carefully, 'and to do that she will have to be prepared to take up opportunities and accept the risk that some opportunities are better than others.'

'Shouldn't you minimise the risk?' Bill asked.

'Of course. Isn't that what most parents do? Let their children take risks but try and limit the potential damage?'

'So you don't think that going to America is risky for Annie?'

'No.' Ben's reply was quick and confident.

'And you don't think that sponsorship with *Spiked* is risky?' Bill continued.

'That's not what I said.'

'You can't pretend that going to America has nothing to do with sponsorship from *Spiked*,' Bill said, trying not to sound cross.

Ben turned back onto the main road. 'Going to America is, I feel, a good risk even though I agree with you that sponsorship with *Spiked* -'

'Is bad,' broke in Bill.

'Is not ideal. But.'

'But?'

'But it is a risk nonetheless worth taking.'

Bill thought of the cynical marketing of a drink through healthy attractive young sportsmen and women who probably didn't touch the stuff but implicitly encouraged less able and talented children to drink it and dream. And what about the spiking of *Spiked*, the expansion of premises onto conservation areas, the takeover of large parts of East Wolds, the corrupting of the council, the domination of the cricket club, the threats to himself. But none of this need impinge on Annie or her parents.

They'd already arrived at Bill's garden gate. 'So you're saying that the ethical issues here are not important,' Bill persisted.

'You've placed me in a very difficult position, Bill,' Ben answered him.

'Does that mean you're going to delete those documents?' Bill asked and slammed the car door closed.

21

'You're late.' Susan didn't say again. 'Dinner's just a Morrison's fish pie. Shall I heat it up for you?' She was watching the stars from *New Tricks* being interviewed on *The One Show*.

'It's all right, love, I had lunch with Ben. I'm not that hungry. I'll just make a cup of tea.'

'With Ben?'

'Yes I met him after my meeting. I rang him up and he invited me out to lunch.'

'Well, how nice.'

'Yes, I suppose it was,' Bill said.

'How was the meeting with that woman and Mike, or Mark or whatever he's called?'

'Susan?' he questioned tentatively.

'Yes, dear?'

'Would you accept a bribe if it meant you'd get one of those new Minis, love?' he said into his tea mug.

'Don't be ridiculous,' said Susan.

*

At four o'clock Bill gave up trying to sleep. He dug around quietly trying to find a jumper and his slippers and then tiptoed out of the bedroom, shutting the door carefully to Susan's exasperated cry. 'Can't you tiptoe more quietly?'

The house was cold. Armed with The Worlds Best Grandad mug of tea he shuffled into the sitting room. He opened the curtains but it was dark outside so he shut them again. Then he peeped through them and watched a shadow shimmering under a tree. He switched the light off to get a better look. But there was no shadow, at least there was no shadow now.

He'd had more than enough evidence to cause a huge scandal. *Spiked* would have had to shut down. The cricket club would have had to demolish their pavilion without being able to afford to build a new one. Annie wouldn't be going to America with the chance of becoming a national tennis star. So what if a child drank extra spiked *Spiked*? Children were obviously drinking it all the time and nothing dramatic had happened as far as Bill knew. Not that Bill would know anyway. He'd been too busy rushing around on his bicycle to read local or national news, and too busy to listen to anything or anyone.

He took a slurp of cold tea. *Spiked* was a major jobs' provider. It funded local projects and facilities. It developed derelict property. It was going to save the cricket club from ignominious decline into a scratch team playing on a small pitch against other small village teams.

He wondered whether he should finish the job and destroy the post-it notes as well. But someone was singing opera in a very loud and melodramatic way. Then the operatic singing turned into Susan shaking him gently and asking him if he wanted more tea.

She opened the curtains wide before Bill could protest and they both looked out on the early morning of a bright winter day.

'Is that our wheelie bin?' asked Susan.

'I don't know. I can't see from here,' said Bill from the sofa.

'It is you know,' said Susan indignantly, 'it's our paper bin and the wretched thing's been knocked over and there's paper all over The Avenue. It'll be those kids from number 5.'

Bill joined her at the window. Or perhaps it had been the shadow hovering around the garden at four in the morning. But there weren't any papers in the paper bin. In fact all the evidence had probably now been deleted from Ben's email account. Although Bill had told Julia and Mark that he had copies. Had someone been inside his house that night and having failed to find the copies ransacked the paper rubbish? Didn't they understand that Bill was beaten, not by *Spiked* but by the avidity of his own family.

*

By half past one Bill had had enough of waiting miserably for the evening's cricket club meeting. So setting off on his bicycle he decided to look for sympathy further from home. He started with One Shot.

'There was a lot of trouble on Thursday,' One Shot greeted him on the doorstep. Delicious smells emerged from the kitchen but Bill wasn't invited in.

'Oh,' said Bill uncertainly.

'Janet got a ticking off.'

'Ah,' said Bill. Not another Summers out of work because of him. He looked down at One Shot's shoes, not liking to meet One Shot's sorrowful gaze.

'They didn't like it that she couldn't be bothered to put the rubbish in the bin. They said it attracted animals and broke health and safety regulations.'

'Oh,' said Bill.

'And that she'd better not do it again.'

'Ah,' said Bill, 'hang on a minute, so she didn't get the sack?'

'No. Why should she get the sack?'

'Well.' Because Sadie did and you looked so downbeat. Although that was One Shot's habitual expression. Bill smiled broadly. 'Well then, that's all right then isn't it,' he said cheerfully raising his gaze from One Shot's shining shoes to One Shot's dreary countenance.

'All right,' exclaimed One Shot indignantly, 'it's not all right. Janet doesn't like being ticked off.' One Shot lowered his voice. 'I wasn't allowed out last night and I'm only allowed to go to the meeting tonight because she wants to go too.'

'Geoff, who's that you're talking to? You can't stand in the door like that letting all that cold air in,' came a voice from the kitchen.

'Look, you'd better scarper, Bill. If she sees it's you it'll set her off all over again.'

'But you're coming to the meeting?' asked Bill remembering that what seemed like a long time ago now One Shot had shared Bill's negative view of *Spiked*.

All One Shot said was, 'Coming dear, what a nice smell.'

So Janet was a domestic tyrant after all. Bill launched off in another direction and headed for John Bailey's. As Bill raced up The Crescent he failed to notice an old man in pyjamas waving at him and shouting, 'I'm with you son, all the way.'

John Bailey was in his garage with an upside down bicycle. When he saw Bill he beckoned urgently for Bill to hide in the garage while he checked nervously to see if Bill's arrival had excited any interest from inside the house.

'That woman you rang,' John began still waving Bill into the garage and still nervously checking the house.

167

Bill looked puzzled.

'You borrowed the phone and rang some woman,' said John.

'Oh yes,' said Bill. How did John know that he'd rung a woman? Even Bill hadn't known that he was ringing a woman at the time.

'She kept ringing back and Barbara thinks I'm having an affair.'

'Ah,' said Bill inadequately.

'And if I tell her that it was you who rang the woman then she'll think that you're having an affair and she'll tell Susan and the whole town besides.'

'I'm not having an affair,' said Bill.

'You're not?' questioned John, 'well, that's grand then,' he added uncertainly.

'It was just some woman I had to meet.'

'Well, that was just it. That's what she kept saying to Barbara. Barbara got quite cross and told her she could keep her scheming hands to herself and find a husband of her own.'

'I don't think Julia wants a husband,' said Bill, although despite himself he sounded sorrowful.

John Bailey took the cue and looked disappointed himself. An affair with someone called Julia didn't come in a man's way all that often.

But this wasn't getting Bill anywhere. He took a deep breath and said. 'She's an executive for *Spiked* and she wants me to stop making a stand against *Spiked* buying out the cricket club.'

A long silence ensued while John's brain tried to switch gear. He twiddled a bit with the upside down bicycle as if that would help. 'Are *Spiked* buying the cricket club?' he finally asked.

'No, they want to sponsor the cricket club and make us all wear red cricket whites with big black logos on.'

'I thought they were just giving us money to rebuild the pavilion?'

'No they're not giving us money they're sponsoring us which means -'

'We get a new pavilion and there's lots of new members now. That Shaun Bean who was hanging around here the other day seemed to know all about it. Useful fast bowler by the sounds of him.' John stood up large and straight. 'You know, Bill, I'm glad you popped by and cleared things up about that woman and so on. Eh, it's a grand day an' all. I'll be seeing you, Bill.'

Which was Bill's cue to launch himself back onto his bicycle and leave. 'At the meeting tonight,' called Bill.

'Oh, ay, the meeting, I'd nearly forgotten clean about that. We'll be there, me and the wife.'

Bill waved back at John as he sped blindly past the enthusiastic support of the pyjamaed old man. It seemed that he was not wanted anywhere so he bicycled in the direction of the village green.

22

The cricket pitch was a sad sight despite the fine day. Tyre marks were still deep in the waterlogged western perimeter and sodden leaves covered half the pitch. The wicket had rough tufts of grass growing where the crease had got worn over the previous summer. The nets in a far corner hung low and sagged at several points where there were gaping holes in the fabric. Bill leant his bicycle against the pavilion wall and wondered if wicket keepers were just a thing of the past. And then his eyes caught a big council sign pasted on the rotten panelling of the pavilion. UNSAFE BUILDING. Dereliction Order no. 638. Issued on behalf of East Wolds Council Planning Dept. The windows were boarded up and a large plank was nailed across the door. It would seem that the dereliction order had been issued and was in process of being enforced.

The key however was still in its old hiding place. Bill fished it out, ripped the plank off the door, his shoulders doing their stuff with a great deal of pleasure, and let himself in.

Fumbling for a light switch Bill was surprised to discover that the electricity hadn't been switched off although from a fire safety point of view the electrics were probably the only thing unsafe about the building. Apart from a sad damp feel the pavilion was reassuringly familiar. Bill sat down at the long table which hosted cricket teas and committee meetings. There was a cabinet of trophies against the wall. None sadly from the previous summer. Photos of past captains hung on the walls. There was even a painting of the founder of the East Wolds Cricket Club dating from 1903, who looked suitably illustrious and sported a large cricketing beard. Unfortunately the pavilion didn't date from 1903 as if it had it would probably have been protected by a preservation order. Not that preservation orders would have stood in the way of *Spiked*. The current pavilion had been built in 1951 on a wave of post war enthusiasm funded by a government eager to rebuild local communities and public buildings. On the cheap of course. The building from 1903, which it replaced, was still going strong as several garden sheds in the gardens of long forgotten members, such as Bill's pyjamaed friend.

But the pavilion that Bill had grown up with was this one and he was almost enjoying sitting in the gloom of the single light bulb being sentimental. Sentimental enough in fact to go into the little office at the back and start to rummage amongst the old archives. Happy days. A match report from 1981 kept him busy for a long time. They'd been playing some pucker team from York in the cup final and the pucker team from York had opened with an ex-Yorkshire batsmen which was bad form as the ex-Yorkshire batsman was a 'guest' player and didn't live anywhere near York. Bill had caught him out with a cracker of a catch going away from the off-stump as Bill dived four yards to his right and ended up in a heap with first slip. Miraculously the catch was still in his glove when they all managed to extricate themselves and the 'guest' player was sent back to the pavilion. Bill took three more catches in the game and scored an undefeated 25 that took East Wolds to victory and into the archives of the club's history for winning the Cup in three successive years.

In 1988 he'd had a hairline fracture in his left thumb and had had to abandon his wicket keeping gloves. Instead he batted with a thumb brace and became the most successful spin bowler of the season.

Then there was that memorable fifth wicket stand with One Shot in 1994. And look at this, just three years ago John Bailey knocked off 51 and Bill caught another four heroic catches to snatch another cup victory. All the more precious as such victories had become much rarer in recent years. This time it had been against Beverley.

Bill pulled out more match reports and carefully archived statistics and laid them out on the desk in the little office. There were newspaper cuttings too. Mostly from the *East Wolds Gazette* but some of the cup matches had warranted three lines in the *Yorkshire Post* and a regional match against a team from Durham County had occupied half a page in *The Northern Echo*.

Surely this was the kind of material that he could use for an emotional appeal against sponsorship. The kind of thing he could have used to get support for a stance against *Spiked*. Perhaps it wasn't too late. He could use these examples of past triumphs and make a final plea against sponsorship at the meeting this evening. So that's what he decided to do. He might have handed over the responsibility of whistle blowing to Ben but it didn't mean that he couldn't argue against sponsorship of the cricket club.

His selection of suitable data was accompanied by a lot of banging outside the pavilion and if Bill had been less absorbed by planning his grand speech he might have identified the noise as being the bangings of a hammer against large nails. Because when Bill finally decided he'd got just the information he needed and that it was time to go home for his early tea he couldn't. The door was nailed fast and having the key was no help against six-inch nails on the other side.

It was half past five. Bill was locked in the pavilion, or perhaps barred in the pavilion was a more accurate description, doors and windows being well and truly boarded up. Furthermore he'd left his mobile at home. At which point the electricity switched off. Or the fuse blew. Or someone cut it out.

'Oh dear, Susan's not going to be too happy about this,' said Bill.

He said 'Hello' a few times in a friendly way. Then had a go at the door in a less friendly way. Bill, after all, had the right shoulders for the dramatic smashing in of doors. Although the reality of such action was less effective than the drama. Many years ago, when he first joined the fire service, Bill had been trained to break doors down and rescue people from burning buildings. This door however was not budging. It opened outwards and the planks nailing it shut must have been hammered into the only bit of sound cladding in the whole building. Bill retired with a bruised shoulder and felt`his way to a chair at the table. A few chinks of light glimmered through holes in cladding that was rotting. But a few chinks of light at five thirty on a winter evening didn't help much.

Bill sat calmly thinking of all the great escape films he'd seen and decided that on balance there must be a way out, which of course there was. There was a back door into what would have been a cloakroom if the pavilion had run to such luxuries. Bill felt his way along the walls and a picture of a former captain landed on his knee as he knocked into it. There were also a few loose nails that caught on his hands as he felt his way to the storage-cum-cloakroom. The panelling in this back room must have been rougher because there were more chinks of light and the room was shadowed rather than pitch black.

Bill felt over the door. It was locked but he couldn't make out what sort of lock it was. There must be a key somewhere and the best place for that key would have been in the lock itself, but the key wasn't in the lock. Bill paused in his fumblings to listen to the distinct sound of a car engine outside. He held his breath, let it out, listened again, said 'Hello' loudly, held his breath again. Nothing. The car had probably gone.

'This will be bloody *Spiked*,' said Bill, 'locking me in to make sure I can't get to the meeting.' He had been kidnapped after all.

The chinks were letting very little light in now. Bill couldn't see his watch and he had no idea whether he'd spent an hour trying to bash doors down or ten minutes. He had a go at this new door but his shoulder was too bruised to go to it with any great enthusiasm. Finding the key would be an easier solution. There were various places that the key could be. The pegs on the wall of the storage-cum-cloakroom were a possibility. Bill felt his way through several old garments and cobwebs before giving up. A drawer in the desk in the office was another possibility. This time he nicked a hole in his trousers as he made his way back to the office. But he did find a key. Back to the storage-cum-cloakroom. The wrong key.

Bill felt his way to the far end of the small room and gave his heart a little pat for safe keeping. He then opened his lungs to make some primeval berserk attacking sound and went for a full paced Shaun Bean fast bowling run up at the door. The compact velocity of Bill's solidity combined with Shaun Bean's speed ended in a most fantastical cascade of noise and dust. The whole wall fell down. Bill ran out of the pavilion. He put a hand up to his head and felt the protection of his bicycle helmet still reassuringly in position. He blessed Susan for all her nagging and ran for his bicycle. He had no idea what the time was but his best option was to get to the big new *Spiked* sports hall at the school as fast as he could.

In the ecstasy of the assault Bill failed to notice that there was now a gaping hole in the demolition ordered pavilion. That large pieces of rotten cladding and nails stuck out at all angles as if a bull had just charged through. And that under the deluge was a once sleek black Audi Sportback.

Bill burst into the *Spiked* sports hall just as Mark Hammond was saying. 'If no one else has anything to say I think we can move on -'

'I've got something to say,' said Bill.

A gasp echoed around the hall and if Bill had listened really hard he would have heard a familiar sharp intake of breath (Carol) and a groan somewhere between indignation and pity (Susan). But he didn't. What he did realise was that his disreputable state, camouflaged during his race through the dim streets, was now illuminated by the bright lighting of the sports hall. He was covered in a grey film of dust and rotten wood and a large nail stuck out of his bicycle helmet. Luckily he couldn't see the nail and concentrating on getting everyone's attention he repeated. 'I've got something to say.'

Standing at the back of the hall was as good a place as anywhere to command the room's attention. Everyone had to strain their necks and turn around to listen which meant that no one could look at Mark Hammond for guidance, or at the Chairman who anyway looked at Mark Hammond. Neither could Bill see the sober suits and dark briefcases of the *Spiked* legal team. He'd no idea what had already been said but decided anyway that it was irrelevant to what he had to say.

'I've just come from the cricket pavilion,' said Bill. 'The pavilion, our pavilion,' here he caught the eye of John Bailey, 'is a grand place. An institution that is more than the sum of its rotten walls. And I agree they are rotten.' He didn't add that a large chunk of the wall was now missing. 'But East Wolds' Cricket Club is not rotten. Maybe times are lean but we are not desperate. Our members have kept us going for three even four generations and I'm proud of that. And so should you be. I'm too proud to accept a quick fix when times are hard. And so should you be. I'm too proud to hand over all I believe in – sportsmanship, ethical standards, healthy young people – to anyone for the asking just for money.'

Someone, possibly Shaun Bean, yawned loudly and started a bored shoe stamp. Bill held up an imperious heroically battered arm and no one else joined in.

'And I hasten to add that even I would consider a donation from *Spiked*. But this is not about donations it is about,' he looked straight at Mark Hammond, 'bribery and sponsorship. The way I see it sponsorship like bribery is a buy out. We get money and the sponsor gets control over us. I'm not against donations and neither am I unrealistic enough not to see that sponsorship is perhaps the only way forward.'

'Then for goodness sake cut the crap,' someone interjected. Shaun Bean?

'But I cannot agree to sponsorship from a spiked energy drink that cynically promotes itself to children, makes them believe that they will be as energetic and talented as the best and most hard working of our sporting heroes and addicts them to caffeine and sugar at the most dangerous of levels.'

A lawyer made a careful note.

'Because that is exactly what *Spiked* is.'

Bill's head was starting to spin and his heart joined in the confusion. The hall was quiet until someone at the back of the room applauded quietly. People looked anxiously from Bill to the Chairman to Mark Hammond to the quietly clapping person until a loud voice said.

'What a load of bunkum.'

Relief rippled through the crowd. Some people started to laugh. Bill was after all only Bill and looked more like something out of a comedy sketch than a public orator.

Mark Hammond licked the cream. 'As I was saying before we were interrupted if no one has anything to say shall we move onto a vote?'

The Chairman roused himself and the Secretary read the proposal. 'All those in favour of accepting sponsorship from *Spiked* please raise their hands.'

The hands went up, row after row of them.

'Abstentions?' asked the Secretary.

Susan bravely proffered a lone hand and Bill's heart burst with love and gratitude and palpitations.

'And those against?'

Bill's hand shot up wafting rotten wood in a great swathe around him. Another hand was raised. The loan applauder. Dr Adams! Bill's heart dropped down a notch or two in due reverence and then along with everyone else was distracted momentarily by a striped hand at the end of a row held up quiveringly by a pyjamaed man.

The Secretary said that the motion was duly passed and Bill collapsed in a heap on the floor. The nail attached to Bill's bicycle helmet embedded itself into Bill's skull and a dramatic amount of blood poured out through his helmet and around his ear.

Soft ministering hands tried to soften the blow and Bill heard someone saying 'Call an Ambulance please,' before he passed out completely.

23

The hospital curtain fluttered gently in the spring breeze. Bill shifted in the token armchair by the bed and watched the clock creep towards 2pm. A small holdall containing all his hospital belongings rested by his feet. He'd spent all morning hoping for a quick getaway but as neither the doctor had appeared to sign his discharge papers nor his family arrived to collect him Bill remained trapped on a neurology ward. He had been back again to the hospital for yet more tests. Although this time he was in the confident belief that everyone would agree with him that he was in full working order again.

Pre-visiting hour footsteps disturbed a flurry of activity from the staff office and after a hushed dispute Ben appeared in the doorway to Bill's room. Both men stared at each other embarrassed.

'Why have they sent you?' Bill didn't mean to sound disgruntled.

'Susan had some kind of crisis at work.' Ben sounded apologetic. 'And I have business in the area.'

Bill looked up suspiciously but said nothing.

'Carol's making a welcome home dinner for you,' Ben tried to smile, 'and I'm going to drop you off with her before my meeting.'

'We'll have to wait,' Bill said. He must have sounded belligerent because Ben swallowed a desire to protest. 'The doctor hasn't seen me yet.'

'I thought Susan said you were being discharged this morning. I'd have come sooner if I could.'

'It wouldn't have made any difference, Ben, apparently the doctor's supposed to sign me out and until he does we're not going anywhere.' Bill pointed to his notes still fastened to the end of the bed.

Ben looked at his watch. 'But I thought that you'd got the all clear finally. No heart problem and no permanent damage to the head.' Ben looked embarrassed again no doubt conscious of the family's female verdict on what constituted damage to Bill's head.

Another assertive female joined them now. 'I've already explained to the other gentleman that the ward is currently closed to visitors,' she said to Bill, 'some of my patients are trying to sleep.'

Although there were no other patients in Bill's room. Bill smiled. 'We're just waiting for the doctor,' he said.

The nurse looked at the clock which was now creeping towards the half hour. 'I'll see where he's got to,' she said and left them.

*

An hour or so later Ben's SUV was taking the Hull Road at 90 mph. A less gentle man would have been swearing vociferously as well.

'I'm going to be late,' he pronounced unnecessarily to Bill.

'Must be important,' Bill said.

'Yes maybe, I don't know, but it doesn't help my clients' case if I don't show for a meeting.'

'Can I ask who?'

'I'd rather you didn't.'

'Can't you just go straight to your meeting? There's no need to take me to Carol first. I can wait in the car. It's a nice day. I can stretch my legs a bit.'

'Aren't you meant to be taking it easy?' Ben said negotiating a double bend.

'Oh no, fighting fit me,' said Bill.

'Carol said that you'd be off work for a few weeks yet.'

Bill shrugged which Ben didn't see as he was overtaking a tractor.

'I thought you weren't taking me home?' Bill said a short while later as they hurtled round the East Wolds' ring road.

'I'm not, although I should because I don't want to get you -' He didn't need to finish his procrastinated sentence because a familiar approach road suddenly alerted Bill to their destination. *Spiked.*

Ben shot into a parking space rather too close to a brand new Audi Q7.

'That looks expensive doesn't it,' Bill said squeezing out of the car door.

'Bill, I really don't think,' said Ben, then he looked at the gleaming Audi. 'It does doesn't it.'

'You see,' said Bill, 'when the plumber turns up in the latest Mercedes you know you're using the wrong plumber.'

'I'm not quite following you, Bill.' This apparent irrelevance distracted Ben sufficiently to take his eye off Bill's in-swinger which guided Bill nicely up the pitch and towards the entrance to *Spiked*.

'You know, a plumber who can afford a fancy car is charging too much.'

'Or is a good plumber,' said Ben.

'Do you think Mark Hammond is a good Managing Director?'

'I don't know.'

'Or that *Spiked* is a good product?'

'It doesn't have to be good to make money,' Ben said.

'It's a lousy product, it cheats its customers and it has no ethics,' Bill said excitedly.

'Now look here, Bill, I haven't got time for this, please don't -' Ben tried to interrupt.

'Added to which it cynically poisons children by addicting them to an unhealthy product just to make money.'

'Bill, stop right there.' As they were within a few yards of activating the sliding entrance doors Ben was speaking literally rather than figuratively. 'The whole *Spiked* thing is over and my being here on behalf of Yorkshire Water has nothing to do with your issues with *Spiked*.'

Bill did stop. 'You're not representing *Spiked*?'

'Why would I be representing *Spiked*?'

'I just thought. Everyone,' Bill said inconclusively. 'Hang on a minute if you're not representing *Spiked* then you're representing clients with a case against *Spiked*!' As Bill had moved close enough to the glass doors to open them he walked through into the familiar marble of the reception area.

Ben was stopped from physically forcing Bill back onto the outside of those doors because they were both obstructed by a life sized poster which dominated the open area. The poster was of a sleek made-up woman. The woman held a tennis racket in an inviting feminine sort of way. She was wearing a tennis skirt styled to reveal an enormous length of cosmetically tanned leg and the tightest of *Spiked* t-shirts designed to emphasised a cleavage and a tempting view of trained midriff.

179

'Can I help you?' the skinny young man from reception appeared from behind the poster where it hung from a chrome beam and floated enticingly in the middle of the marble floor.

'That's Annie,' Bill and Ben said in unison. Then Bill continued, looking hard at his son-in-law. 'Now that,' he said ignoring the young man, 'is what you young people call a game changer.'

The young man was trying to work out which public face he should be presenting. His local one for interested but annoying local residents or the welcoming professional one for the tall distinguished looking man kitted out in expensive clothes for the country.

Ben recovered first. 'I have a meeting, although I'm sorry I'm late. It was scheduled for four o'clock.'

The young man checked on a computer screen. 'Yes of course, Mr Whitby Jones.' He looked at Bill meaningfully. Bill had a bald patch on the side of his head and a deep scar was still clearly visible. Both Ben and Bill ignored the man's unspoken inquiry.

'Perhaps you would let Mark Hammond know that Ben Whitby Jones is in reception and apologise for my tardiness.'

'Yes of course, sir,' said the young man rushing back to the telephone behind the reception desk trying to work out if Tardiness could be the name of Mr Whitby Jones' companion. After a hushed exchange he called over to Ben. 'Mr Hammond will be with you shortly.'

Bill and Ben were now half concealed by Annie's poster.

'We'll just have a little look around while we're waiting,' Bill called out in his best posh Yorkshire. He dragged Ben down a marble corridor.

'Bill, can you please stop this,' Ben tried to protest.

'You see what they're up to? You see what sponsorship really means?' Bill hissed urgently then dragged Ben into the gents to avoid someone who looked alarmingly like lipsticked woman. 'You know what goes on here, Ben, you read those documents. Now you chose to do nothing. I chose to do nothing. Because of Annie. But I've had a long time to think Ben and that poster. Maybe we were wrong. So as we're here officially we, you Ben, can have a look around.' Not giving Ben time to respond Bill just charged him on down the corridor, through a door which required a code that Bill had already cracked on a previous visit and into the production room. He even managed to propel them both into the middle of the industrial space before Shaun Bean charged up to them. Then incidents in fast sequence were only just averted by Ben finally finding his voice.

'Shaun, good to see you,' he said extending smooth long fingers, 'so this is where it all happens?'

Shaun Bean took Ben's hand hurriedly. His eyes fixed on Bill but they kept hopping round to look at two huge vats of bubbling brew in a far corner then back to Bill again. There didn't seem to be anyone else around. Perhaps because it was late on a Friday afternoon.

'Have you met my father-in-law?' Ben asked ingenuously.

'Yes,' said Shaun Bean. He didn't extend his hand to Bill.

'We did a bit of net practice together,' Bill said.

'Shaun, you must be as keen as Bill. You were down there the other day again with Danny, weren't you?'

Shaun Bean's eyes fixed on Bill. 'I thought you were?'

Bill ignored him. 'It's pretty impressive all this isn't it, Ben?' he said and moved towards the bubbling vats.

'Now just watch it.' The big man moved in close to Bill.

'It is indeed. We've heard so much about *Spiked*. It's rather interesting to see it in the making as it were. I suppose there's a bottling plant as well?' continued Ben.

'Canning plant,' grumped Shaun Bean. 'It's through there.'

'I don't suppose we could just have a quick look could we?' asked Ben.

'So the *Spiked* stuff is syphoned off those big vats through pipes into the next room?' asked Bill.

Shaun Bean clenched his hands into two large fists.

'And those pipes run along the canal side of the building?' Bill looked meaningfully at Ben. 'We couldn't have a sample from one of them there vats now could we?' pressed on Bill.

A further incident was nearly beyond Ben's control. Shaun Bean had Bill by the collar of his anorak and though Bill was not tall he was at least as broad as Shaun Bean. Luckily just as Ben contemplated the unpleasant task of both having to intervene and explain to Susan why Bill had been re-admitted into hospital the door to the marble corridor opened and a splash of light was cast on the crisis.

'Hello, Mark Hammond,' said the rescuer. 'You must be Ben Whitby Jones. Good to meet you at last.'

They didn't get further than Mark Hammond's white office decorated with a large modern painting and smelling of freshly ground coffee because Ben's mobile burst into life. Bill recognised Carol's voice on the other end. He more or less made out the words 'where the hell are you' but it might have been less cross and more wifely. Ben predictably didn't answer. Another blast from Carol including the words 'Annie' and 'GCSEs' inspired a response from Ben. 'Ah,' he said. Something more distinctly cross again ended the conversation.

Ben turned to Mark Hammond. He looked completely unruffled. 'Terribly sorry about that. I'm afraid we'll have to rush to another appointment. Running a bit late you know. I'm glad we've met at last albeit briefly and because of the helpfulness of your staff I've seen what I need to see for the moment. Either my clients or I will be in touch.'

Bill enjoyed the flurry of responses that flickered across Mark Hammond's face. He scuttled after Ben across the marble floor and out through the sliding glass doors. Both men had taken a last look at Annie staring at them from her poster before squeezing themselves past the Audi Q7 and into Ben's Land Cruiser. It wasn't until they drove out onto the bypass that Ben finally explained what was happening.

'Apparently I'm meant to be collecting Annie from her training today,' he said as the SUV cruised up to seventy. 'Her training doesn't normally finish this early, does it?'

'I don't know, but it used to be on Tuesdays and Thursdays not Fridays if you mean that Australian who's an expert in personal training and prevention of injury,' added Bill.

'Is that where she is then?' asked Ben. 'At the university?'

'I don't know,' said Bill. 'She could be at the tennis bubble in Leeds.'

'Really? Christ, I hadn't thought of that. No, I'm sure Carol said York.'

For want of further argument they continued to hurtle back towards York.

'She doesn't have any other training in York, does she?' Ben worried again.

'Not that I know of, but I haven't really been told anything for the past month or so,' Bill answered. 'Anyway,' he continued brightly, 'York's more-or-less on the way to Leeds isn't it, especially if you go this way.'

As Ben obviously wasn't going to clarify the situation with Carol they continued driving towards York. Bill didn't mind. He'd been in and out of hospital for weeks and he enjoyed being out again now, noting the signs of spring in the flashes of blackthorn flowering in the hedges as they rushed past. A new cricket season almost upon them.

'Can I come to the next meeting you have with Mark Hammond?' Bill asked.

'I haven't managed to have any meetings with Mark Hammond yet, and for goodness sake, Bill, of course you can't. I should never have let you anywhere near that building. What has Shaun Bean ever done to you?' said Ben.

'You had one today,' said Bill, choosing to ignore Ben rather than get into his dealings with Shaun Bean.

'I ended up having an informal fiasco of a meeting,' Ben responded, obviously feeling that the brief informal nature of the meeting had been Bill's fault rather than his.

'Yes, but you said.'

'I doubt it, Bill.'

'That you'd got all the information that you needed for now and that you'd be in touch.'

'A form of words.'

'Mark Hammond took it as more than a form of words. He looked quite upset and he takes a bit of ruffling up.'

Ben didn't say anything.

'In fact I think we did quite a good bit of ruffling up,' Bill tried to continue provocatively.

'Antagonising Shaun Bean was not a good bit of ruffling up,' Ben said.

'But he was ruffled. He was right ruffled when I mentioned those big vat things. So this client of yours, Yorkshire Water eh?'

'Please don't push me on client confidentiality, Bill.'

'Does that mean there's a water pollution case against *Spiked*?'

'There isn't anything against *Spiked*.'

183

Bill wasn't listening. 'You know what I think, Ben?'

Ben said nothing.

'I think that those big vats are the spiked *Spiked* and that Shaun Bean does the spiking when it's quiet like on a late afternoon and then they get canned up and sent out with all the rest. Which means that a random percentage of all *Spiked* products are even more addictive and unhealthy than the normal product.'

'Does it need to be spiked to be unhealthy?' Ben said, conceding Bill a few words.

'Well no, but,' Bill paused, 'I think that's what they do anyway.'

'And somehow or other the food standards agency just happens not to have tested *Spiked*?'

This time Bill was quiet.

'I'm running this particular file, Bill, not you. It is a suspected pollution case which has been running on for a few months. Although there's nothing concrete to link it with *Spiked*. *Spiked* is one of the cleanest set-ups I've come across. All the paper work is in order.'

'Yes, and we know why, don't we?'

'No, Bill, we don't know why. You can't just -'

'I have it,' Bill said turning an excited face towards Ben, 'those big vats aren't tested they are, um, hang on a minute.'

Ben hung on.

'They spike them but when the inspectors come they empty them into the canal. Yes, that's it! The canal is just by that side of the building. They pour the spiked *Spiked* into the canal if there is an unannounced inspection and then the canal flows into the river and then Yorkshire Water finds contaminants.' Bill was so pleased with himself that he leant on a button and his window rushed down.

'Of course, Bill, anything is possible. I've had cases you wouldn't believe but this isn't one of them. Speculation and circumstantial evidence might aid an out of court settlement but wild speculation and no evidence doesn't have any use or significance. There is no case against *Spiked*, Bill.'

Bill fiddled with the button until his window wound back up again and they both endured an awkward silence as Ben drove into the University car park. Thankfully Anne was there. She was sitting

184

on a grassy bank chatting to a bronzed man and drinking water from a *Spiked* water bottle.

Ben parked the car. 'There is one thing that does worry me about *Spiked*, though,' he said.

'Oh yes?' Bill held his breath in a rush of cautious optimism.

'Annie,' he replied ambiguously, because just at that moment Annie was running across the car park to meet them.

Bill dropped out of the Land Cruiser and waved at Annie. 'Hi Gramps, wow you're home. You look weird. Should you be out driving and stuff? Shouldn't you be at home in bed or something?'

'I just collected Gramps from hospital,' Ben interrupted her, 'and he seems in good form to me.'

Simon strode over to join them. He shook Bill's hand. 'How's it going, mate?' he said. Bronzed tattoos rippled beneath a torn-off t-shirt. He made Bill and Ben look over dressed in anoraks and winter shoes.

Annie turned back to Simon and hung on to him as much as it was possible to hang onto someone without actually touching them. Ben joined them.

'Have you two met?' said Bill.

Simon stretched out a hand. 'No.' Simon was frowning too. 'You're not from *Spiked* are you?'

His voice sounded unusually flat for him and without the lilt the words became threatening.

'I'm Annie's father,' Ben said with equal suspicion and Bill noticed suddenly how tall he was, taller than Simon.

'Annie's father? Pleased to meet you at last.' It sounded critical. 'I've been Annie's personal trainer for a while now. I've met this fella here.' A playful punch landed on Bill's broad shoulder. 'But we haven't met before have we?' The lilt returned to Simon's voice.

'I'm glad you both showed up. I was worried that -' Annie didn't finish her sentence and a sudden cloud puckered across her face. It was as though something unpleasant had just come amongst them.

Simon looked uncertainly at Annie. 'It's none of my business really,' he said, 'but that *Spiked* bloke comes along sometimes and -'

'What *Spiked* bloke?' Ben got the question out even faster than Bill.

'Mark what's his face,' Annie said quietly.

'Mark Hammond?' now Bill sounded threatening.

'Like I said, it's nothing to do with me, and your wife,' Simon looked straight at Ben, 'seems to encourage him, as far as I can see.'

'It is probably something to do with the sponsorship,' Ben said mildly.

It was an inadequate comment and the three men stood awkwardly around Ben's car while Annie seemed to shrink away from them as if brooding. She gave a little shiver and Bill was struck once again by how much she seemed to have changed. Perhaps it was because he hadn't seen so much of her while he'd been going in and out of hospital that the changes suddenly seemed more apparent. There was the troubling image of the glamorous poster girl, the girl confident and radiant from training (or a little love struck with Simon, but Bill's intuition didn't extend to love struck teenagers) and the girl who for a moment looked small and vulnerable until she turned an angry pink face towards them.

'You're all so stupid,' she said, her anger flaring quickly, 'and this is so typical of you, Dad. First you don't show up. In fact you never show up. Now when you do finally turn up you have Gramps with you and Gramps should probably be tucked up in bed somewhere. I mean he looks like some bionic invention with that scar all over his head. Then because you're late Mum was going to.' She stopped abruptly for a second time then opened the back of the Land Cruiser and flung her kit inside.

None of them attempted to say anything. They just waited for the tears which didn't come.

'And have any one of you given any thought to the fact that I have my first GSCE exam next Tuesday? That I'm taking nine GCSE subjects, training more than I've ever trained in my life - as if that was possible - and -'

She swept a look at them, making it clear that not one of them had a hope in hell of understanding her. Then she marched round to the front passenger side of the Land Cruiser, climbed in and banged the door shut.

Bill meekly climbed into the back seat and Ben wondered impotently how to exert his authority. Driving home was a first safe option. Annie kept her face pointedly turned away as if the view out of the passenger side was rivetingly novel. Bill kept a miserable silence and nursed a growing exhaustion while he wondered what he'd done wrong.

'Annie,' her father began mildly, 'do you want to talk about any of the issues raised in the past fifteen minutes or?'

'Or not,' mumbled Annie.

Bill opened his mouth to see if anything constructive would come out of it. 'Ben,' he managed to say, 'why don't we talk about it first.'

'Talk about what?' Annie's head spun round.

'*Spiked.*'

'Bill.'

'Mark Hammond.'

'Bill!' Ben finally found an authoritative tone.

'I don't mean now,' said Bill.

'Don't mind me,' said Annie.

'We will not say another word for the rest of the journey,' Ben said. 'Annie, send Mum a text message to say we're nearly home.'

'Does that count as saying another word, or not?' asked Annie.

Ben started to speak but changed his mind. Annie's mobile bleeped out a message and a blast of some heavy metal music startled them all as Carol's reply came back.

'I only use that ringtone for Mum,' Annie said as a slice of humour slipped back into her voice.

When they finally got there the Whitby Jones' home was surrounded by vehicles and Ben had to drive past their entrance and pull onto the pavement outside the neighbours.

'What's going on?' Ben and Annie both sounded cross.

'We're coming for tea,' Bill said uncertainly. 'My home coming tea apparently,' he added sadly.

'Yeah right, since when did Gran drive an Audi?' he heard Annie say as she banged her car door shut.

Bill struggled to get out. His head was aching and even he was beginning to think that he should still be tucked up in bed taking it easy. He struggled after the others and joined a small party on the doorstep where Carol was trying to invite Mark Hammond in and Shaun Bean out. Had Mark and Shaun become usual guests in his daughter's home? Bill would have wondered about what else had been going on if he hadn't desperately needed to sit down quietly somewhere.

'You'd better all come in,' Ben said, remnants of authority still ringing in his tone.

In the background Bill heard two boys give a whoop of delight. Carol tried to say, 'But Ben,' and Bill, in his desperation to find a chair, herded them all over the doorstep and into the house. As his manoeuvre had been surprisingly effective he carried on ushering until they were all standing in the kitchen. Annie dumped her training bag by the washing machine and Susan appeared in the kitchen with a large dob of cream on her nose.

'There you are,' said Susan as if she might have been anxious and Bill assuming that the words were directed at him, opened his arms out yearning for some marital sustenance.

Carol went back to a vicious looking machine anchored on her kitchen work bench which could have been mistaken for a small instrument of torture if it hadn't been bedecked with flour and Ben found several bottles of beer in the fridge.

Bill clutched at a bottle of beer and fell into a chair. Shaun Bean wouldn't sit down and Mark Hammond gravitated over towards Carol.

'Something smells nice,' he said. Bill wondered how flour could smell nice. Mark Hammond was enjoying himself. 'I was just telling Carol,' he continued, 'that I could have easily popped over to York to collect Annie.'

Annie, still in the corner by the washing machine, went very still.

'Especially as you two seemed to be so busy,' Mark carried on without a hint of sarcasm.

'Which two?' Either Carol or Susan or both said this.

Bill and Ben looked guilty.

'Nice place you've got,' said Mark waving his beer bottle at Ben.

'We like it here,' said Carol.

'I should be -' said Shaun Bean.

'Oh, sit down,' said Bill.

'I think Shaun's right,' Carol said. She obviously didn't like using his first name. 'It'll be past Danny's tea time now.'

'Mummy, Mummy, can't Danny stay for tea?' Will and Danny had crowded into the kitchen doorway.

'No, there won't be enough,' said Carol.

'I don't see why not if Danny's Dad doesn't mind, I'm sure there's plenty,' said Susan.

'I'll come back later,' said Shaun Bean.

'Yeah!' said the two boys.

'I'm getting out of here,' said Annie.

'How's it going, sweetheart?' said Mark Hammond softly. Did he touch her as he positioned himself so that she had to squeeze past him to get out?

Everything had happened so quickly that the only thing Bill did register clearly was that Ben followed Shaun Bean out to the front door. When Ben came back into the kitchen he still hadn't said anything.

'I really don't see why,' Carol began.

'Not now,' said Ben.

'I'll be getting off,' said Mark Hammond.

Carol hurriedly dried off her floury hands and followed him out. Ben sat down at the kitchen table and looked meaningfully at Bill and they all listened to Carol from the doorstep.

'Thank you so much, Mark, it was so thoughtful of you.'

'Any time. Just give me a ring. You've got my mobile number? I can pick her up any time.'

'Over my dead body,' muttered Ben.

Bill looked in surprise at his mild quiet-mannered son-in-law.

Ben caught his eye. 'What did you call it, Bill? A game changer?' He couldn't say anything else because Carol had come back into the kitchen.

*

An Italian dinner later Bill was finally tucked up in his own bed at last with his Worlds Best Grandad mug of tea.

'Do you think there's something going on,' said Susan sipping from her own Worlds Best Grandparent mug.

Bill concentrated on his tea and the luxury of being encased in soft downy pillows and duvets.

'Are you going to pretend you didn't notice?' asked Susan. 'This Mark Hammond person. He is the man from *Spiked,* isn't he?'

'Yes,' said Bill, not really caring given that he was now exhausted by the trail of unscheduled events which had plagued his discharge from hospital.

'Does Ben think he's having an affair with Carol?'

Bill spilt tea on the clean duvet cover. He hadn't thought of that. All sorts of things seemed to have been going on while he had been stitched up, wired up, drugged up and punctured during a string of endless tests at the hospital.

'Because I'm sure he's not,' continued Susan.

'How do you know?' The question slipped out without Bill meaning it to.

'Bill Reeves, you can't think that your own daughter would be unfaithful to her husband.'

'Well,' said Bill again.

'What were you up to today anyway? You can't have been at the hospital all day. Weren't you supposed to be discharged this morning?'

'Nothing,' Bill said too quickly.

Susan went quiet.

'Ben had a meeting at *Spiked,*' Bill said.

'Oh, Bill!'

'To do with a client of Ben's,' he finished.

'Is that what all the atmosphere was about this evening?'

'Oh no, not at all. We were invited up to Mark Hammond's office to have coffee, but then Carol rang.' Bill stalled.

'We? What do you mean we?'

'I think,' Bill tried again then paused. 'How do you think Annie is these days?' he said deflecting Susan's question.

'She's got a lot on what with exams and training. Carol and I have been talking about it at lot. I think that was why Carol just wanted a quiet dinner with family only. Carol's not entirely -' but Susan didn't finish what she was trying to say. She just looked worried.

'I just think that Annie's looking a bit, well you know,' Bill tried to say.

190

'Thin,' Susan whispered.

'Is she?' said Bill surprised.

'Haven't you noticed? She didn't touch the trifle.'

'Well, trifle's not very healthy.'

'No,' said Susan. She looked at Bill, still worried.

Bill scratched his scar. 'I haven't seen her much for the last few weeks of course.'

'It's just, Bill, well we see a lot of girls her age at the Health Centre with eating disorders,' Susan looked miserable as she voiced the idea.

'You think she's got anorexia!'

'There's no need to shout,' Susan said. 'I don't just mean anorexia. But a girl training as much as she does needs to eat enough calories for the body to both function and grow. At the same time she's developing a more female shape and she, well, she might not like it. She might also feel the peer pressure of squeezing into the latest skinny legging jeans things.'

'And of looking glamorous for a poster,' added Bill.

'A what?' said Susan.

'A poster. There's a big poster just when you go into the *Spiked* new building bit of Annie looking, well, looking glamorous. Too glamorous.' There was no way a grandfather was going to use the word 'sexy' when describing his granddaughter. As Susan didn't say anything Bill went on, 'It's this sponsorship deal you see, they can use Annie to promote *Spiked*. It's just the very thing I've being trying to get everyone to understand. Carol and Ben, the cricket club.'

'Bill, are you bringing this back to you and that wretched cricket club of yours?'

'No. But. I'm just making a point.' Bill rushed on before Susan went further onto the attack. 'I think that's what was bothering Ben tonight. The poster and Annie being exploited by *Spiked*.'

'Is that what Ben thinks?' Susan sounded surprised.

Bill stared unhappily at his empty tea mug. He wasn't sure. Too much had happened that evening. And of course it wasn't Carol's relationship with Mark Hammond that particularly bothered Ben. It was Mark Hammond's relationship with Annie. If Bill had had the courage to expose *Spiked* properly. If he'd got the cricket

191

club to believe him. If he'd persuaded Carol and Ben not to accept Annie's sponsorship with *Spiked*. If he'd been organised and calmly presented facts at the cricket club extraordinary general meeting. If he'd had any clear message at all. If.

Whatever else he had a strong feeling that somehow it was all his fault. From the first day when he stole that document and failed to take responsibility for it. You can't do something bad to achieve something good, he thought. Or perhaps said out loud because Susan turned sharply in her pillows and looked at him. However if he had spoken out loud she didn't respond to his words. What she did say was, 'As you're home now are you going to go to the grand opening then, Bill?'

'The grand opening,' Bill said carefully.

'Don't be disingenuous, Bill Reeves, the grand opening of the new cricket pavilion.'

24

The next morning Bill decided to test ride his bicycle. He waited until Susan had gone off to Morrisons and appeased his conscience by putting on a new helmet which was waiting for him on the kitchen table.

He planned to avoid the village green but as if of their own accord his legs pedalled in that direction. He'd missed the snowdrops and the early crocuses and the gardens he cycled past were already full of displays of daffodils and primulas. Hardly ten minutes had passed before he was inspecting the condition of the wicket, and then it was too late to avoid noticing beach flags fluttering in the spring breeze alongside the completed shell of a super modern club house. The beach flags were red and black and unsubtly suggested that *Spiked* now owned the cricket club. 'Along with the rest of East Wolds,' Bill muttered crossly, scuffing his shoe at a bit of lush green grass on the leg side of the wicket.

Two large vans proclaiming East Wolds El Co were parked outside the new pavilion. Overtime if they were working on a Saturday. The whole thing must be costing a fortune. The club would never be able to pay *Spiked* back if it came to a falling out.

One of the electricians emerged from the new building, noticed Bill then waved, uncertainly. It was Matthew Watkins, the reserve wicket keeper. Now no longer the reserve, a very nice get well note had informed Bill. It wasn't however young Matt's fault and if Bill ignored him now it would look like he minded. And minding was a very private business.

Bill pushed his bicycle over to the new club house and the younger man stopped what he was doing and looked pleased and embarrassed.

'Wicket's looking good,' Bill said.

'Yes,' said Matt, 'should be in good shape for next Sunday. You're on your feet again then,' Matt continued uncertainly.

'Is that the first match of the season?' asked Bill.

'Yes, after the big opening next Saturday. Are you?' began Matt then stopped.

Another man appeared in the doorway of the pavilion. 'Have you found that extra wire or what, Matt?'

Bill peered round the man into the modern interior of the new pavilion.

'Would you like a preview?' the man said. 'Bit modern for my taste but -'

'No thanks,' said Bill, 'I'd better not hold up the good work. Things to do,' he said and cycled on to Ben and Carol's.

'Poor chap's obviously gutted. They've picked me, you know, as wicket keeper, at last.' Bill heard Matt say to his boss before he managed to get out of earshot.

Carol answered the door.

'It's very quiet,' said Bill following her into the kitchen, trying to decide whether to accept an offer of a cup of coffee if such an offer was made.

'Everyone's out. How are you feeling, Dad? Is Mum with you?' Luckily Carol hadn't seen the bicycle and Bill had had the wit to leave his helmet out of sight with the bicycle. No coffee was offered. 'William's gone off on his bicycle,' she added implying, with years of practice, that this was Bill's fault, 'and Annie's out.'

'She's not training again, is she? I thought she was studying today?'

'She's doing a photo shoot.'

'She's doing a what?'

'A photo shoot, Dad.'

'You mean?'

'It's part of her sponsorship deal with *Spiked,* and Mark says she's particularly photogenic. So they are using her more than the other kids.'

'Is that meant to be good?'

'Dad, for goodness sake.'

Bill took a deep breath of self-control. 'I suppose Ben's taken her to wherever it is, then,' he said calmly.

'Leeds. Oh no, Ben's doing the weekly shop.'

'How's she got to Leeds then?'

'Mark's taken her.'

'Mark Hammond?' This was not said calmly.

'Of course Mark Hammond. Who else?'

'And does Ben know?' This was now shouted.

'Dad, I really think -'

'Can I borrow your car?'

194

'Can you what?' At least this stumped Carol's indignation.

'Can I borrow your car?' Bill repeated.

'Is that why you came? To borrow my car?' Carol was too puzzled to be indignant. 'Why? Where are you going? Are you okay to drive? Dad?'

During the course of the above conversation Bill had worked his way into the entrance hall which meant he was now in arm's reach of the keys neatly hanging on hooks behind the hall table.

'Are these yours?' he asked grabbing at a large set of keys which looked like they might belong to Carol's SUV, a smaller, older model than Ben's.

'Dad!' Carol began.

'I won't be long,' Bill said trying to sound normal and appeasing. He rushed out to the road where Carol's SUV was parked. He'd managed to stab at the unlock icon on the key ring, open the door and climb in before Carol found her outdoor shoes and ran out to try and stop him.

Bill found the ignition and the SUV splurged into a big rattling diesel engine starting noise. Carol opened the car door.

'Dad!'

'Where's the handbrake?' said Bill.

By the time Carol had sent a text message to Susan saying 'What's going on? Dad just stole my car,' Bill had worked out how to use the automatic gear and had launched himself out onto the open road.

It was exciting driving a large car at high speed along the M62. Bill had wonderful views of the sweeping flat landscape and whooped with pleasure when he crossed the Humber over a high mini suspension bridge. In fact his venture was so exhilarating after being restrained in hospital that he was hurtling through a maze of motorways all claiming to be heading into Leeds City Centre when it finally occurred to him that he didn't know where he was going.

Bill had assumed without really thinking about it, that he was heading to the specialist sports facilities at Leeds Met where Annie did her sports training. However she wasn't training, she was at a photo shoot. Whatever that meant and wherever that was. The important information from Bill's point of view had been that she was with Mark Hammond, not what she was doing.

He swung into a petrol station and switched the engine off. He could hear Susan's voice in his head. Probably right now sitting down having a cup of coffee with Carol. What was he playing at? He rubbed his head.

Someone tapped on the window and he started guiltily. As if in possession of a stolen vehicle. He didn't know how to open the window so he opened the door.

'Are you going in the carwash or what?' A man in a loud sweater asked him.

'Carwash?'

'Yeah,' the loud sweater said sarcastically.

'No, I'm going to a photo shoot.'

'You don't say.'

'I don't suppose -' Bill began optimistically.

'Do you mind just moving your frigging over sized tank?' the loud sweater interrupted.

'It's not mine,' Bill said unhelpfully. Although he did have the wit to close the door and manoeuvre the SUV to another part of the garage forecourt.

He felt in his anorak pocket and miraculously found his mobile.

'Now then,' Bill said when Ben finally answered his phone.

'Bill?'

'Hello,' said Bill. 'How's things?'

'Just a tad busy right now. I'm at the check out in Morrisons. Can I ring you back?'

'No!'

'Is there a problem?'

'I'm in Leeds but I don't know where she is.'

'Where who is?'

'Annie.'

'What about Annie?'

'Annie's gone off somewhere with Mark Hammond and I'm trying to find them.'

There was some kerfuffle at the other end then Ben came back on the line. 'Bill can you just say that again a bit more comprehensibly.'

'I went to your place on my bike. When I got there no one was home apart from Carol and she said that Annie had gone to Leeds for a photo shoot and that Mark Hammond had taken her.'

'Mark Hammond?'

'Yes, that's what she said.'

More disturbance at Ben's end then Ben said. 'I thought I'd made it clear that Annie was not to be out at all hours whenever *Spiked* decided.'

Bill couldn't remember any such edict. 'I don't know about that but I'm in Leeds so I can collect her from the photo shoot, but I don't know where she is.'

'Yes, I'm being as fast as I can,' Ben suddenly said down the phone. 'Bill? Bill? Are you still there?'

'Yes, I'm here,' said Bill.

'Just wait while I finish here.'

Ben's phone went all smudgy as if he'd muffled the mouthpiece or put the phone in his pocket.

'Bill?' he finally resumed after a minute or so.

'Yes.'

'Where did you say you were?'

'I'm in Leeds but I don't know where Annie is.'

'But how did you get to Leeds?'

'I'm in Carol's car.'

'How on earth -. Let's get this straight. You called by home, ascertained that Annie had gone off for a photo shoot with Mark Hammond. You decided that this was a bad idea, so you took Carol's car so that you could drive to Leeds and collect Annie and bring her back home despite the fact that you are probably not fit to drive a car?'

'In a nut shell,' said Bill, impressed.

'And you've never collected her from a photo shoot before?'

'No, just from the Met's sports grounds a while ago now.'

'So you don't know where to go?'

'I haven't a clue.'

'And I've never been - but hang on a minute. You're in Carol's car?'

'Yes.'

'Have you tried the sat nav?'

'The what?'

'The navigation.'

Bill said nothing.

'On the central console just above the gear stick,' started Ben.

'This bit in the middle?'

'Yes. Is there a button that says navigation or some such thing?'

'I've pressed a button that says nav,' said Bill.

'Has anything happened?'

'Yes, there's a map. It shows a petrol station and a blob. How clever. Just like the set up in Mark Hammond's car.'

'Bill?'

'Yes?'

'On the screen is there a memory option?'

'A what? Oh yes. Shall I click something? I get it, but now that map's gone and there's just a list of addresses.' Bill sounded disappointed.

'Brilliant,' said Ben.

'Oh,' said Bill.

'Is one of those addresses somewhere in Leeds?'

'No. Hang on a minute I can scroll with this button can't I? There's the Leeds Met address and, yes, here we are, another one, 12-18 Lowrie Road, Leeds.'

'That'll be the one. Now click on it,' said Ben.

'Hello? Hello?' said Bill several times until he realised that his phone had run out of battery

But when he clicked on the Lowrie Road address a nice woman said 'Your route is being calculated,' and the map came up on the display again. The nice woman then said 'Please make a U-turn if possible,' and a big blue line appeared on the map.

'Well I never,' said Bill, and he and the nice woman set off in the direction of Lowrie Road, Leeds.

Bill was feeling pretty smug when he noisily barged through a door which said, 'Filming in progress. Please do not enter'. A girl with a clipboard came rushing up to him. Someone said, 'Gramps!' and someone else said, 'Mr Reeves, Bill.' The girl with the clipboard said, 'How may I help you?'

Bill said nothing. Annie was revealing a lot of fake tanned leg, a lot of fake tanned breast and a lot of fake tanned six-pack.

Black and red silk fluttered around her. She leant towards a camera, bottom posed out, lips pressed into a kiss and breasts exposed to the shot. A red transfer blazoned across her forehead.

An annoyed voice said resignedly, 'Let's take a break,' and Mark Hammond appeared from the direction of the camera lens and said, 'I'll deal with this.' He walked over towards Bill. Annie joined them. Bill had still got no further than the door.

'Gramps what the?' Annie said. She was trying to pull her shirt over the six-pack and her skirt down to hide her tanned thighs. The red transfer looked like an assault.

Bill puffed himself out. Broad shoulders, big chest. 'I've come to take you home,' he said loudly.

Someone sniggered. Annie hunched her shoulders and her eyes darted round to see who was laughing.

'Bill,' Mark Hammond didn't quite say old chap, 'that's very dedicated of you. There's really no need. I'll pop Annie home when we're finished.'

Bill failed to fill an appropriate pause with appropriate words.

'Don't mention it. It's no trouble at all,' Mark Hammond answered him anyway.

'I mean,' said Bill, 'I'm going to take Annie home now.' He looked at Annie huddling next to him and felt large and protective. He slipped his anorak off in a grand gesture and folded it over Annie's quivering shoulders.

Annie shook it off. 'Gramps, for god's sake,' she said.

'You get your things and we'll go home,' Bill said, less loudly.

'Gramps, just go away,' Annie turned her head and gestured to the room behind her. 'You're so embarrassing,' she hissed.

Bill opened his mouth and moved back towards the door. Mark Hammond stepped into the breach. 'We won't be much longer,' he said. He nodded into the room and Annie returned to the camera. He opened the door for Bill and held out his hand. 'Nice of you to come, but everything's under control here. Don't worry, we're taking good care of your golden girl.'

Bill wanted to hit him. He certainly didn't take the proffered hand but he did back out of the door. The air felt dirty inside and out and Bill felt polluted. That's our little girl, he whispered to Carol's car as he climbed into the driver's seat. He picked his mobile off the passenger seat and punched the redial button to speak to Ben again. His phone of course was dead. He leant his head against Carol's neck support and lurched the diesel engine into noisy life again. The automatic gear launched him out onto Lowrie Road and Bill drove round Leeds three times before he managed to find an exit onto the M62 heading eastwards.

All Bill could think about was Mark Hammond's sleek face and where he would land the punch. So he was a bit taken aback when he pulled up outside Carol and Ben's house behind an Audi Q7. Then when he marched in without knocking found that self same sleek face sitting in Carol's kitchen looking even riper for a punching. He went straight over to Mark and stood over him his knuckles clenched into position. Someone said, 'Hello.' Someone else said, 'Dad, what have you been doing?' And a third person said, 'Gramps, I don't believe it.'

Bill said, 'Where's Ben?'

A third mug for coffee was not produced. Bill's question remained unanswered and Annie said pointedly, 'I'm going to revise now. Just in case anyone remembered or cared.' The fake tan on her chest had gone blotchy and her blond hair had gone limp and over-washed.

'Darling,' said Carol, 'of course we all -' and she rolled her eyes as if they all did whatever it was that she thought they all should.

Bill found himself backing down for a second time that day. He dropped Carol's car keys on the kitchen table and retreated head first into Ben who was just opening the front door. Bill stepped back and looked up at his son-in-law. He jabbed his finger towards the kitchen, then at Ben.

'You won't be killing him, Ben,' he said, 'because I'm going to have a go first.'

Ben was a maze of questions, but Will was pushing in behind him and Bill continued with his own push to get out of the house. Stultifying again, polluted, his head throbbing under the scar. Ben turned back in the open door, his question mark taking in the Audi Q7 and Bill grappling with his bicycle at the side of the house. Bill pushed his bicycle along the lawn and paused by Ben. Will's voice boomed from the kitchen.

'Gramps is really impressive when he's in a funk, isn't he?'

Bill raced home longing for several pillows and a cup of tea but Susan was out, he'd forgotten to take his key with him and his mobile could just as well have been left on the kitchen table.

By this time Bill was ready to take a swing at anyone. How could Susan have gone out and left him alone on his first day properly out of hospital? She couldn't possibly still be at Morrison's and Bill couldn't remember her saying she was going anywhere else that day.

Self pity sent him to the Pub. Given that it was only five o'clock The Cricketers Arms was surprisingly popular. Perhaps the cricket club had been training for the opening match of the season the following weekend. Bill shuffled to the other end of the bar and managed to exchange greetings with his ex-fellow cricketers without any of them actually doing any greeting. You'd think head wounds were contagious. He was briefly cheered when he spotted One Shot Summers but One Shot didn't catch his eye and hung onto the in-crowd with an eye to a few free drinks on the strength of past glories.

Bill ordered himself a pint of best bitter. Decided he didn't want to talk to anyone anyway and took his drink off to a dark corner.

About ten minutes later he watched Ben go through the same procedure, but when Ben turned to find a quiet corner he found Bill.

'Didn't think you should be here,' one of them said as both looked accusingly at their watches.

However when Ben took Bill's pint off for a re-fill it suddenly looked as if they had planned to meet each other instead of being the excluded losers and they were both happy to sit in the gloomy corner together. It didn't occur to Bill that Ben becoming an excluded loser was a monumental shift in perspective. Bill was more interested in seeing the bottom of another pint. When he saw the second bottom approaching he finally acknowledged Ben.

'Not exactly your scene this, Ben, is it,' he said.

'A third mug of coffee to include me in the love-in with Mark Hammond was not forthcoming,' Ben said, regretting that he'd only bought himself a half.

'Ah,' said Bill, 'same again?'

Ben agreed, and as Bill bought him a pint this time he had no cause for regret.

'Now if my wife,' Bill began two pints the braver.

'I'm not bothered about Carol.'

Which careless statement should have bothered Bill, but he drank more instead of responding.

'The most risqué any of Carol's flirtations get is to accept a second glass of wine. She gets pleased with herself but always ends up in my bed.'

Bill needed more than three pints to be comfortable about discussing sleeping arrangements with his son-in-law.

'But I don't trust the guy,' Ben continued, 'and I thought you'd gone to Leeds to collect Annie anyway.'

Bill remembered that he was miserable again. 'She wouldn't come with me.'

'She what?'

'I mucked up again, Ben. I embarrassed her. And that smarmy -' Bill was talking quite loudly and a couple of the cricketers plying One Shot with free beer turned to peer into the dark corner where Bill and Ben were sitting.

'I'll get you another drink,' said Ben quickly.

Bill watched Ben go to the bar and accidently caught the eye of the couple of men paying him some slight attention. 'It'll all end badly,' Bill said generally, darkly and loudly. Which was about when Shaun Bean arrived on the scene, because Ben bought him a drink too.

'That,' said Bill, starting on his forth pint, 'is fraternising with the enemy.'

Ben had just joined him again. 'Carol doesn't think of him as the enemy.'

'I don't mean Carol, I mean you. He represents the enemy,' said Bill pointing at Shaun Bean.

Bill was neither in the mood nor sufficiently sober to worry about Ben's silence and discomfort and Shaun Bean was not one to avoid a fight. Shaun Bean toasted Ben with his pint, stood in the middle of the room and turned his back on Bill to gloat over cricketing prowesses with the in-crowd. Bill was up beside Shaun Bean ready to buy another pint before Ben could formulate a more peaceable plan.

'There's only one way our cricket club's going now and that's down hill,' said Bill.

'Oh come on, Bill,' several people said.

'Sour grapes,' Shaun Bean said.

'You've all sold out to *Spiked* and no good will come of it,' Bill said, though not as steadily as he believed.

'No good in the form of a spanking new club house and a massive increase in membership, and enough kids training to form two teams in the youth leagues.' It didn't really matter who said this as Bill assumed it was Shaun Bean anyway. In fact in some re-tellings of this little piece of club history there were claims that Ben was the originator of these statistics.

'I'd rather come bottom of the league than sell out to *Spiked*,' Bill continued. 'All of you, the whole town.'

'We'd better be getting home,' Ben said at his elbow.

'Corrupted,' Bill shouted.

Someone was pulling on his sleeve and he swung around to shake them off except a chair got in the way and Bill thought that the chair was Shaun Bean and as Shaun Bean was the closest he was going to get to Mark Hammond that evening Bill dropped his empty glass and landed a huge punch somewhere in the vicinity of Shaun Bean's chest. Somehow or other Bill then followed his glass to the floor only to find that Ben was already there. The damage stopped there as the publican was a large man and Ben managed to get himself to his feet quickly enough to take care of Bill, apologise for the mess and push Bill out of the door before the publican did and before any further threats or bannings were able to be issued. It was drizzling outside and inside someone cheered.

The two men were silent. The rain sobered Bill up a little. Ben tried to straighten them both out and a cut on Bill's hand suggested that the glass Bill had dropped had broken. Ben looked at him sadly.

'None of this is helping Annie, is it,' he said.

25

After a restless night in the spare room Bill woke up the next morning with a throbbing hand and a head that throbbed in more than one place. Susan said he should have stitches in his hand but after looking pathetic and hangdog enough he managed to persuade her to tape it up. Bill spent the rest of the Sunday morning tucked up in the spare bed looking at a cold cup of tea. The Worlds Best Grandad. If only. Bill had ended up in hospital and everyone had become much happier. The cricket club was flourishing. Annie was a star. She was signed up for junior Wimbledon a year ahead of schedule and the 'face' of Britain's coolest newest brand.

Annie. His granddaughter had become the sex symbol for a crap product which harmed children. And for whose benefit? Did the children benefit from pouring large doses of sweetened caffeine and God knows what else down their throats? Did Annie benefit from being pushed to achieve results? Did the cricket club benefit from having a ridiculously fine clubhouse and lousy values?

'No,' said Bill, so loudly that he made himself jump. He looked around the bedroom guiltily, wondering where Susan was hiding out. 'No,' he whispered, because the word was so reassuring. 'I'll tell you who benefits,' he said to the bedroom, 'middle-aged men like Jonathan Andrews and yes, Mark Hammond. Because even Mark Hammond, for all his gloss, is a middle-aged man closer to forty than he is thirty. A middle-aged man drooling, drooling,' Bill shouted, 'over my granddaughter.'

'Who on earth are you talking to?' said a voice from the bedroom door.

Bill jumped again and guilt froze his lips into a smile. 'The dog,' he said limply.

'We don't have a dog,' said Susan. 'Bill Reeves, were you talking to yourself?'

Bill tried to look calm, in control and normal and with a nonchalant wave of his bandaged hand he spilt the cold tea all over the spare duvet.

'Really, I don't know what to do with you. I've had a nice quiet few weeks knowing exactly where you are and what you're up to, but now when you're supposed to be back to normal look at the state of you.'

'I'm,' Bill started to say, 'it's Annie.'

'What do you mean, it's Annie? Don't start blaming anyone else just because you're in a state with yourself. It's the cricket club isn't it? They're doing well. They're opening the new clubhouse next weekend and they're starting the new season without you. And whose fault is that?'

'It's not the cricket club,' Bill said violently. It was hardly his fault that he'd ended up in hospital, or if it was his fault it hadn't been intentional.

'If you're going to start shouting at me as well then you can get yourself up and out of bed and leave me in peace to make dinner. And just in case you've forgotten, it's Sunday, and we're all going to sit down together this evening and have a nice family dinner.'

'Right,' said Bill.

'Right,' said Susan.

'Okay,' said Bill and flung off the wet duvet.

He shuffled his feet into some slippers and went to hide in his little office. He switched on his computer and while it warmed up he noticed that it was a lovely day outside. A day he would normally have spent at the nets practicing for the first match of the season. A day when he would have come home and bored Susan all evening with a detailed analysis of how the team would function and what each individual needed to do to win matches. He would have made Boycott look tongue-tied.

The computer buzzed into life and after another three minutes his inbox opened. He had no new mail. Not even anyone who wanted to sell him Viagra. He opened up Google and typed in Mark Hammond. There were quite a few Mark Hammonds. Bill clicked on a link which mentioned *Spiked*. There wasn't much. Nothing he didn't know already about Mark Hammond. Nothing to suggest why Mark Hammond in particular should be shadowing Annie.

Was he shadowing Annie? Was that what he was doing? Turning up all the time. Collecting her from training. Taking her off to photo shoots. Surely an executive wouldn't normally take such an interest in any particular sponsee. If Mark Hammond was shadowing Annie then that clearly wasn't right. None of this was helping Annie, Ben had said.

'Well, I'm going to do something about that,' said Bill. 'If he, that smarmy bastard, is shadowing Annie then I'm going to shadow him.'

He typed in bt.com and did a domestic search for a local telephone number. And there he was. Living in a cottage in a village about five miles away.

'Gotcha,' said Bill, just as the house filled with noise downstairs and he realised that his family had arrived for Sunday dinner.

Bill bounced downstairs to greet them. He felt a much happier man and ready to comply with all Susan's edicts. He crowded into the kitchen with them all and everyone was being particularly friendly until Will asked Susan, 'Why is Gramps still in his pyjamas? Is he still poorly?'

26

As Bill had survived the weekend he decided that a long bicycle ride would do him good. It was a fine morning. A tonic for any convalescent.

First he went to the *Spiked* car park to check that the Audi Q7 was parked there then he headed south towards Woldsby. Woldsby was a bleak East Riding village made popular by its position vis-à-vis the M62 rather than any pretty features.

The landscape was flat, but Bill had grown up with it and liked it. It was good for bicycling. The hedges on either side of the B road he trundled along were straggly and unkempt, attacked with a flail once or twice a year but not cut back or laid into useful purpose any more. The trees that had been allowed to grow out of them were ash. In the old days it had been a pleasant jaunt out to the pub in Woldsby which had had a reputation for cheap beer and lax closing hours. Now it had tried to expose a few beams, hang bits of old harness on the walls and offered adventurous meals like seafood risotto and venison in prune sauce.

Within half an hour Bill was scootling past the pub looking for Wolds View Cottages. Wolds View Cottages was now one cottage with an awkward array of windows in the front as it tried to pretend that it only had one front door and that that one small front door was a main entrance into a spacious dwelling. Bill didn't quite have the nerve to prop his bicycle up against the garage at the side of the cottage so he went back to the pub and parked his bicycle there.

No one was about so Bill decided that an open approach to Wolds View Cottages was the best and marched up to the front door and knocked loudly. Assuming that no one would answer his knock he then had a pretext to wander around the building and have a good snoop. However, just as Bill was heading off for his snoop, someone did answer the door. It swung open and a thin dark haired woman looked at him with a startled expression.

'Er,' said Bill helpfully.

'Is something wrong?' the woman asked.

'Is Mark at home?'

At least the woman looked less startled now. 'No,' she said.

'I suppose he's at work,' Bill said.

'So do I,' said the woman. 'He's often not at work,' she continued and a distinct whiff of alcohol wafted into the air between them.

'It was just about the East Wolds Cricket Club,' said Bill, suddenly inspired.

'I don't think it's cricket leading him astray,' the woman said. 'I'd love to have a husband who was only led astray by cricket.'

It was difficult for Bill not to warm towards this poor lonely woman who longed for a cricketing husband. So when she asked him if he'd like to come in and have a drink he said yes.

The cottage had a surprisingly homely kitchen. Bill didn't expect the wooden units and the Aga, given that the current rage seemed to be the marble and granite that Carol and the Andrews favoured. A door was open from the kitchen straight onto a little patio. This patio looked out over a large garden and a tasteful array of native flowers and a riot of spring bulbs. The patio caught just enough of the early sunshine to be warm enough to sit out on.

The woman brought cushions for two solid teak chairs and drinks on a tray. A cold beer, American style, for Bill and a glass of wine for herself.

'Well,' said Bill, 'cheers.'

'What did you want to see Mark for?' asked the woman.

'Well, cricket,' Bill said unconvincingly.

'Is he after your wife?'

'No, he's not after my wife,' Bill said, but he sounded defensive and the woman knew immediately that she was onto something.

'You've come on behalf of a friend?' she continued eagerly.

'No,' Bill shook his head.

'A relative,' she was starting to guess wildly, 'a daughter?'

'No, my granddaughter,' Bill let slip and immediately regretted it. The woman screamed in fury and threw her wine glass to the far end of the garden where it smashed dramatically against a stone water trough.

'I'll make a cup of tea,' said Bill.

'I hate tea,' the woman said, but Bill went into the kitchen anyway.

208

Bill didn't do hysterical women and the kitchen was a safe haven from broken wine glasses. There was a kettle already warm on the Aga so Bill lifted up one of the Aga's covers and put the kettle on the hot plate. Various teas were lined up on a narrow shelf and Bill found something that said Yorkshire Tea. As this was bound to be strong and black he pulled two tea bags out of the box. Mugs were in a cupboard over the ceramic sink. Carol would have called them French country style. Bill was just impressed by their size. The kettle was already making a lot of noise on the Aga. Bill assumed that this meant it was boiling and poured hot water over the two tea bags. He then squeezed all the blackness out of them both and poured in a big dollop of milk. Sugar was hidden in a cupboard with general baking supplies, but not so hidden that Bill didn't manage to find it. He added generous teaspoonfuls to both mugs. By the time he had presented the woman with her strong cup of sweet tea he had also felt at home enough to successfully forage for biscuits.

The woman grimaced painfully when she sipped at the syrupy liquid but she didn't hurl it across the garden and she also took a biscuit.

'Well,' said Bill.

'What do you mean, well?' said the woman. She still didn't sound as calm as Bill would have liked.

'Umm,' said Bill cluelessly.

A question might have roused the woman's suspicions but cluelessness set her talking.

'We moved here a couple of years ago and you're the first person who's sat at this table with me and had a cup of tea.'

Bill made another clueless noise.

'It was meant to be a fresh start.' Her hand swept to the table in search of the habitual wine glass. It found the tea instead. She took another sip, grimaced but carried on sipping. Her hands closed around the mug as though discovering such comforts anew. 'New job, new product, new part of the country, new friends, new -' Wild eyes suddenly locked onto Bill's and she carried on in a whisper. 'When we first met I had an abortion and since then nothing. Not a sign now, bloody hell, when we'd actually like a baby.' The word baby sent her hand looking for the glass then back to the mug.

Bill opened his mouth but even clueless was inadequate to describe his hopelessness in the face of such trouble.

'At least I wanted a baby, but Mark, he just wants, what do you call it? His tottie.'

Poor Bill. One person's tottie could be another person's granddaughter.

'It started with my friends. An arm around the shoulders, a whispered joke, a slow dance. The arm moving to the small of the back and then a meeting, deliberate and secret. Time and time again why do these women fall for it? Every time.'

Bill looked at her and she looked at him.

'I suppose I did,' she said.

'He did marry you,' Bill ventured bravely.

She ignored him. 'And I've got older. He's got older. But only in theory; in practice he still thinks he's bloody twenty-five. So the girls get younger.'

Bill went very quiet.

'A couple of years ago it was the daughter of a friend. That's why we moved here. Bloody hell, I'm not really drunk enough to be telling you about all this.'

'What do you know about *Spiked*?' Bill said.

Her head jerked up and Bill adjusted his expression several times before failing to look clueless.

'Not a lot.'

Bill said something that was something and nothing. But she was lonely. She liked to talk.

'Mark wants to make money. He intends to make money out of *Spiked*. There's some property. He doesn't talk to me. I just see the post sometimes. He says the locals are stupid clodhoppers and he likes to have them eating out of his hand. Apparently there was one bloke, something to do with the cricket club?' her voice rose as in a question.

Bill held his breath and hoped that his earlier reference to the cricket club was forgotten.

'But he hasn't mentioned anything for a while. I remember,' the booze was wearing off and the memory was kicking in, 'he said he'd well and truly castrated this bloke. So it must have been a bloke mustn't it? I suppose if it had been a woman he would have just shagged her into submission.'

210

She was wandering back to what was obviously her favourite subject with regards to her husband.

'So this bloke?' Bill said tentatively.

She shrugged. 'People usually submit in the end,' she said. 'Look at me. All fire in theory, but in practice I'm shit scared he'll leave me for some stupid bimbo just out of school.'

'Is there anyone in particular, at the moment?' Bill said, baulking at the image of bimbo and schoolgirl.

'You mean your granddaughter? There's always someone at the moment.'

Bill finished his tea. He ought to go.

'Mind you,' she started again, 'although Mark claimed to have wiped the floor with this local opponent, from the state of his car at the time it looked more like someone had wiped the floor with his nice Audi.' She smiled. Her fingers were still wrapped around the half drunk mug of tea but her eyes showed a longing for something stronger. 'I wouldn't mind meeting the guy who wrote off that Audi.'

Bill coughed. 'Well,' he said and stood up. 'It was nice meeting you.'

'We could have another drink?'

Bill shook his head. When he went back into the kitchen the telephone rang.

'Bloody hell,' the woman swore from the patio. 'Be a dear and get that on your way out.'

Bill half turned back to the patio, made several impotent gestures with his arms then, as the telephone was on a wooden worktop just where he was standing, he picked it up.

'Hello,' he said.

'Vicky?' a man's voice said uncertainly.

Bill recognised the smarmy undertones immediately.

'No, shall I get her for you?'

Pause. 'Who is this?' Aggressive, not smarmy.

'The gardener.' Not Bill's most inspired untruth. He called out to the patio. 'It's your husband.'

Vicky came to the patio door. 'Tell him I'll ring him back,' she said.

'She says she'll ring you back,' Bill said and clicked the off button on the telephone.

211

Vicky stood in the open door and smiled a slow purring smile. 'Did he want to know who you were?'

Bill nodded.

'And what did you say?'

'I said I was the gardener.'

She looked at him for a long intimate moment then threw her head back and laughed in sheer unalcoholic delight.

*

Bill didn't manage to get through to Ben until late that evening. He shooed Susan up to bed. She would have been suspicious if she hadn't been tired. Bill pressed the redial on Ben's number on his mobile while he lurked in the kitchen with the lights turned off. Ben answered after the first ring.

'Bill? Isn't it really late?' It sounded as though he was lurking too.

'He likes girls,' Bill whispered back, 'young ones.'

'Susan, where are my shoes?'

It was Tuesday morning. Early. Susan was still trying to enjoy a cup of tea in bed before having to get up for work. 'What do you mean where are your shoes? I expect they're where they usually are.'

Bill appeared in the bedroom doorway.

'Are you wearing your suit?' Susan raised herself up on her elbows to get a better look. 'Why on earth are you -'

'So I need my best shoes,' said Bill.

'But,' then Susan gave up asking why. It was quarter to seven so she might as well get up anyway. 'How should I know where your shoes are,' she said and locked herself in the bathroom.

Luckily when Bill dived into Ben's car five minutes later he was wearing a half decent pair of black lace-ups.

'Did you manage to arrange a meeting?' Ben asked as he pulled out into a thin but steady stream of traffic heading for the M62.

'Not yet,' said Bill happily. He pulled his mobile out of his pocket and waved it at Ben. 'It was a bit late last night.'

'That's what I tried to -' but Ben gave up. He hoped his own diary hadn't filled up since yesterday and he was due in Court later that day to settle a dispute on fishing rights.

'What time shall I suggest?' Bill continued unperturbed.

'The earlier the better I should think,' Ben said.

'A breakfast meeting?' Bill said hungrily.

Ben said nothing. Bill failed to notice that this was out of irritation and was not strategic. He scrolled down a few dozen messages on his mobile and finally found his exchange with Julia.

'Hello Julia,' he wrote, 'I wonder if we could have another meeting? Breakfast in just over half an hour? 8am say? Bill.' He pressed the send button.

'Of course she might not be in Leeds,' he said to Ben.

His phone beeped.

'Sorry, who is this please?' the message said.

'Bill,' Bill typed into the phone. 'Bill Reeves the local East Wolds,' he paused, wrote 'cricketer', changed his mind and wrote 'activist', was very pleased with himself and pressed the send button.

213

He read his message out to Ben. They both waited with some interest to see what came next. Bill's phone beeped.

'Armandes at 8,' it said.

'Armandes at 8,' Bill said.

'Armandes?' said Ben. He stopped changing lanes at ninety miles an hour and almost smiled at Bill. 'I hope she's paying.'

Bill sent a message back. 'Okay, see you there.'

Julia was sitting up at the counter of a space age breakfast bar about ten minutes walk from Ben's office. It smelt of almonds and patisserie. Julia had a cup of something very foamy and deeply aromatic. She had prepared a welcoming smile for Bill but obviously hadn't expected him to come with anyone else. Ben met her less welcoming smile and introduced himself. Ben Whitby Jones, QC. It didn't help the atmosphere.

Bill rubbed his hands together hungrily. 'Where shall we sit then?' he said.

Bill sat down at a table for three and watched Julia and Ben move more slowly to join him. He had the distinct and gratifying feeling that they'd caught Julia on the hop. Just as she'd tried to catch him last time they'd met. This time, however -

'Have we met before?' Julia was saying.

'No,' answered Ben.

'It's just that the name seems familiar,' Julia continued as she sat down, carefully placing her foaming cup on the table first.

'My daughter is in the *Spiked* young talent sponsorship scheme,' said Ben as he helped slide her chair back into position. 'Are you eating Julia?' he continued smoothly.

'I'll just have orange juice,' Julia passed on this order to a waiter who had followed them to the table.

'Bill?' Ben continued taking charge.

Bill was silent. He was wondering how to order a bacon butty in French.

'I'll have an almond croissant and an espresso,' said Ben.

'Yes, I'll have one of those,' Bill broke in quickly, 'but no coffee. I'll have tea,' he finished.

'It's very nice to meet you Mr Whitby Jones but I can hardly think a meeting arranged as a matter of urgency was just to congratulate us on the generosity of our sponsorship deals.'

214

'Congratulate', 'generosity' and 'sponsorship' reminded Bill that he was an activist and not a hungry Yorkshire man. 'Sponsorship deals are not generous,' he said loudly, 'they are entirely in the interest of the sponsor and pay no regard to the long term benefit of the sponsored person.'

'Miss Whitby Jones is currently benefitting from our sponsorship to the tune of, at a rough estimate £10,000. Does that sound a fair guess Mr Whitby Jones? And I therefore find it hard to believe that that has no impact on her long term sporting opportunities.'

'Numbers always sound good, but my granddaughter is being exploited.'

'Bill,' exclaimed Ben and the waiter interrupted them all as a black tray bedecked with a white cloth distributed orange juice, coffee, tea and almond croissants.

'I can only repeat,' Julia said coolly sipping orange juice, 'what is it that you really want to talk about?'

Ben looked uncomfortable and Bill had just been silenced.

'Mark Hammond,' one of them finally said.

'In which case,' Julia caught the waiter's eye, 'I'll also have an almond croissant,' she said, 'does anyone else want anything?'

'A bacon butty?' put in Bill quickly and quietly. But no one heard him, or at least no one acknowledged that they'd heard him.

Then there was silence because Julia was waiting to hear what they had to say and Ben always waited to see what anyone else had to say. Which left Bill, who was hungry and wasn't sure if he liked almond croissants.

'Do you know what Mark Hammond is doing?' Bill finally asked.

'He's our CEO based at our main production site and he's doing very well.'

'But do you know what he's getting up to?' said Bill loudly.

'CEOs don't 'get up to' anything. They manage companies and in this case manage companies rather well. Mark's track record was immaculate when he came to us and we can see why.'

'It's not what his wife said,' muttered Bill.

'Perhaps, however, people in East Wolds get up to things and then find someone else to blame. Isn't that what people do in small communities?' She was sneering, distinctly sneering. 'If I remember aright you, Bill, were getting up to rather a lot last time we met. In fact I think you were trying to blackmail us.'

It was such an onslaught of body liners that Bill could only duck helplessly.

'Mark has also shown great sensitivity to the needs of the local community which I must admit I hadn't expected. He was very generous in particular with the amount of time and resources he allocated to you, Bill.'

'So I'm meant to be grateful am I when he sets his heavies on me?' Bill said attempting a quick single.

'We're not actually here to talk about Bill or East Wolds but to raise a concern,' Ben broke in gently. He smiled. A handsome self-deprecating smile. 'My daughter has as you say benefitted a great deal from her sponsorship deal with *Spiked*. And we are, as is the local community, grateful for all the support, not least monetary, which has gone into local projects.'

'Now hang on a minute,' said Bill, accidentally waving away the waiter who was trying to deliver more croissants.

Ben looked at him and Bill remembered that Ben was a successful and experienced barrister. Bill sat on his hands and the waiter delivered the croissants.

Julia smiled a slow smile at Ben. 'But?' she said, the smile lingering between them.

'It doesn't strike me as usual, or perhaps advisable for a CEO to take a particular interest in one of the sponsees.'

Julia went silent and Bill started listening. Ben continued.

'It might cause bad feeling and arouse jealousies if one person is singled out of a group. It might also lead to unrealistic expectations on the part of the person being singled out.'

'And your daughter is being singled out?'

Ben nodded.

'Perhaps she is particularly talented,' Julia said, coolly.

Bill gave up listening and butted in. 'Talented has got nothing to do with it. She's being picked out for photo shoots not tennis matches.'

'Then perhaps she has a particular talent which lends itself to photo shoots.'

'Now look here young lady -' began Bill before Ben silenced him with a look.

216

'Or she's just good at pushing herself forward,' smiled Julia.

Her deliberate antagonism worked and Bill flailed his bat wildly over the breakfast table.

'Annie's not doing any pushing. The only pushing going on around here is Mark Hammond. And from what I hear he is good at pushing himself on women.' Bill spoke so loudly that the waiter came over looking solicitous. Ben indicated that everything was under control. Julia started to gather her things together.

'So that's what this little meeting is all about? You're accusing Mark of being what? Too friendly towards your daughter?' she deliberately addressed herself to Ben.

Bill said something loud. Ben said nothing. Julia stood up and swung her bag onto her shoulder.

'It often happens,' she said, 'the girls are keen to get on and older men are easily tempted.'

Ben shot a look over to Bill just in time to stop Bill's chair from making a dramatic dive to the floor.

'May I take it then that it is company policy to ignore such complaints?'

Julia hovered by the table and raised an eyebrow. Bill decided to listen again.

'And that if there is fault it is assumed that it is the girl's?'

'Are you putting words into my mouth?' Julia asked.

Ben shrugged.

'How old is your daughter?' the question was asked coldly.

'She's only sixteen,' exclaimed Bill.

'Ah,' said Julia, 'then I certainly can't see the problem. If she chooses to have a relationship with our CEO then I agree it is not advisable but I'm not sure what it has to do with me or *Spiked*.'

This time Bill's chair did fall down. The waiter came rushing over. Julia moved away from them and Bill moved as if he intended to block her way.

'You would then advise, even recommend that we do nothing about this?' Ben said, still calmly sitting down.

Julia said nothing.

'I take it that this is *Spiked* policy?' he continued.

Julia leant over the table. 'And I take it that this was a without prejudice meeting conducted in the spirit of our policy to liaise with local communities and to always make ourselves

217

available to answer questions and concerns. Now if you'll excuse me I have work to do.'

Bill watched her retreating back. 'Aren't you?' he said to Ben.

'No,' said Ben.

Bill picked up his chair, 'But,' he began.

Ben finished his coffee and shrugged again. 'She wasn't happy. She'll give Mark Hammond a rollicking,' he paused, 'but.'

That was all. But. Nothing to be done. Except pay the bill which Julia hadn't picked up after all. It was nine o'clock when they set foot outside again.

'I'd better get on,' said Ben.

Bill said nothing. He grunted at Ben and set off in the opposite direction scuffing his feet on the pavement.

Half an hour later he was still muttering bloody hell to himself like a mantra. However somehow or other he'd managed to get himself to the station and in the station forecourt was a café where old has-beens were more than acceptable and bacon butties a must.

28

Bill was, as his mother used to say 'cruising for a bruising' and taking all the trains and buses he needed to take to get back home was a long time to be cruising a bruising.

Firstly he missed the 10.12 train to York and had to wait half an hour for the next one. This was entirely the fault of the bacon butty which in turn had to be washed down by some genuine British Rail tea. But as Bill reasoned it, if he'd been allowed to have a proper breakfast in the first place then he wouldn't have had to waste time eating bacon butties at the station. Bill caught the next train chuntering to himself about morals and ethics. 'In my day people like that would have got the sack,' he finally concluded loudly.

'Aye, lad, thee's right there. The sack,' came a voice from the seat next to Bill's.

Bill looked up at his companion startled and without recognition. He hadn't noticed him sit down and therefore he hadn't noticed that he was wearing pyjama bottoms. The old man had a whiskery face and tufts of hair sticking out of his ears. He then mimed a wicket keeper's catch and shook his head from side to side.

'Eh, but you were good, laddie, the best,' he said.

Bill couldn't think who the man was but the sympathetic gestures being made cheered him up. So it seemed quite natural that when they got off the train at York they caught the East Wold's bus together and shared the front seat. A couple of youths sat behind them sniggering and a woman carrying the kind of basket that indicated country living and poshness had to make do with an inferior seat further down the bus.

Bill carried on grumbling. He was enjoying the fact that he now had an audience.

'It's people like that that are giving this country a bad name,' he announced.

The old man nodded sagely.

'People don't have morals or ideals anymore. It's all about money and sex,' Bill continued bravely.

The woman with the basket tried to look out of the window indignantly and the youths blushed.

'Sex,' agreed the old man loudly. 'It's just the same with my neighbours,' he continued enigmatically.

'And I'm damned if I'm going to just stand by and let him, them, get their own way with everything.'

'You have to stand firm,' agreed the old man.

'Do you know,' Bill leant into his companion and whispered loudly, 'it's happened before. This business with girls. Everyone just accepts it. It's not right.'

'No, it's not right.'

'And that poor wife of his,' Bill carried on.

'Wives,' said the old man sadly shaking his head.

'I'll show them,' said Bill punching one fist into the other hand.

'Aye, you show them,' said the old man.

By the time the bus dropped them all off in the High Street in East Wolds Bill had honed up his anger quite nicely and his companion was delighted. Bill took long determined strides in the direct of the village green. The old man took a tight hold of his pyjama bottoms and scuttled after him.

The green was surprisingly empty of activity and there were no vans loitering around the new pavilion. Bill waved his hands in the air and howled into the pleasantness of the midday breeze.

'And all for this!' he waved at the new pavilion.

Bill didn't hear his companion whisper, 'It's a travesty.' Nor did he notice the pyjamaed sleeve which emerged from the old coat to wipe away the tears getting caught in the whiskers. Neither did Bill notice which of them tore down the beach flags proclaiming *Spiked* first. But the beach flags were torn down, scrumpled up and pushed into the bin on the edge of the green. The one which said 'Dog waste only'. Neither did Bill notice the man in working overalls who appeared out of the Pavilion shouting, 'Oy, you there,' nor the two fingers that his companion joyfully raised to cover their retreat.

Having put the High Street between them and their pursuer Bill and his friend solemnly shook hands and parted company.

Luckily when Susan arrived home later she laughed so much at the sight of Bill's indignation, his suit rebelliously hanging open and his tie pulled half off like a school boy that they actually sat at the kitchen table together. And not only did Susan stir sugar into The Worlds Best Grandad's mug but she also put the chocolate digestives on the table.

'Oh, and something else funny happened today,' she said, 'which might interest you.'

'Oh?' said Bill, 'funny funny or funny peculiar?'

'Both I suppose. Old mad Bob has been out again and apparently vandalised the green.'

'Oh,' said Bill, looking up in surprise.

'Yes, apparently he tore down the *Spiked* flags by the new pavilion and put them into the doggie-do bin.'

'Oh,' said Bill, alarmed and suddenly very interested in his chocolate biscuit.

'So you see you do at least have one supporter.'

Bill kept his head down and mumbled something unintelligible into his tea.

29

'Bill, Bill,' Susan shouted up the stairs. 'I've got to go. Don't forget you've got a check-up with Dr Adams this morning.'

'That's tomorrow,' Bill shouted down from his pillows.

'It is tomorrow, I mean it's already tomorrow,' Susan shouted back.

Bill appeared at the top of the stairs. 'Is it Wednesday already?'

Susan nodded up at him. She smiled. 'You won't go out in your pyjamas will you? Like mad Bob.' Then she turned to go.

'Susan,' Bill called out after her, but quietly as though he didn't really want her to hear the question, 'I don't suppose anyone else was seen with old Bob were they?'

Susan didn't turn back but he heard her pause. 'Don't insult my intelligence, Bill,' she said and slammed the door shut.

'What is that supposed to mean?' Bill said to himself.

Bill got himself ready and out of the house in record time.

Dr Adams was pleased with his progress. 'I can't see any reason why you shouldn't start playing cricket again. From what Su...I mean it is good for you to be out and about.'

Bill didn't like the idea that Susan gossiped about him with his doctor. 'Do you know Vicky Hammond?' he asked suddenly, in the vein of gossiping.

Dr Adams looked up at him. She was no longer smiling. 'I didn't think she knew anyone around here,' she said carefully.

'I met her the other day,' Bill said.

Dr Adams said nothing.

'You know her husband,' Bill began.

'Really, Mr Reeves. Although I will say that Vicky Hammond could do with a friend or two. But -' she stopped.

'Is he a patient here too?' Bill tried to look innocent.

'No, *Spiked* provides its own health care for all employees.'

'As if that should surprise me,' Bill scoffed.

'I'm sorry, Mr Reeves, Bill, but I have a long patient list today.'

'But *Spiked* hides everything, controls everything. You know they're up to no good,' Bill looked at her desperately. Vicky Hammond wasn't the only local in need of a friend.

Dr Adams got up and opened the door so that Bill had to follow her. 'I really can't pretend to know anything of the kind, Bill.'

'But you agree with me that *Spiked* is poisonous stuff and shouldn't be let loose on an unsuspecting and naive public.'

'Yes, but just because the product is bad doesn't mean that the company is bad.'

Bill shuffled past her. 'That's what you think,' he grumbled. The trouble was that that was what everyone thought. He turned just before she closed the door. 'I really wanted to ask you about Annie,' he said.

'Look, I've already said.'

'I know, but?'

Dr Adams hung on to the door. She looked suddenly sad and shrugged. 'She doesn't come to me anymore. All her health care goes through *Spiked*.'

'Bloody hell,' said Bill.

'Quite,' said Dr Adams and shut her door.

Bill retrieved his bicycle and set off in the vague direction of the council offices, The Cricketers Arms and the village green. He landed at the green. The remnants of mad Bob's vandalism had been removed and as he looked out over the green he had to admit that it almost looked like a cricket pitch again. Unfortunately the new clubhouse didn't look like a cricket pavilion anymore. Deciding to turn his back on it all and return home his eye caught sight of a large wheelie bin overflowing with paper rubbish. Bill had just got his head immersed into the bin when a man in overalls appeared.

'Now then,' said Bill innocently.

'Now then,' the man replied cautiously.

'This bin,' Bill said, 'you won't be wanting all this stuff in it?'

The man shook his head.

'So you won't mind if I have it?'

The man shrugged, uncertain, and as the man turned back to get on with his work Bill assumed that the uncertain shrug meant help yourself. Five minutes later at least three of Susan's friends saw Bill bicycling down the High Street, one hand on the handlebar of his bicycle and the other gripping onto a large green wheelie bin which slowly trundled after him.

Bill had an irrational expectation that wheelie bins of paper waste contained clues to conspiracy theories and confidential documents. With these delights in mind Bill enthusiastically emptied the contents of the large green wheelie bin all over the kitchen. The shed being too dark and the outside being too windy.

What Bill was going to find was notes and memos referring to prospective deals and sales. A conspiracy to sell the village green to *Spiked.* Then people would listen. Or how about match fixing? Yes, that was why he was out of the team, because the matches were being fixed. *Spiked* was paying people to lose. Or win. Bill didn't really know how match fixing worked. He knew there'd been a big scandal in Indian cricket.

What the wheelie bin did contain was cardboard packing from flat pack furniture, plastic, which although environmentally inconsiderate was not Bill's area of expertise, bunkers of match scorecards going back to the sixties, which Bill tried to get cross about and twelve cigarette ends, which Bill decided self-righteously was a fire safety issue. He was just considering the protocol which might allow him, as Chief Fire Officer for East Wolds, to make an unannounced site inspection of the new pavilion when a greater disaster struck. Susan came home.

'I was just going to put the kettle on,' Bill said to her gasp of horror.

'And I'm just going to go back to my car, walk down The Avenue, come back and then try walking into my kitchen again. By which time all this -' she finished and headed off back up the path to the front gate.

Bill wasted precious seconds agonising over whether to put the kettle on first or whether just to start clearing up the mess. Paper, cardboard and plastic not to mention a few random bits of post, which got caught up in the frenzy, were hurled to the door and then stuffed into the big wheelie bin. As time was of the essence the odd scorecard from 1962 which floated into the roses was an acceptable sacrifice. The big bin was full again and Bill parked it outside their gate innocently lining it up with their other bins. Luckily Susan had got waylaid by the Andrews' dog which must have escaped again. This dog was an enterprising Cairn Terrier called Rufus.

Melanie Andrews arrived on the scene at the same time as Bill. 'That's a nice big paper bin,' she said, eyeing up the big green wheelie bin, 'how did you manage to get that?'

Bill didn't manage to look Susan in the eye but he did manage to look pleased.

Rufus was quietly escaping again but Melanie ignored him. 'Did you just ring the council or what?' she asked.

'Well,' said Bill standing firm and pulling out his shoulders with all the self-importance he could muster, 'I suppose one could ring the Refuse Department.'

Susan pushed him through the gate and Melanie remembered that she was supposed to be capturing her dog.

'I suppose one could ring the Refuse Department,' Susan mimicked Bill as she carried on pushing him until they were inside the house. 'Alternatively one can just -'

'I didn't steal it,' said Bill, 'I asked and the man said I could take it.'

'And when are you taking it back?'

Bill put the kettle on. Melanie Andrews was right, it was rather a nice big new green wheelie bin. It hadn't been that easy getting it here and it wasn't going to be any easier getting it back. Anyway building sites always lost things like wheelie bins.

'How did you get on with Dr Adams?' Susan asked sitting at the table so that Bill had to carry on waiting on her.

'Alright,' said Bill.

Bill solicitously plied The Worlds Best Grandma mug with several spoons of sugar and Susan wondered if there was any husband actually capable of waiting on his wife.

'You know that Annie doesn't go to the health centre any more? That she gets all her health care through *Spiked*?' Bill continued after the solicitous sugar pause.

Susan nodded her head so sadly that she almost enjoyed the overly solicitous tea.

'I didn't know.' Bill sounded indignant.

'What was there to know?' Susan asked tiredly.

Bill said nothing.

'Should I ask why I got three text messages from people in the town? All three confirming that you had been seen making off

225

with a large bin from the new pavilion site? And should I ask why?'
Susan finally braved, bolstered by all the sugar.

'Well,' said Bill, 'I was looking for evidence.'

'And?' said Susan but the 'and' denoted more lack of interest
than a question.

'Nothing.' Bill realised sadly. 'Apart from -' He suddenly
jumped up. 'That's it,' he shouted, 'an unannounced inspection.'

Susan just looked at him.

'I've got to ring Ben,' said Bill and dashed out of the room to
see if he could find his mobile.

30

Bill needed a camouflage outfit. He had abandoned a pair of jeans (which Susan banned him from wearing anyway on the grounds that men over a certain age shouldn't wear jeans unless – and the conversation never got further than unless). He had also abandoned a pair of black Lycra cycling trousers with accompanying jacket on the grounds that this might be espionage but he wasn't James Bond (and nothing whatsoever to do with the fact that Carol had given him them for a birthday present some years ago and that Susan had laughed for a week after he'd tried them on). The current outfit was his best corduroy trousers which happened to be a useful muddy brown in colour, a muddy brown shirt and a green puffer jacket that Ben had given him because it had been both too short and too wide for Ben. Plus a woollen hat, which might have been more convincing if it had been winter and not spring.

The current outfit would have to do because he now had less than an hour to get into position. He sent Ben a text message to say that he was on his way and Ben confirmed that he would send a message when he was in the *Spiked* car park and about to make his unannounced inspection.

Because Bill's plan, and Ben had been surprisingly amenable to it, was that Ben was to make an unannounced inspection of the *Spiked* premises supposedly in connection with his pending case with Yorkshire Water. Bill's theory that *Spiked* was polluting the river by ditching illegally spiked *Spiked* could have a link with Ben's pollution case for Yorkshire Water. Bill's theory, moreover, also assumed that someone, probably Shaun Bean, was under orders to do this ditching immediately anyone appeared at *Spiked* who looked important enough to carry out an inspection. Bill was sure that Ben could look important enough.

The thing that concerned Bill now, however, was his own lack of a decoy. He had his bicycle, but that made him immediately recognisable and he wanted to be unrecognisable to anyone happening to be keeping a look out from *Spiked*. He had several empty plastic bottles hidden in a rucksack but he didn't have a convincing cover if someone found him loitering along the canal outside *Spiked*. Which was when Rufus appeared. His dangling lead attached to Rufus but not to his owner.

'Well, I'll be blowed,' said Bill. He scooped up Rufus's lead and pedalled up The Avenue with the dog excitedly running at his side. Neither of them heard Melanie Andrews shouting crossly in the distance.

The plan was, having bicycled a good way up the canal path towards *Spiked*, to leave the bicycle discreetly hidden behind a few scrubby bushes below the embankment made by the *Spiked* car park. Bill would have been better camouflaged if his bicycle had been left further away but in the event of requiring a quick getaway he had decided that the closer his bicycle was the better. Having abandoned his bicycle Bill was then going to loiter along the canal path up behind the *Spiked* buildings which housed the production unit and Shaun Bean's big vats of brewing (theoretically spiked) *Spiked*.

With Rufus in tow Bill's disguise was complete. He could saunter along the canal bank innocently, stop and pat the dog, talk to the dog and as a matter of necessity also constantly have to bend down and untangle the dog.

When Bill estimated that he was about parallel with Shaun Bean's vats he started to do a lot of dog patting and unravelling which allowed him to rummage in the undergrowth behind the building. Bill was confident of finding a large pipe discharging, or about to be discharging spiked *Spiked* into the canal. This evidence was going to both give Yorkshire Water a counter claimant and Bill the ammunition he needed to re-open his own case against *Spiked*. And this time the evidence was going to be whistle blown across the national press.

On cue his mobile beeped. 'I'm going in,' the message said. Bill started to rummage more frantically, forgot to take account of Rufus who gave an expert tug at the right moment and rushed away from Bill.

'Damn, damn, damn,' said Bill. 'Come on boy, there's a good boy then.' Of course Rufus ignored him. He was having a merry old time of it scrabbling and digging on the muddy bank of the canal. Bill launched after him, scrabbling about in the mud himself trying to regain control of Rufus's lead, which was why Bill failed to notice a large figure coming along the path towards him. The large figure was carrying a crow bar. Rufus saw the man before Bill did and suddenly jumped back onto the path and started barking and Bill looked up to see Shaun Bean being savaged by Rufus.

Bill tried to stand up in the mud on the side of the canal. He was shouting at Rufus. 'Good dog. Bad dog. Shaun. He doesn't mean any harm.' But Shaun Bean did. He kicked at the small dog with a large booted foot and having caught him off balance he picked him up by the scruff of his neck and hurled him into the canal.

'Oy!' said Bill.

'You're next,' growled Shaun Bean and strode off the path into the mud which was still hindering Bill's progress onto firmer ground. Shaun Bean raised the crow bar and Bill not quite believing what was happening just stood staring at his attacker as the crow bar was swung from the fast bowler's right arm. The mud however was also sucking at Shaun's feet and his action weakened at the point of impact with Bill's shoulder. Bill trained to stop leg byes grabbed the crow bar and pulled. Shaun Bean fell sideways into the mud and Bill fell into the canal still clutching the weapon. Shaun Bean crawled back to the path. Bill tried shouting help but his mouth was full of murky water. Rufus was frantically swimming and trying to climb out onto the slippery bank. Bill flailed with his arms, one hand still clutching the crow bar and his feet slowly sinking into the mud at the bottom of the canal.

Shaun Bean grinned. 'Your finger prints are all over that crow bar,' he said. 'Trespassing and in possession of a weapon. Planning to make a break-in and steal more company documents perhaps? Someone paying you for trade secrets? Won't look good in court, Bill,' he jeered.

'Shaun, wait. Stop. The dog. He'll drown. I'm sinking.' Bill was sinking. The mud clutched at his ankles. He dropped the crow bar and clutched frantically at loose tufts of reeds growing out of the bank. It was impossible to get a purchase and in one frantic effort he fell sideways and felt the water close over his head. He had forgotten to hold his breath and the water sucked into his nostrils. Then as his hands floundered in the slimy water they hit something hard sticking out of the bank. It was a modern black plastic pipe, with a corrugated surface which his fingers could grip onto. He pulled himself up along the length of the pipe until he reached a firmer footing in the mud under the water. Here sturdy clumps of vegetation gave enough purchase to allow him to haul himself slowly upwards. He lay sprawled on his stomach with one arm still trailing in the canal. He tried to call out to Rufus but his lungs were retching with the water. Sharp claws and a wet mess of fur scrabbled at his hand and with one last heroic effort Bill grabbed the dog and pulled him to safety. Bill then turned back in the mud ready to face Shaun Bean's next assault, but Shaun Bean had gone. He had gone without waiting to see if Bill would manage to pull himself out of the water. Bill was too overcome with shock to think until his mind suddenly registered the implications of the pipe which had saved him. A new pipe leading into the canal from the direction of *Spiked* and Shaun Bean's vats.

'Good boy, Rufus,' Bill shouted, 'we'll get the buggers yet.' He moved back towards the canal bank and put both hands on the pipe and pulled it up as far as it would go. The pipe was disgorging a thick dark reddish liquid into the canal.

'Bingo,' whispered Bill. He filled his six plastic bottles with the stuff while Rufus, apparently fully recovered, happily lapped up the spillage soaking into the mud.

When Bill finally managed to get himself and Rufus to Carol and Ben's Will was the only person home.

'Gramps, look at you! Cool dog, whose is he?' Will said.

'I don't know,' said Bill who couldn't be bothered to think about the dog.

Rufus had escaped again and was chasing his tail round and round in the garden. Will joined him. Both getting more and more hysterical.

'What's his name, Grand...Gramps? Are you going to keep him?'

Luckily Bill didn't have to answer any of these questions as Ben's big Land cruiser appeared at the bottom of the street.

Will dashed into the house with Rufus. Bill decided that he'd better not go into the house. Rufus would be depositing enough mud all over Carol's kelim carpets. He waited for Ben by the door trying not to shiver and spitting the occasional mouthful of mud into Carol's terracotta pots. Ben slammed the SUV door closed behind him.

'What a complete waste of time,' he said not looking at Bill. 'We, and I wish I hadn't had the bright idea of taking the solicitor along as well, looked ridiculous. An unannounced inspection on behalf of our clients.' Ben did look at Bill now, accusingly. 'We just spent nearly an hour sitting in a plush office drinking espresso being invited most politely to admire *Spiked's* bomb proof environmental policy. Mark Hammond and a woman with a lot of lipstick told us we were welcome anytime, but that they had busy schedules and it would be more helpful if next time we could make an appointment, but seeing as I was local and because of the family connection etcetera, etcetera. Meanwhile the solicitor just sat there drinking espresso and clocking up hours of fees.'

Bill was rendered speechless by Ben's sudden vociferousness but the abrupt pause shook him to his senses. 'But it did work,' he finally managed to say and produced one of his bottles of dark red liquid.

Ben was silent, not his natural silence but a stunned silence.

'I've got six of these beauties,' said Bill.

Ben opened his mouth, but opted for more silence.

'I found the drain, just as I expected leading straight from Shaun Bean's big vats. Though, Ben, there's something else.'

'Have you tasted it?' Ben asked.

Bill looked nonplussed. Ben took the bottle and before Bill had the sense to object Ben tasted it. Then he smiled, a slow smile which straightened all the way through his long back.

'That's *Spiked*,' he said.

Will was standing in the door behind Bill. 'Dad, are you drinking *Spiked*? Can I have some?'

Both men shouted no and a mad Cairn Terrier tore out of the house worrying a large sheepskin boot which about thirty seconds previously had proudly borne a discrete label saying *Uggs*.

'William, what are you up to in there?' Ben said sharply.

Will pulled an innocent expression worthy of his grandfather. 'Nothing,' he said.

'Where's that dog come from?'

'Oh, the dog,' Will replied, 'that's Gramps' dog.'

They all three of them stood and watched while Rufus finished off Carol's *Ugg* boot. Will slipped back into the house and Bill clutched Ben's arm to get his attention. 'As I was trying to say, Ben, there's something else.' He glanced at the house to make sure that Will really had gone back inside. 'Just after you'd sent your message there was an incident.'

231

Ben took a step back from Bill as if noticing for the first time that Bill was covered in mud, wet and smelly. 'You didn't fall in did you? You should be careful. This whole thing, it's not worth getting hurt for. Especially not again for you, Bill.'

'Yes well, it's too late to worry about that now,' Bill said. 'As I say there was an incident with Shaun Bean.'

'An incident? You didn't say anything about Shaun Bean,' Ben sounded suspicious.

'Shaun Bean appeared and it got a bit nasty.'

'Bill, why are you always provoking Shaun Bean?'

'I wasn't provoking Shaun Bean. He appeared with a ruddy great crow bar and.' Bill made an extravagant bowling action, Ben caught the ruck sack of samples and Carol swept up to park by Ben's SUV. Annie poured out of the passenger side almost before the car stopped. Carol quickly followed her, about to pick up the remains of an argument when she saw Rufus shredding apart something that looked distinctly like a large brown rat all over her garden.

'Is that my?' she gasped.

'It's nothing to do with me,' said Ben and vanished into the house clutching Bill's bottles secretly to his chest.

'Come on, boy,' Bill whistled to the dog, 'better get you home.' The boot being quite dead by this time Rufus happily obliged his new owner and allowed himself to be retrieved from the strange garden.

Annie managed a squiffy rather vicious smile directed at her mother. 'Cool dog,' she said to her grandfather before she too vanished into the house.

Bill didn't wait to see what happened. He felt old and vulnerable but didn't, as usual, seem able to confide in anyone. He set off on his bicycle dragging Rufus behind him until he realised that he really was dragging Rufus so he had to stop and pick the little dog up. Rufus had gone from killing machine to wet rag and Bill had to bicycle all the way home with the poor creature huddled on his knee.

When Bill realised he didn't have a key and that it was Susan's knitting night he almost wished that he was back in hospital again. The only positive thought that he could muster was that at least he still had his decoy with him. Five minutes later he was knocking on Melanie Andrews' French windows, mouthing the word 'key' and waving Rufus at the knitting club. Opting not to confide in anyone else about the incident he hoped Susan wouldn't notice that he was dressed in his smartest casual clothes and covered in mud.

31

Friday was a day of atonement. In fact after his near death experience Bill felt curiously re-born. He put his destroyed clothes in the washing machine and then forgot about them. He discreetly left the coveted large green wheelie bin outside Melanie Andrews' garage. He went into the council offices to suggest that he started work again the following week. Furthermore if he'd understood the significance of the *Ugg* he would have offered his daughter a new pair for her birthday. He promised Susan a fish and chip supper and headed off home early to find some husbandly task to perform.

When.

An Audi Q7 roared past him up the High Street almost knocking him off his bicycle. Up the High Street in the direction of York and in the opposite direction to Woldsby. In Woldsby awaited a drunk wife and in York was an impressionable sixteen-year-old due to finish her personal training session and in need of a lift home.

Bill notched up a few gears and followed the Q7 at top speed. When he got to the top of The Avenue he reluctantly gave up the chase and charged off home. Ideally he would now resume the race in a car. However he had no car. Susan wasn't home yet.

Luckily Bill had his house key and he had his mobile. He sat himself down at the kitchen table and decided to be sensible. He rang Carol. 'I'm sorry I can't take your call, please leave a message,' said Carol's phone. He rang Ben. 'I'm sorry the number you are ringing is unavailable or switched off,' said Ben's phone. Annie's repeated the same message. Who else could he ring? He charged upstairs. He waited the longest five minutes of his life and did another search on BT for Mark Hammond, Wolds View Cottages and a telephone number. Bill rang the number. The number rang for a long time.

'Hello,' said an uncertain voice.

How drunk was she?

'Who is this?' Vicky was sober enough to ask.

'Bill,' Bill said unhelpfully.

'Am I supposed to know you?' said Vicky

'We met earlier this week,' Bill couldn't remember which day and his brain was too frozen on Annie to think clearly.

'Oh?'

'I'm from the cricket club,' he suddenly remembered.

Another oh.

'You know,' inspiration at last, 'the gardener.'

Vicky started to laugh. 'Of course,' she said, 'what do you want?'

'Is Mark at home?' Bill asked innocently.

'What do you bloody think?'

Bill imagined her reaching for a drink.

'Of course he's not home,' she continued.

'I don't suppose you -' Bill said inconclusively.

'Well, you and he suppose wrong, I know exactly where he is,' said Vicky.

Bill waited. There was a pause.

'I spy on him.' Did she hiccough? 'What do you call it? Hacking? I hack in on all his messages. Of course he doesn't know that I do but I'm not so stupid that I don't know how to work out whatever stupid passwords he might be using at any one time.'

Bill waited, trying not to get hysterically impatient.

'So what do you want to know?'

'Do you know where he is now?'

'Yes, at least.'

More waiting.

'He sent a mail to someone called Carol saying, now let me get this right, 'Don't worry I'll collect Annie tonight,' and the Carol woman, stupid bitch, said, 'That's so kind,' and he said 'It won't be a problem if we're a bit late back will it? Got some things to pick up. I'll make sure Annie gets fed,' and stupid bitch replies, 'Of course not,' and sends some kind of smiley message. Then -'

Bill gulped on the other end of the phone. Could there be more?

'Then he sends a message to some Annie bitch, and I'm guessing she's the bimbo, 'Collecting you tonight after training, babe, and dinner afterwards on me'.'

'Did?' Bill managed to squeak.

'No, Bimbo didn't reply.'

Bill was now frozen in limb as well as thought and had forgotten that he was still clutching his mobile to his ear when the voice on the other end suddenly changed and said.

'I forgot you were from the cricket club.'

'Oh,' said Bill.

'Is that the East Wolds thingummy?'

'Yes,' said Bill.

'So you'll be going to this big bloody *Spiked* booze up tomorrow. Is it tomorrow?'

'Yes,' said Bill.

'I'll go if you're going to be there.'

'Yes,' continued Bill.

'So I'll see you tomorrow?'

'Yes,' said Bill and suddenly realised that he was looking out of the window of his little upstairs office and watching Susan park the car. 'Yes,' repeated Bill and pressed the red button on his phone.

He met Susan at the back door, seized her car keys said either that he was in a hurry, or that he'd see her later or that he'd explain why later or that he'd pick up fish and chips on his way home. Susan said nothing, more through lack of opportunity than inclination because most of Bill's hurried explanations were taking place when he was already in the car speeding off up the main road in the direction of York.

The Audi Q7 was already occupying two spaces in the university car park. Bill parked in front of it blocking it in. Just in case. He wasn't quite sure whether it was hot or cold as he wiped a hot or a cold sweat off his forehead. He squared his shoulders. He was in time. The Q7 wasn't going anywhere in a hurry now. Unless it was someone else's Q7? No, he mustn't be ridiculous, who else parking in a university car park could afford an Audi Q7?

The scene which met him in the gym was much more complex. Annie wasn't there, but Mark Hammond was. So was Simon. Simon's back was turned away from the entrance to the gym so he didn't see Bill come in. Neither did he turn to see who it was. He was concentrating on Mark Hammond. His muscles rippled along his snaking tattoo. Bill had the distinct impression that Simon was about do to what he'd been longing to do all week. Send one heavy delightful punch straight into Mark Hammond's smiling smarmy mouth.

Mark Hammond, however, did see Bill. He looked surprised, alarmed, relieved. 'Bill,' he said loudly and jovially.

It had the desired effect. The tattoo loosened and Simon swung round to face him.

'Bill, am I glad to see you,' he said at the same time as Mark Hammond said, 'Bill, whatever are you doing here?'

Bill didn't say anything. A good trick learnt from Ben because it meant that someone else had to fill the gap and that someone else was Mark Hammond.

'I'm collecting Annie. Carol asked me and as I was in the area I was only too happy to help.'

'I'll bet,' Bill couldn't help growling softly.

'Sorry you've had a wasted journey,' Mark continued.

'Sure someone's had a wasted journey,' Simon butted in.

Bill couldn't quite work out whether Simon was still inclined to go for the punch-up or if he'd now gone back to professionally laid back Australian.

'Where is Annie?' Bill suddenly asked.

Both the younger men looked surprised and again they both answered over each other.

'I guess she's still in the shower.'

'She's getting changed.'

On cue Annie appeared. Getting changed was a most inadequate description of the transformation which had taken place in the girls' changing rooms. What Bill noticed was lots of leg, lots of hair, lots of make-up and, well, lots of girl.

Mark Hammond smiled smugly as if he'd told them so. The tattoo rippled. Bill was about to make the sort of cold water remark that grandfathers and fathers make when they see teenage daughters looking unacceptably attractive. Then he remembered the last time he'd been on a mission to rescue Annie. Annie hadn't wanted to be rescued.

All three men had turned to face Annie and she coolly, inscrutably looked back at them all.

'Jeez,' said Simon.

'How nice,' murmured Mark Hammond, smoothly moving towards her.

He didn't get very far because several shoulders got in his way. Some tattooed and some just rather solid and broad. Someone said, 'Not so fast, mate.'

Mark paused but Annie didn't budge an inch one way or the other. If Bill had been less pre-occupied with shoulders and the

237

chance of throwing that one big punch he might have stopped to wonder why she was trying to hide a smile.

'Look, I don't know what's eating you guys,' Mark began in his best placatory, condescending tone, 'but I need to get on.' He turned to Annie. 'Your mother knows I'm here and she knows I'll get you home safely.' He moved closer to her. No one intervened. 'I squared taking you out for dinner with her, too,' he said softly, to Annie only. Although he didn't apparently care who else heard him. He put a practiced hand on Annie's back and steered her towards the door. Past the broad and tattooed shoulders. Past the notice board in the entrance with warning posters on good hygiene and girls always training with a buddy. On her way past Bill she dropped her kit bag silently. There was no word either for him or for Simon.

Simon obviously didn't know which way to run, away from the stupid girl or to her rescue. Bill put a hand on the tattoo where it ended on Simon's upper arm. Then he calmly picked up Annie's bag and indicated that Simon should follow him out to the car park.

In the car park Mark Hammond was looking cross and officiously taking the registration number of a little Honda which had blocked him in. Annie was standing to one side smiling again. In fact not smiling but trying very hard not to laugh out loud.

Bill bustled up to Mark Hammond. 'There's no need to bother taking numbers or anything. This is my car.'

'Then what the?' Mark was losing his cool.

Annie looked slyly at Simon and moved towards Bill. Simon's tattoo stopped rippling and a big smile started to spread across his face. The big muscled arm was raised but it landed a friendly punch on Bill's back. Nowhere in the vicinity of Mark Hammond. Mark Hammond looked at Annie. It wasn't an entirely nice look. Annie moved closer to Bill.

'Nice to see you guys getting to know one another. I don't suppose you invited Simon to your big *Spiked* bash tomorrow did you, Mark?' she said.

Mark tried to look cool. 'It's an open event for the whole community. Of course anyone can come,' he said uninvitingly.

'Well then,' Annie was looking at Simon.

'I haven't got anything else on tomorrow,' he replied cautiously.

'East Wolds village green at 2 o'clock,' Annie said, trying to sound indifferent.

Simon gave her a long look and slowly nodded his head. Annie was hiding a huge smile.

'Hey, Gramps,' she said, 'shouldn't we be getting home?'

32

Bill had been so confused about what had been going on that he completely forgot all the husbandly niceties he had promised himself he would perform for Susan. The next morning he was still confused and a little bit cross because his brown corduroys for some reason were still damp even though he distinctly remembered washing them the day before. Susan wasn't sympathetic.

'I don't know why they were in the washing machine because I didn't put them there and neither do I know why you should suddenly want them today. After all *you* aren't going anywhere, are you?' All this was said very pointedly with a vicious stab of sarcasm attached.

Bill said nothing. He went into the sitting room, put the television on and fiddled with the Skybox in the hopes of watching England's test match against New Zealand.

At lunchtime he made himself a sandwich because Susan was getting changed. At a quarter to two he decked himself out in damp brown corduroys and a nice blue checked shirt that Susan had bought him for Christmas and which still had the label on. Then he waited by the kitchen door for Susan to come down. A couple of minutes later she did appear. She looked casually smart in simple trousers not unlike Bill's and she was wearing a tweed jacket where the dull brown was rescued by weaves of red and orange. She had a soft orange scarf clipped with a broach around her neck. Bill was a bit taken aback.

'Where are you going?' he asked.

'What do you mean, where am I going? I might just as well ask where are you going. And by the way the label is still on that shirt.'

Bill tried to find the label so that he could pull it off. 'I thought I was going to the opening of the new pavilion with you,' he said.

Susan looked at him for a long moment. 'Now hang on a minute, Bill, you have made it quite clear that you are not going to any opening today and definitely not going to anything which has anything whatsoever to do with *Spiked*.'

'I never said I wasn't going.' Bill sounded hurt.

'Bill Reeves, you distinctly said that you were not going anywhere near this opening today.'

'No, I never.'

'I really don't know what to think anymore, Bill, but I wish you'd said something before because quite frankly I'd much rather have gone with you than with the Andrews.'

'You're going with the Andrews?' Bill's shoulders bristled indignantly.

'I didn't want to go on my own. Oh, Bill, it's no use standing here and arguing now. Melanie and Jon are picking me up at the end of The Avenue in one minute.' She looked at him and he lapped up the glimmer of wifely forgiveness in her glance. 'Why don't you come with us? I'm sure they won't mind.'

'I'm not going with Jonathan Andrews.'

The glimmer of wifely forgiveness faded. 'Then you'll have to go on your own,' she said.

'I'll take my bike.'

Susan rolled her eyes. 'Come on then, we'd better both get a move on.'

Susan locked them both out of the house and marched on up The Avenue while Bill fiddled with his bicycle. He caught her up just before she reached Jon and Melanie's waiting Mercedes. She turned to him with a sudden anxiety, looking down at her smart jacket and smoothing out the soft orange scarf.

'I haven't overdone it?' she asked Bill.

'No, you look very nice.'

'Really?'

Bill was cleverly balancing on his bicycle. Not quite stopping but maintaining just enough motion not to have to put his foot down to steady himself.

Susan turned as she opened the back door to climb into the car and smiled at Bill. 'So do you,' she said.

'So do I what?'

'Look very nice.'

Bill wobbled and smiled.

'What made you decide to come after all?' she asked sinking into the backseat.

'I'm meeting someone there,' Bill said, still preening himself and smiling smugly.

'You're what?' But the car door had to close and the Mercedes pulled carefully around Bill who waved through the windows as they went slowly past. It then lurched up a few gears and charged up the main road with Bill in hot pursuit.

Vicky Hammond was waiting for him by a newly erected beach flag. She was teetering on inappropriate shoes and smelt strongly of mints.

'Bill, I wasn't sure I'd recognise you,' she said the moment he appeared, scarcely giving him time to dismount from his bicycle. She wobbled so much that she had to put her arm through his.

'Oh,' said Bill.

The Andrews and Susan were just arriving, having spent some time finding somewhere to park. Lots of loud music was emanating from the new pavilion. Lots of children were buzzing like wasps around a simple awning proclaiming loudly, 'Free *Spiked*'. Men and older boys were sporting brand new *Spiked* cricketing outfits. It took Bill a while to pick out faces in the crowd but he noticed Ben, Carol and Will in the same moment that he picked out Mark Hammond and Annie. All of them, including Susan and the Andrews, were looking at him. Apart from Annie who was looking out for someone else.

Vicky propelled him forwards and before he was able to take any kind of control of the situation he was thrust into the bosom of his family with Susan and the Andrews closely behind him and Mark Hammond homing in from the leg side. Vicky was enjoying herself.

'Mark, darling, I believe you already know Bill,' she said smoothly enough, although her legs were shaking and she kept a tight hold onto Bill.

'I didn't, however, know that you did,' Mark said to his wife and then, unable to resist the nastiness, continued, 'in fact I didn't know you knew anyone.'

Vicky wobbled a bit more and faltered.

Bill squared his shoulders and took a firmer hold of Vicky's arm. 'In a small community like ours everyone knows everyone,' he said pompously. 'Vicky,' he continued, 'meet my family. This is Vicky Hammond,' he announced with a loud and relishing emphasis on the Hammond. Susan shook hands coolly. Vicky Hammond was after all holding tightly onto Susan's husband. Ben stepped forward with refined gallantry and Carol managed to smile with her mouth.

Annie didn't really notice what was going on and Will made the most of the distraction to slip away from parental control.

The circle widened to include the Andrews and in just a few minutes more Vicky was charming a large number of new beaus whilst still clinging onto her first one. Mark Hammond gave up. No amount of polite veneer could disguise the contempt he felt for his wife and he anyway had more important things to do than get embroiled in any further doings with Bill Reeves.

As Vicky was seemingly so adept at small talk Bill was able to keep a look out on the wider proceedings. One annoyed, indignant and worried glance took in all the children under sixteen who were buzzing around the free *Spiked* tent. Another glance made a mental note of the various local dignitaries who exchanged familiar handshakes and congratulations with Mark Hammond. He noticed Ben noticing too. During this general noticing another familiar face appeared in the crowd around him and Vicky Hammond. Tattooed Simon, both discreetly with and not with Annie.

'This, Simon,' Annie was saying through the general mêlée, 'is Mark's wife.'

Mark's wife latched onto the words with all the sharpness of the alcoholic. 'My name's Vicky,' she said, 'Vicky Hammond.'

Bill felt her eyeing up the sudden competition, the attractive girl. The reference to 'Mark' rather than to Mark Hammond.

'And you must be the -' Vicky Hammond continued.

'My granddaughter and her personal trainer,' Bill broke in loudly.

The word 'Bimbo' was hanging on Vicky's lips. However the words personal trainer distracted her and the bronzed rippling Australian looming before her drowned out the bitterness and instead of saying 'Bimbo,' Vicky Hammond finished her sentence with, 'personal trainer.' She loosened her grip on Bill, lurched towards Simon and said, 'Don't I just wish I was sixteen again. What's your take on older women then, er -?'

Simon looked from Annie to Vicky. 'Simon,' he said, 'the name's Simon.'

Bill backed away quickly. He heard someone, possibly Carol, say in a stage whisper, 'Is that woman drunk?' and backed even further away. The *Spiked* cricketers were hovering around the wicket as if some kind of friendly match was going to take place.

Bill wondered what on earth had possessed him to come. The only obvious refreshments were *Spiked* and going in pursuit of anything more wholesome meant entering the enemy's territory. Although the enemy's territory was cordoned off with a red ribbon. Bill sidled up to the edge of a group of ex-cricketers including One Shot and someone rang a loud bell.

Mark Hammond stood on a box by the red ribbon and made a pretty speech about the importance of local community ties with local businesses. What a great pleasure and honour it was for him to now not only represent *Spiked* in the donating (Bill made a careful mental note of the word donating) of this cricket clubhouse erected for the benefit of the whole community but to also feel that he was himself a representative of the community in grateful receipt of such largesse. A lot of posh Yorkshire voices said 'Hear, hear,' and Fred Carstairs suddenly emerged from the fawning crowd wielding a large pair of scissors. (There was one dissenting voice lurking at the back of the new pavilion also wielding some vicious object approximating to scissors, but no one took any notice of him.)

The ribbon was cut. Bill was caught on a tide of hungry enthusiasts and swept into the bright newness of prefab pine and ergonomically designed chairs and a long Ikea table loaded with food. Several minutes later Bill was standing outside the new pavilion leaning against its now solid weather-proof wall and tucking into a pork pie. His neighbour exchanged views on the weather, England and the first over just hammered down the newly prepared wicket by Shaun Bean.

'And that young wicket keeper is doing a grand job too,' someone in the group said.

Bill bit off a large chunk of pastry and nodded. He might just as well swallow his pride along with the pork pie.

'Reckon they'll do alright tomorrow,' said someone else.

'Tomorrow?'

'First match of the season.'

'Oh aye.'

It took several more studied observations on the cricket from the oldies before they noticed that there was something going on by the ropes at the bowlers end because the commotion had now spread onto the pitch itself. Shaun Bean sent a nasty googly at some poor gangly youth just as one of the umpires uncertainly held up an arm.

This delivered several confusing messages both to the players on the pitch and the ex-players off the pitch. Eventually everyone realised that it meant the game should stop. Then all eyes turned to the commotion which had attracted a large crowd.

The trouble seemed to be centred around a lot of children screaming and for the first time that afternoon Bill noticed Dr Adams amongst the crowd. Dr Adams was running towards the centre of the upset. Along with everyone else Bill took several steps in the same direction. A girl was dragged passed him screaming hysterically

'But the little boy is dying,' she was shouting.

'Little' and 'boy' gripped Bill like a nightmare. He couldn't see Dr Adams any more but he saw Susan also rushing towards the epicentre of the hysteria. Some poor mother was screaming, 'Can't someone do something. Why is everyone just standing around. Please do something.'

Bill started running. Someone caught up with him and clutched his arm. Annie. He used his broad shoulders and cut a space through to the centre of the crowd. Annie was still holding on to him.

At the centre of the heaving mass was a little boy having an epileptic seizure. Dr Adams was administering first aid and pulling the boy into recovery position. Susan was ringing emergency services on her mobile and Ben, who had somehow or other got there before them, was pushing back the crowd. Bill was so certain that it was his own little boy, Will, that when Shaun Bean pushed past him he held him by the arm to keep him away. Shaun Bean shook him off so violently that Bill thought he was going to assault him again.

'It's Danny,' he heard Annie whisper as her fingers pulled at his arm and brought some sense back into his brain.

'Danny?' he questioned. But as he looked down at his granddaughter and saw the horror in her eyes he realised that she too had thought that it was Will lying there. For all they knew dying.

Then they both saw Will hiding behind Susan and peering round her at his friend. Although Danny was no longer recognisable as his friend because his face was smeared in vomit and his cheeks had gone blue. Shaun Bean was shaking Dr Adams and shouting at her. Ben stepped forward and forced him away from the child. Dr

245

Adams, Bill noticed, was now talking into Susan's mobile exchanging instructions and information with some emergency service and Susan had taken over care of the fitting boy. Bill spread out his arms and made slow steps backwards forcing the unruly crowd to back off. Another pair of broad shoulders (these ones tattooed) did the same on the other side of the crowd and a wave of silence spread over the onlookers.

Annie went over to Will and held on to him. Whether to support him or her or to stop him running away was unclear because several people were now hurling questions at him. Ben stepped away from Shaun Bean and put an arm around his son. Shaun Bean was angrily hurling abuse at everyone but Susan gently pulled on his arm and insisted that he help her nurse his child rather than excite the situation further. Bill caught a brief glimpse of Carol standing on the edge of the drama not quite able to cope with the hysteria of a woman weeping onto her shoulder. Mrs Bean perhaps? Bill reverted his attention to Will who was still being questioned by everyone.

Dr Adams addressed her questions via Ben. 'We need to know what, exactly what, Danny has eaten or drunk today. If he's had anything he shouldn't have had. You won't get into trouble, William, but can Danny have taken any drugs or anything like that?'

Will looked confused as though he didn't understand her question. Ben repeated it and Will looked him in the eye and shook his head before a great hiccough of tears overcame him.

Ben waited and indicated to the other eager questioners that they should do the same.

Will rubbed a sleeve over his face and sniffed. 'Honestly, Dad, just *Spiked*.'

Dr Adams broke in urgently but Ben silenced her.

'When you say just *Spiked*, William, can you explain what you mean by that?' he said.

'Just *Spiked*,' Will hiccoughed.

Ben waited, holding up an arm to stop anyone else interrupting.

'Quite a lot of *Spiked*,' Will said made uneasy by his father's silence.

'Be more specific,' Ben said quietly.

'It was free and you could just help yourself so we did. Although to be honest I don't like it that much so Danny drank mine as well.' Poor Will finally broke down completely. 'Is Danny going to die and is it my fault?'

33

It was a good half hour before they heard the ambulance sent from York Hospital speeding down the High Street, its siren blazing and it took a further ten minutes before it barged its way past the new pavilion and across the cricket pitch to the dwindling knot of people surrounding Danny Bean.

Danny was still in status and Susan and Dr Adams were obviously getting increasingly worried about him. Dr Adams insisted on going in the ambulance with him and Ben stepped forward and insisted on taking Shaun and Mrs Bean to the hospital, promising that they would be right behind the ambulance the whole way.

Little knots of people now regrouped. Everyone wondered guiltily whether it was okay to eat pork pies again, enjoy second helpings of cake, resume the cricket match or even to make the most of the free *Spiked* on offer. The cricket match was abandoned but people still tucked into the tea and Bill noticed Mark Hammond re-immerging from some prudent background to encourage people to enjoy the festivities. After all the over indulgence of one child shouldn't entirely spoil the fun for everyone else. There was no sign of Vicky Hammond and Bill re-grouped with his own family.

Susan was holding Will's hand. Annie was standing a little way away from them, as though about to have a quarrel. She looked at her grandparents and her mother and her gaze swept further afield until it included Simon. Bill noticed for the first time that she was wearing a *Spiked* t-shirt and headband. Her cool gaze finally settled on Bill.

'Don't think that this changes anything,' she said, 'because it doesn't.'

Bill looked at her puzzled. She turned her back on them all and marched off home. Bill referred his puzzlement to Susan but she just gave him one of her warning looks.

'I'll take William home with us,' she said to Carol. 'Why don't you come too.'

'But,' said Carol.

'Leave Annie,' said Susan.

'It's much further to walk to your house. Why did Ben involve himself in that way? Really, it was so unnecessary.'

248

'The walk will do us good,' said Susan and marched them homewards.

Bill still hadn't moved. Simon came over to join him.

'Jeez, is it always this exciting in these parts?' he said.

Bill wasn't sure how to respond.

'No offence, mate, but -'

Bill still didn't know how to respond.

'I guess you know the kid?' Simon continued.

Bill nodded.

'I don't want to butt in.'

'What did Annie mean?' Bill finally managed to find his voice.

'Ah, well,' just as Simon seemed to lose his.

'You said that it wasn't possible for her to make it without a big sponsorship deal,' Bill continued.

'I did,' Simon said carefully.

'Because this *Spiked* stuff,' and Bill suddenly realised that he was really angry. That he had been angry all week, all year. That everything had been leading up to this. That this tragedy had been inevitable. That someone had to get hurt.

'I'm just a personal trainer,' Simon broke in on Bill's anger.

'That's no excuse,' shouted Bill.

In fact he shouted loudly enough for several people to wonder if another drama was about to unfold.

'People have to make their own decisions about -'

'Do you think Danny Bean made his own decision?' Bill carried on shouting.

'I'm not talking about the kid, Danny Bean or whoever he is,' Simon said calmly.

'Well, I am,' continued Bill. 'This isn't just Mark Hammond and poor Shaun Bean and the whole bloody *Spiked* shemozzle, it's all the rest of you. You make Annie into a superstar and some simple boy like Danny Bean will pay the price. Every time.'

Bill didn't wait for further comment. He wasn't anyway having a conversation. He spun away from Simon and a growing group of spectators and made his own dramatic exit.

On his way out he nearly had a nasty accident with a man in pyjamas wielding the vicious object approximating to scissors. Fortunately the man's objective was the *Spiked* beach flags which he

249

attacked with such gusto that a policeman had to restrain him forcibly.

34

The next day Bill and Susan met by the kitchen door, both on their way out. Bill was shining in full cricketing whites. Susan was more modestly dressed.

'You off out, then?' Bill asked.

'I might ask you the same question,' Susan said. She looked at him, a slight worry making her look cross.

'Lovely day,' said Bill.

'Yes. I thought I'd walk over to Ben and Carol's and see if they've heard anything from Danny's parents.'

'Will they have done?'

'I don't know do I, but Ben did take them to the hospital yesterday.'

'Oh yes, I'd forgotten that.'

'Bill?'

Silence.

'Bill, where are you going?' The cross, worried look pulled at the smile lines around Susan's eyes.

Bill smiled, looked guilty, fiddled with his immaculate white sleeve, pulled at a kit bag bulging with bats and pads.

'You know you're not in the team. Everyone knows you're not in the team.'

Bill smiled tensely. 'They'll be a man short now, won't they.'

'What do you mean?'

'Shaun Bean won't be playing will he, not today, not -'

'Bill! How can you even think of it.'

'They haven't cancelled the match.'

'No, but,' Susan picked her words carefully, 'they'll have a twelfth man. That's what he's there for. As a substitute, in case.'

'That dozy chap from the butcher's who couldn't catch a toffee apple if you dropped it right into his hands. Or even, God help them, Ben.'

'Bill.'

'No harm done if I just pop along.'

Susan sighed. 'Shall we just pop along together then.' If Bill was going to face humiliation at least she could face it with him.

'Well now, that would be grand,' said Bill.

251

'You'll have to walk.'

'I don't mind walking,' said Bill.

It was pleasant strolling up The Avenue with Susan marching on one side and his kit bag swinging on the other. Rufus, setting off on urgent business of his own, made time to greet Bill warmly as he ran past. Bill whistled *Land of Hope and Glory*.

'You're not going off with the Andrews again today then?' Bill asked jauntily as he waved Rufus on his way.

Susan caught his eye and suddenly smiled. 'Apparently Melanie and Jon had a bit of a fall out yesterday.'

'Oh?'

'Jon spent most of yesterday afternoon and evening in The Cricketers Arms with that woman you were with.'

'Vicky Hammond? Really? Well I never.'

'Poor Melanie.'

'Poor Vicky. Shall we take the short cut?'

Bill led them down the snicket which cut through to the village green. A couple of men were practicing at the nets but most of the team were huddled around the new pavilion. Bill set off straight for them until Susan tugged on his arm so hard that he couldn't ignore her.

'Bill, you know. You know they have another wicket keeper now.'

'Yes, I know. The young lad that works for the electricians. He's not bad, not bad at all. He's coming along quite nicely in fact.'

'But Bill,' Susan gestured with a wide arm at the other cricketers already gathered at the ground. They were all blazoning *Spiked* colours over every available arm, leg and head.

'Don't worry, love, I'm not going to wicket keep. Anyway it's a bowler they've lost if Shaun Bean doesn't play.'

'Isn't he a fast bowler?'

Bill didn't have to answer her because he had now marched right into the middle of the anxious knot of men hovering around the new pavilion, his whites making him look like a victorious angel. Or an avenging one.

'Now then, lads, what's the damage?' he announced.

Alarm, embarrassment and relief flashed over several expressions. Then Ben emerged from the pavilion sporting a *Spiked* top and looking hugely uncomfortable.

'Bill!' He nearly hugged his father-in-law. 'Are you playing then? Thank goodness I won't have to and I can get this awful stuff off.'

'I just thought I'd help out,' Bill said modestly.

'Isn't that grand,' said a voice from the back and when big John Bailey started patting Bill on the back they all had to. Apart from the captain who finally stepped forward trying to regain his authority which wasn't easy in the face of the angel.

'Now, look Bill, we don't need a wicket keeper,' he said.

'I'm not going to wicket keep,' Bill announced for the second time, 'and if you don't mind I'd like to do a bit of net practice before we start.'

'But -' But it was no use butting Bill. He was already out of earshot.

'Don't you worry about Bill,' John Bailey broke in again, 'just give him a few overs here and there.' John winked at the crowd in general. 'Aye just give him a few overs.' He started to chuckle. 'And by God they won't know what's hit 'em.' John made a slow overarm swing with an exaggerated spin in his fingers as he let go of an imaginary ball. 'Eh, I've waited a long time to see Bill bowl again. Wasted behind the wickets he is, wasted. Well, what a grand day it is, lads,' he finished.

Then because an old man in pyjamas sitting modestly out of the way said in a very loud voice, 'hear, hear,' everyone else did too.

35

A week later Bill and Susan had to abandon their plan to walk to Ben and Carol's because it was pouring down with rain. They were being treated to a takeaway to give Susan a week off from the Sunday roast. Also Annie refused to leave her room unless she had a GCSE to sit. And the old bad Chinese takeaway had just been taken over by a good new one. Bill didn't like Chinese but Susan insisted that he would both have to eat Chinese food and go in her car. The same rain had also led to the cancellation of several cricket matches including East Wolds' second match of the season.

The Whitby Jones household was rather muted. The children were hiding in their bedrooms, Ben was preparing a case in his study and Carol was doing the *Sunday Times* crossword.

'Are we early?' Susan asked anxiously, as she and Bill joined Carol in the kitchen.

Bill sidled over to a rack of cooling biscuits and rubbed his wet hands over them.

'Dad, they're for later. You can have a drink now if you like,' said Carol.

'I thought we were having takeaway.' When Susan said the word takeaway it sounded like a lament for Sunday roast.

'We are. Look, you choose what you want from the menu.' Susan pointed to a menu on the kitchen table, 'and then -'

Susan and Bill looked at the menu suspiciously.

'Really Gran and Gramps, you're so prehistoric sometimes,' said a voice from the door and Annie came into the kitchen. She sat down between her grandparents and as she enthusiastically listed all the things that they should eat Bill caught Susan looking at him with a big smile in her eyes. Annie showing a healthy interest in food. Annie sitting at the table close to them. Annie holding her grandmother's hand. A look which Ben also interpreted happily as he entered the kitchen behind Annie.

Annie paused in her ordering of the food and looked up at them all. It was a long time since Bill had felt so close to her.

'By the way,' she said casually, at least she would have said it casually if she hadn't spoken so loudly, 'I'm giving up the *Spiked* sponsorship.'

254

Two parents in several tones of voice responded. 'You're what? You can't.'

'It's not up for discussion,' said Annie.

Bill inched himself just a bit closer to her. Broad shoulders. Protective. Ready for a fight.

'But you can't just,' both parents continued until Carol got a head start on Ben. 'You can't give up just like that, Annie. This isn't up to you. It's up to us. *Spiked* has made everything possible for you. After all these years. After all I, we've given up.'

'Mum, this isn't about you.'

'Annie, look,' broke in Ben, 'it's not that simple. We've signed contracts. We've made commitments. Deposits on your school fees in America have been paid and I've -'

'I've spoken to Simon about it and he -'

'What's it got to do with Simon?' Carol raised her voice above the others. 'And Mark Hammond has been such a -'

'Fucking bastard.'

'Annie,' shouted several shocked voices.

'What I mean is,' continued Annie unfazed, 'that Simon agrees that I can break off the contract.'

'Annie, it really isn't that simple. I've already thought about it,' Ben said quietly.

'Ben, what do you mean?' exclaimed Carol.

'Really, Dad?'

Ben nodded.

'I'm going to make a complaint of sexual harassment against Mark Hammond and break off the contract at the same time. So you see, they'll make a deal to keep me quiet and we'll get out of the sponsorship thing.'

Ben shook his head sadly. 'He's not likely to go for it, Annie. It has too many implications for his career. He's much more likely to let you push it to tribunals and then make you look young and impressionable. You have no evidence against him and what is more your mother, and I,' he added hastily, 'have encouraged Mark to play a role in allowing him to take you to training sessions and -'

'Oh, I think we might have some evidence,' said Bill deciding that it was time to join in the fun.

This shut everyone else up.

255

'A few messages here and there, hacking into his emails, past history you know, that sort of thing.'

'Bill/Dad you can't hack into someone's emails,' lots of people said.

'*I* won't do any hacking but I know someone who can,' Bill said. It was hard not to sound smug. 'Then there's the evidence of spiked *Spiked* not to mention several cases of intimidation and one incident of attempted gross assault.'

A general tumult erupted around Bill but Annie just shrugged and held up a muscled tennis arm. 'I don't think we need to make a big deal out of this, Gramps. Simon and I reckon that Mark Hammond will be happy to settle everything as quietly as possible.'

'Perhaps now at last we should make a big deal out of this?' Bill looked at Ben but Ben was fiddling with cold beers by the fridge and Carol was butting in on the argument.

'Annie this isn't something you can just do on your own and on the advice of a personal trainer. It's madness.' Carol's voice sounded shrill. 'It's tantamount, ' and she emphasised tantamount as though she enjoyed the word, 'to giving it all up.'

'I'm not giving anything up.'

'Junior Wimbledon,' wailed Carol.

Annie faltered slightly. 'This year, but not next year.'

No one said anything until Ben spoke quietly. 'Annie you know we can't afford to pay for anything like the sort of training you've had for the past year.'

'I know.' Annie went quiet too. 'I Googled a bit. Energy drinks and stuff. There are guys out there making a stance. You know there's a big international snowboard event held in Norway every year and energy drinks are banned. It was all started by this really cool sounding dude Teridifficultnamesomething Haakonsen.'

'What on earth has all this got to do with some godforsaken little snowboard event?' seethed Carol.

'Let her finish,' Ben was still quiet.

'The point is they put together a whole competition paid for by, I don't know, charities and stuff who sponsored a campaign called *Drink Water* to sponsor this event.'

'*Drink Water*,' said Bill.

Ben coughed modestly. 'It just so happens,' he said when an angry voice interrupted him from the doorway.

'How can you all sit and discuss this as if Annie's tennis stuff is the only thing that matters? My best friend nearly died and none of you care.' Will was unable to disguise that fact that he'd been crying.

'He didn't nearly die. Don't exaggerate,' said Carol.

'Will, Billiam,' said Bill.

'Don't call me that,' shouted Will, 'I'm not a baby any more.'

'Look, Will,' Annie said, moving from her haven between Susan and Bill, 'I'm doing what I'm doing because of Danny. I agree with you, nothing is as important as what happened to Danny. So I'm risking my whole future as a tennis player because of that. I'm not,' and she swung round to face both her parents, 'not going to feel responsible ever again for something like what happened to Danny.'

Bill looked down at the list of chop sueys, sweet and sour dishes, chef's specials. 'I suppose *Spiked* is off the menu then,' he muttered quietly to himself.

Epilogue

A year later the Whitby Joneses and the Reeveses set off to London. They were going to watch Annie compete in her first Junior Wimbledon. Bill had even been allowed to spend a day at Lords watching the test match.

Annie didn't win, but on her way to the semi-finals she knocked out two *Spiked* competitors. She looked grand in a simple white tennis skirt and polo shirt and after her matches she wrapped up in a large black hoodie proclaiming across her back the logo *Drink Water* and in smaller letters 'sponsored by Yorkshire Water'.

Danny Bean was still on medication for epilepsy and an arrhythmic heart. Tests on possible brain damage were inconclusive but Will knew that he wasn't and never would be quite the same Danny that he'd known at primary school.

A lot of settlements were shrewdly made out of court so that *Spiked* could continue making money and increasing its share of the energy drinks market and a few local business men also profited accordingly. Amongst them Jonathan Andrews who made so much money that he had to buy an apartment on The Algarve.

Spiked did mysteriously often suffer from small acts of vandalism. However the chief suspect was usually seen either on his bicycle far away from the crime scene or playing cricket in his new roll as 'Swanny' Bill. Thus the real culprit, occasionally spotted wearing a sort of striped convict outfit, happily continued to mar an otherwise unsullied outlook for yet another baddy who got away with it.

Proof

Made in the USA
Charleston, SC
24 November 2015